About the Author

Tim's advent thriller in *The Advent House* follows forays in other genres. Tim's published works include plays, chancel dramas, and novels of historical fiction. His play *Bonhoeffer* was first produced in 2004. The dozen chancel dramas are available online through Amazon. His novel *Mrs Keckly Sends Her Regards* is set in the Lincoln White House. The novel *The Night Is Far Gone* is set in the household of the Imperial Romanovs, during the last years and days of Nicholas II, Alexandra, and their children.

Tim and his wife are by no means housebound. Except perhaps during the summer monsoon season, they're always able and eager to get out and about, exploring the forests, mountains, canyons, and Indian ruins that bedeck their home territory in Arizona's high country.

THE ADVENT HOUSE

TIM JORGENSON

THE ADVENT HOUSE

Vanguard Press

VANGUARD PAPERBACK

© Copyright 2023

Tim Jorgenson

A CIP catalogue record for this title is
available from the British Library.

ISBN 978 1 80016 453 6

*Vanguard Press is an imprint of
Pegasus Elliot Mackenzie Publishers Ltd.*
www.pegasuspublishers.com

First Published in 2023

**Vanguard Press
Sheraton House Castle Park
Cambridge England**

Printed & Bound in Great Britain

To the Adrianas & Adans
Everywhere

Santiago de Cuba

1.

The first steps toward a journey come via the imagination and revelation; her boss was always saying that. Her job, he said, was to fire the imagination through revelation. Creating enticing photos would draw travelers to *Cuba Hermosa* – Beautiful Cuba, a Cuba beyond the ordinary. That's what he meant by *imagination.* But his words were more revealing than he imagined. She was to learn the ordinary *was* extraordinary in ways no travel poster could convey. And these extraordinary ordinary things weren't the sorts of thing CubaTur or state security would want bandied about.

For starters, when Gabriela decided *not* to leave Room B-153, Adriana had just died. Not to leave the room was a no-no; Gabriela was supposed to report the death immediately. But as she came to the door, she turned and returned to the bed where Adriana lay. In a twinkling, Gabriela had changed from a model citizen into... what? Could she change back? Any delay in reporting the death might yield an 'unpleasant situation,' a term her father often used. State security, after all, labeled Adriana a 'person of great interest.' That's why Adriana had been assigned as the only patient in Room B-153. That's why Gabriela had been assigned as a 'volunteer' to aid Adriana in her dying days. Had Adriana believed Gabriela was merely a volunteer? She must have; she had entrusted so much to her. Too much in a way. But in that doorway moment, Adriana's trust – and perhaps more – had triumphed. Was this a betrayal of the revolutionary state?

That's a silly question, Gabriela told herself. But state security, like her father, would surely think otherwise. A second cousin in state security – not her father – had opened the door to visiting her sick brother. He'd now been imprisoned for a year and a half, having been convicted of distributing Bibles. Roberto, or Beto, had been repudiated by almost his entire family. Beto hadn't repudiated them, certainly not his dear sister, Gabi. Yet Beto was proud of his 'new family,' as he referred to his brothers and sisters in faith. He stubbornly refused to repudiate them or his new faith. And Gabriela had refused to disown him.

Ideas confer vision and so do people, she thought. For good or bad, Adriana had opened a door and an outlook that even Beto hadn't been able to open. Gabriela looked down at Adriana's fine-featured face and at the open Gideon *Nuevo Testamento Salmos Y Proverbios* in the dear woman's left hand. Adriana had asked Gabriela – she never called her 'Gabi' – to place the book there as her life ebbed away. She had said, 'This book is for you now. Take it once I'm gone, but hold me as I go; God bless you.' Gabriela had taken hold; she'd taken hold of Adriana's right hand, but she hadn't committed to taking the Gideon. No, she hadn't. How could she? Her father was a party stalwart. That said and that known, she had nonetheless committed to delivering the letters that Adriana had entrusted to her.

She could yet turn them over to state security. Adriana would never know. When she had been a young pioneer, Gabriela might have turned them over without hesitation. But she was twenty-one now. 'Rooted in the Revolution,' she was not unreflective. Adriana had come to mean more to her than almost anyone she'd ever known outside her family. *Why?*

Gabriela kept asking that as she removed the Gideon from Adriana's hand. Without breath, without book, bluish of cast, her dear friend now looked like an unkempt, dead creature wrapped in newspaper, a mere dead fish. *Or is this body now the mere husk of one destined for other shores, as Adriana believed? Can new life, as she'd said, come to bear fruit even in the here and now? Look where such thinking had gotten Beto! But enough.*

At any moment, a nurse or doctor or even someone from state security could enter the room. Gabriela put the *Nuevo Testamento* in her purse. She swept a hand through her hair, retrieved her pocket mirror, hoping to give herself an ordered appearance. An air of indifference to Adriana's demise would hopefully hide the extraordinary tumult awash in her heart and mind and hands. To contain this tumult, she would want

13

herself to be read as a coldly efficient, volunteer patient's aide for this now-deceased 'consort of an enemy of the State.' *Nothing of interest was said or done by this person of interest;* so she resolved to report.

Nothing? Surely, she must have said something, written something. She was a calligrapher! She passed on nothing to you?

Nothing, nothing at all.

No, that wouldn't do. That was hardly credible. She would have to give up something. The letters were so very personal. Four Adriana had written in her own beautiful hand, even as she deplored the results. Finally, when she'd become too weak three days past, she'd dictated a letter to one of *her* brothers, Frederico or 'Kiko,' as she called him. What would Adriana think of her if she handed the five letters over to state security? What would her mother think? But, of course, her mother was now dead, her body given by Gabi's father to serve state purposes.

No, the letters mustn't go to state security. They'd stay tucked away.

But the Testamento? What of the Testamento?

It had been Adriana's dearest possession. She'd never considered her family a possession. A family could only be a gift, she'd said. Her daughter had been retrieved by God at birth. And her husband was awaiting trial and a new sentence. Adriana could accept these losses. But her son, *ai,* her son grieved her. If she died with any regret, it was in giving up her son to Kiko. All the more reason why the letters couldn't be shared with state security.

By such reasoning, Gabriela concluded she'd have to give up the *Testamento. Would that it were otherwise!* Gabriela retrieved the *Testamento* from her purse. Inside the book's front and back covers were inscribed the names of family members she'd come to know through Adriana, the names of Adriana's parents, her two brothers, her brothers' families, uncles and aunts, grandparents, each bearing a birth date and some bearing a death date. In the text of the book along the margins could be found elegantly written words whose full meanings could be discerned perhaps only by the deceased.

What would state security make of all this? Of the Scripture, nothing. Of the script, perhaps something. Something, hopefully, would be enough to satisfy their appetite. *Better the book than the letters. Or herself,* thought Gabriela. The book would be the lesser betrayal. Gabriela snapped the book closed and placed it in her purse. She retrieved the letters and tucked them in her dress. She'd worn a loose-fitting one today.

She'd suspected Adriana would pass away this day. She hated death. That's why she'd chosen a dress she least favored. Adriana, on the other hand, almost seemed eager for death, eager to leave the 'kingdom of darkness' for the 'kingdom of light,' as she called them. She would succumb to the cancer but not to the darkness, she'd say.

Gabriela found that alluring. Her father would be appalled if he knew. But for the first time in her life, Gabriela had become close to someone of religious faith other than Beto, the 'Traitor.' Except that Gabriela, who'd never sought a label for her brother, now saw him in the light of Adriana. What was that light?

The sound of footfalls in the hallway prompted Gabriela to a readiness mode. She would sound the word of demise and would be prepared to pass along the decedent's dearest treasure. She couldn't help but wonder what had come over her.

2.

Adriana's brother Kiko couldn't help but wonder what had come over him or, more accurately, what had come over his school. Here in the magnificent halls of the Icarian, a special school of science and mathematics founded by the Revolution, an incident had occurred that could only embarrass the school or, more crucially, him. He paced back and forth in his office, wondering how he'd navigate this crisis. If he went public with the photo in hand, he'd surely be embarrassed. He had a hunch there was a family connection. But if he ignored the incident, the flames of counter-revolutionary thought might spread throughout the school.

If he'd held a photo of the nation's leader desecrated with graffiti, he could have comforted himself. To be sure, such desecration was awful. But it was almost inevitable among adolescents. Deplorable as desecration was, one could take comfort: the culprit would soon graduate or reveal himself. Past desecrations had played out that way. But what of *this* photo? It was far worse than desecration.

Someone had found incarnate a religious person worthy of admiration. The photo bore the image of perhaps the most storied Latin American in this year

1979, Archbishop Oscar Romero. Kiko had to admit to admiring the man, secretly of course. But he knew admiration was out of order. *Not one step back! The revolution must be totally triumphant!* The person who'd posted this photo in a boys' restroom must be dealt with. The culprit had taped across the photo the type-written words '*¡Necesitamos un Oscar Romero, también!*' We need an Oscar Romero, too!

This insolence could only come from a student. Why had the archbishop become a hero to anyone at the Icarian? Romero was in distant El Salvador. His current fame rested on his speaking out against the powers-that-be in a semi-feudal state. Romero was progressive, yes, but such independent voices of progress were a hindrance and distraction in Cuba. In Cuba, the state itself was the revolution incarnate and the revolution was progress incarnate.

Not that Kiko believed all that. He believed hardly any of it. But it seemed necessary to recite such thoughts because the state, the party, and the leader *were* absolutely necessary. If there was any transcendence truly available to mere mortals, it was in the absolute power and truth of state, party, and leader leading the land to a truly progressive future. Neither Cuba nor any other land could have it better, warts and all.

Kiko would have to damp this conflagration. He must find the culprit or culprits who'd taped this incendiary icon to a restroom wall. Must state security be brought into this affair? Of course not. Doing so might derail his journey of ascent. He headed one of the most prestigious high schools in all of Cuba. As a token of his achievement, his school had just received one of ten Volkswagen microbuses given to Cuban schools by an adoring West German philanthropist.

Kiko could see that one day he might be Minister of Education over all of Cuba. This photo incident would be nothing but a peso dropped in a pond, if properly handled. Surely his brother Carlos could be persuaded to see this. Surely Carlos would discreetly provide a fingerprint specialist. *He must!* For Carlos, too, could be embarrassed if, as Kiko feared, this incident were the work of their own nephew, Tomas. Tomas had been saying many disturbing things recently.

Kiko placed the photo on his desk, setting aside the paper he'd used to handle the evidence. He dreaded asking a favor of Carlos, but who else could he ask? His brother was one of the highest officials in all state security.

As Kiko walked to the window overlooking the courtyard, the telephone jangled. He picked up the handset. The school's receptionist told him two state security agents were headed to his office.

How could this be? No one had called state security, at least not on his authority. Using the paper he'd set aside, Kiko gingerly grabbed one corner of the photo while opening his desk drawer with his free hand.

He placed the photo amid pencils and erasers and then firmly shut the drawer.

Kiko turned away from the desk. He looked out the courtyard window. He must look composed before the agents entered the office.

A man was trimming a mango tree in the courtyard. This had once been a Catholic, boys' high school. The priests and brothers were long gone but some of the old habits lingered, like the trimming of mango trees. The trimmed trees were like emblems of paradise. Paradise lost? *Mustn't think that way.*

'Comrade Marquez.'

When Kiko heard his name, he wheeled about to face two agents, both wearing state security fatigues. That seemed ominous. He had expected agents wearing civilian clothes.

'Yes, comrades, good afternoon. What can I do for you?'

'You must travel across the city. Please come with us,' said one of the men.

'May I ask why?'

'You will learn.'

'Of course. Should I bring anything with me?'

'Nothing,' said the man, waving his hand to the doorway. His partner led the way into the corridor, down the steps, and out the entryway past the receptionist. The receptionist looked rather alarmed, but Kiko forged a smile for her benefit.

The state security men had said nothing, nor were they open to questions. Why the silent treatment? *One can't expect state security to be forthcoming.*

A black Mercedes Benz was idling at curbside, bracketed by motorcycles fore and aft. Tinted windows prevented anyone from peering into the car's interior. One of his escorts opened the back door and beckoned Kiko to take a seat. He could see the suit pants of someone who'd be sharing the back seat with him. As soon as Kiko was tucked into his seat, the escort shut the door and revved up the bike that would follow the car. His mate had already ignited the forward bike.

Before Kiko's eyes could adjust to the darkness, he felt a hand grasping for his.

'My brother, we have business.'

Kiko was relieved, then alarmed. He took his brother's hand and vigorously shook it. 'What are you doing here, Carlos? What brings you to Santiago? Where are we going? And...'

'Slow down and shut up. I'm the one to ask questions,' replied his brother. Carlos had a deep voice and a firm handshake.

'Yes, of course.' Kiko was glad to release his brother's hand. Carlos had cold hands.

When the lead bike turned into traffic, the car and trailing bike followed. For several minutes, this procession sped through the streets of the city without Carlos saying a word. The procession was given a wide berth, but then (as always) there weren't all that many vehicles on the street, at least not vehicles in motion. Along the curbs Kiko saw numerous American cars from the 1950s. *They are honored enough to see the light of day,* thought Kiko.

He said, 'What brings you to old Santiago, if I may ask?'

'Our sister.'

'Our sister? She's in Santiago?'

'In this city. You didn't know.'

The words came dripping with scorn, but Kiko could truthfully reply, 'Why would I know, if she weren't to tell me?'

'That's probably just as well. She was here with her husband when he was arrested last month, in November, for anti-revolutionary activities. She couldn't be returned to Havana with him because she had turned quite ill. Quite ill. They discovered she had end-stage breast cancer.'

'Has she asked to see Tomas?'

'She did. I ordered that that not be allowed, unless she divulged everything she knew about her husband's Bible distribution network. We wanted names. We've had someone with her, but nothing has been revealed… so far. That's why I've decided to take a hand in this situation. That's why I've come to Santiago. I want you to talk with her, to promise to bring Tomas to see her before she dies. She hasn't seen her son in fourteen years. When the wood rots, it becomes more pliable. My

22

wish is that our sister consents before she breaks. Do you understand?'

'I understand, but how can I agree to this? For fourteen years Pamela and I have stuck to the story that his mother and father were both dead. Tomas has called me 'papa' for years. If he were to see his mother, our sister, how would I look in his eyes?'

'Dishonest,' said Carlos. 'For all your scientific integrity you've not been honest. You should have told the boy his parents were anti-social, anti-revolutionary criminals of the lowest order. For his own good and the good of the state, they gave up Tomas and you were allowed to adopt him.'

'Cuba will be the better for this,' said Kiko. 'He is one of the most brilliant students we've ever had at the Icarian. He will go far.'

'But no one can ascend the heights unless he can prove he's fit for the heights, my brother. There can be no exceptions. The earlier he proves his loyalty to the revolution, the surer his ascent will be. Anyway, it's your loyalty that's now being put to the test. Your honor as Tomas's papa was based on a lie. Your honor means nothing to the revolution. But the revolution must mean everything to you, as it must to every loyal Cuban. Everything.'

'Of course,' said Kiko. But what would he say to Adriana? What suasion could he bring to bear that state security with its seemingly limitless resources hadn't already employed? Assuming Adriana could be persuaded to give up information, how could Tomas be persuaded to attend to a dying mother he'd been told had died in an automobile accident with his father so long ago?

For another quarter hour, the two motorcycles and the black Benz wound their way across Santiago to Adriana. The two brothers had little to say to one another. Carlos had no news about their parents, none that Kiko didn't already know. Anyway, Kiko expected to see them late tomorrow when he would be driving the VW microbus to Havana for a two-day educators' conference. Would all this business with his sister make impossible his attending the conference? He wanted to tell his brother he was one of the featured conference speakers.

He said nothing. Kiko was uncomfortable with Carlos in the best of circumstances. And this wasn't the best of circumstances. How long would it take to arrive at the hospital? And what would he say to his sister once they got there? All things considered, as he later told Gabriela, he'd rather have been elsewhere. Soon enough, he was.

As the black car pulled up to the hospital, Carlos broke the silence. 'We have long disconnected ourselves from our sister, each for our own reasons. We now visit her for one reason: as a service to the revolution. Remember that and your sacred career will be secure, my little brother.'

That patronizing tone! Kiko always hated it, along with the cant. *What would it take to be elsewhere?*

One of the motorcyclists opened the door on Kiko's side of the car. The other cyclist opened his brother's door. The limo was now under the porte-cochere of a Mission-style hospital built in the 1920s by an order of nuns long gone from its premises. In the lobby of the hospital hung Alberto Korda's iconic photograph of Che Guevara, bearing a beard and wearing a beret atop a zipped-up jacket. Beneath the huge photo, someone had placed a red banner bearing Che's immortal words in yellow: *¡Marcha atrás nunca!* Not one step back!

How would these words apply to the crippled or the paraplegic? Kiko often had such off-color, off-the-record private thoughts. But for him there was no denying the necessary goodness of the people's dictatorship.

Nor any denying its compelling powers, so evident as hospital functionaries and staff members came forth from their warrens to render homage to an exceedingly important member of the revolutionary state. Not that Carlos looked revolutionary. He had no beard. He wore no fatigues. Instead, he was the very image of the revolutionary technocrat who was guiding Cuba under its leader to a new, scientific future in which prosperity would be, was, and is a given of the state. Carlos looked very prosperous in his trim business suit. Had he acquired it on his last trip to East Germany?

Someday, the fawning attention could be mine, too, thought Kiko. But for now, he was happy enough to run a prestigious school. And even happier he hadn't been thrust into the attentions of state security by that awful photo of Archbishop Romero. For once, he had a secret on his brother.

Carlos frowned at Kiko as a way of signaling he wanted him to join him. As Kiko did so, those who'd surrounded Carlos dispersed, everyone except for one white-jacketed physician.

Carlos stated, 'We've had a disappointing development. Adriana is dead.'

Kiko had almost forgotten his sister. He felt guilty.

The doctor told them, 'A volunteer was with her when she died, a young woman named Gabriela Suarez Paloma.'

'Is she still in the hospital?' asked Carlos.

'She said she'd stay until state security arrived,' said the doctor.

'Excellent. Lead us there.'

'Me, too?' asked Kiko.

'Of course.'

There was no saying *No* to his brother. As Kiko followed Carlos and the chatty physician, his thoughts ran to his sister or, more correctly, to his sister's son, whom he had come to see as his own. Tomas must not know of his mother's death today. There was nothing to be gained by his learning he'd been deceived all these years. There was much to be lost. Surely Carlos would see there was no longer a need for the boy to be exposed to the truths about his mother or father. Once you stepped outside of science or math – the home territory of the Escuela Icarian – there was no telling where truth might lead. That was why the custodians of truth *must* keep a tight leash or lid on things.

Carlos must recognize this, but then you could never tell with Carlos, as Kiko would later admit. You could never tell. There was a perverse streak in Carlos, a streak that perhaps powered his ascent in the state security apparatus. *Best not to think of that.*

Carlos, the physician, and Kiko ascended stairs and walked along several hallways before they reached one where a uniformed state security agent could be seen standing by a doorway bearing overhead the stenciled address 'B-153.' The agent came to attention as the three approached.

Carlos turned to the doctor at the doorway. 'We won't be needing you here. If we need you later, we'll call your office.'

'Of course, comrade,' said the physician, who then turned around and sped off.

'Let us enter, dear brother.'

'Yes,' said Kiko.

Gabriela, who'd been sitting, rose when the two men entered the room.

'You're the volunteer?' asked Carlos.

'I am, sir,' she replied.

'You were here as this woman died.'

'I was.'

'A volunteer. Have you anything to volunteer to the state? This woman, as perhaps you knew, was of interest. Her husband has been a notorious peddler of religious drivel, a relentless demoralizer of the workers and youth of our country.'

'I've already been in communication with state security here in this city. When they arrive…' Gabriela hesitated, 'when they arrive, I have something that may be of interest.'

'I am with state security,' said Carlos.

'But I promised them.'

'I am *them* for you. What do you have?'

Gabriela looked perplexed.

'What do you have?' asked Carlos.

She looked from Carlos to Kiko to the uniformed agent in the doorway.

'What are you waiting for?' Carlos asked in a sharpened tone.

'I promised the chief here in the city…'

'Who works for me. Hand over what you have.'

Gabriela looked down, then retrieved a small black book from her purse. She handed the book to Carlos.

'She left this,' she said.

'Very well.'

'Will I be able to see my brother?' asked Gabi.

'Your brother? What does that have to do with this?'

'I was told if I shared whatever I learned or received from this woman, I would be able to visit my brother, who is at a labor station near Havana.'

'You mean at a penal camp?'

'Yes.'

'We'll see about that.'

Carlos began flipping through the *Nuevo Testamento*. The beautifully penned notes that Adriana had cast around the texts were of no interest to him. What caught his eye were the family names and genealogical tree that appeared on the inside covers. Carlos showed the back-end matter to Kiko.

Kiko was alarmed. He saw his own name, not to mention everyone else in his family, Carlos included (of course). He hated that in death he would be associated with a social dinosaur, a malefactor, a traitor to the revolution. Surely Carlos must have similar misgivings. He asked, 'What can this mean for us?'

Carlos replied, 'It means nothing. It's all family drivel of no obvious interest to the state.'

'May I keep it?' asked Gabriela.

'No,' said Carlos. 'This man here will see to its destruction.'

Kiko nodded at Gabriela. He extended a hand to her. 'I am Frederico Marquez Estaban, a brother to... to...'

Kiko fell silent as he looked for the first time at his sister's face. It was a much-thinned face, bluish now, entirely stripped of the possibility of a smile. He remembered the smiles of their youth and the songs they used to sing together. All this business about this little book and what was written in it seemed beside the point. It seemed cruel and indifferent, not that Adriana would know. It seemed a stain on the very possibility of human dignity, an affront to life, to be wrestling over the fate of a book, when there seemed to be not the least care for what fate had brought the deceased. Here in the room where their dead sister lay, the living were diminishing her significance, treating her as a dead fly, hardly recognizing the humanity she'd shared with them. Or so Kiko thought.

'I'm sorry, Carlos, but I want to look at our dear sister.'

'It's best to remember her when she was a girl, my dear brother. Her marriage to that marine-engineer-turned-Bible-thumper is when she became unhinged. If our father had had an inkling of the shipwreck she'd become, he would have mobilized forces to prevent this misalliance. You and I have been in danger in the eighteen years of her marriage. I cannot mourn her death. Rather, I'm relieved. You should be, too.'

'I'm relieved,' said Kiko, 'but I'm also sad. I should have been here with her when she died.'

'What good would that have done? Anyway, the volunteer was with her,' said Carlos.

Gabriela looked as if she wasn't sure whether she'd been elevated or diminished by that remark.

Carlos continued, 'I personally forbade any contact with family members. Such contact would have only served to spotlight the fact that we've had a black sheep in the family. Now it's over. Almost. Soon, Adan, her husband will be finished off.

'Here, take this thing,' said Carlos, handing Kiko the *Testamento.*

Kiko hesitated, then took the book. 'I can't take it. It meant so much to our sister.'

'My dear brother, she believed in a lot of twaddle,' said Carlos, turning to look out the window. 'This is all twaddle. Nothing more and nothing less. You know that. This must be destroyed.'

'Let time do that work for us.'

'Where would you have time do its work, dear brother?' said Carlos, still looking away from Kiko.

Gabriela interrupted, 'If neither of you want the book, the local state security chief will find it of interest.'

'You don't seem to understand,' said Carlos briefly eying Gabriela. 'I *am* state security. Kiko, you will do what is necessary to this book.'

Footsteps and chattering could be heard approaching the room. Kiko hesitated.

'How will I destroy it? I can't be seen with this book now.'

Carlos, still looking away, said in an angry whisper, 'Use your wits. Put it in her purse!'

Kiko looked at Gabi. 'May I?'

Gabriela smiled and said, 'I'll take it.'

She took the book from Kiko but thrust it under the mattress of the adjacent, vacant bed. She quickly faced the door. Kiko saw what she had done but said nothing.

3.

One of the motorcyclists led two uniformed state security agents into the room. Gabriela recognized an agent. She'd seen him at state security's city headquarters. She'd been called there after interviewing to become a patient's aide at the hospital.

The two city men introduced themselves to Carlos, who didn't need to introduce himself. Carlos didn't bother to introduce his brother or Gabriela. The city men explained they'd been sent to the hospital to search Adriana's room for items of interest.

'Very well,' said Carlos. 'The others, I trust, may leave.'

'Yes, sir,' said one of the city men.

Kiko, Gabriela, and the motorcyclist left. The cyclist took up a position near a cross corridor busy with medical staff and patients. Kiko and Gabriela drifted past the cyclist to where the lively and dead corridors crossed one another. Gabriela leaned against a wall and looked back towards B-153.

'Did your brother see me put the book under the mattress?' asked Gabriela.

'I don't think so,' said Kiko.

'Then they might find it.'

'They might.'

'Your sister would have invoked God's help,' said Gabriela.

'God is helpless because He *isn't,* but then I'm getting into matters of theology for reasons obscure to you.'

'Perhaps not. Your sister has introduced me to a more personal kind of God than I've ever thought of.'

'So, you give theological matters some thought.'

'I hadn't until I met your sister. I've never thought of God as a someone and therefore as someone to worship. I've always thought the world so ordered, beautifully so despite the disease. My family – me excepted – is a bunch of scientists. We're all party, except my brother Beto. He's a doctor. At least, he's been a doctor. If I thought of God, I thought of a force beyond human understanding that brings order to our world.'

'Not exactly a party line of thinking,' said Kiko.

'No, not exactly, but not so far out of line as to get me in danger, not like my brother Beto.'

'What's happened?' asked Kiko. He seemed genuinely interested. But Gabi had no desire to say any more about Beto. She'd said enough.

'Your sister believed in a more human kind of God. Human and humane.'

Kiko raised his eyebrows. 'How childish. Thank God, I'm an atheist.' He chuckled.

'Yes, I know. Your sister talked much about you... and about Him,' said Gabriela, pointing up. 'You can thank the missing God that the city agents must have missed the *Testamento*. They're smiling, as is your brother.'

Kiko turned around. The two city agents and Carlos were walking in their direction. As Kiko would later tell her, Carlos almost never smiled except when he was with other agents. In his element he was happy.

The two city men nodded at Kiko and Gabriela as they headed to a stairwell leading down to the hospital entrance. While the two headed down and out, Carlos instructed his motorcyclist to return to the door of Adriana's room, permitting no one to enter until a guard from the local state security office had arrived.

'We may leave now,' said Carlos.

'Not quite,' said Kiko. 'The book is back in there.'

Carlos whirled around, looking toward the door where his man stood. 'Where is the book?'

'Under the mattress of the other bed,' said Gabriela.

Carlos glared at his brother. 'I told you to put it in her purse!'

Gabriela said, 'That seemed dangerous to me, but then I'm not in state security.'

Carlos turned to face her. 'You ought to be more careful what you say... and do. Those men just indicated you were cooperating with the local office. You'd better keep it up with them... and me.'

'I am,' said Gabriela. 'That's why I need to pass on your sister's Bible.'

'You don't understand,' said Carlos. 'We need to recover that book without arousing baseless suspicions. I can't go back and grope around for the thing. You're so smart, perhaps you can suggest something, comrade.'

'I will. I know your sister's son lives here in the city and attends the very school your brother heads,' she said, nodding toward Kiko. 'She wanted to see the boy before she died. That didn't happen.'

'If she'd been cooperative, it could have happened,' said Carlos.

'Now's the time to make up for past errors,' said Gabriela.

'You're bold.'

'Let the boy see his mother with me. I'll recover the book when he comes.'

Kiko sighed, 'We can't have the boy here. We simply can't.'

'Do you have a better idea?' asked Carlos.

'None.'

Gabriela spoke up. 'I think the boy should see his mother, for the sake of the truth. We live in a society founded on truth, yes?'

Carlos replied, 'Of course, but one of those truths is that human relations founder on truth.'

'Truth isn't the issue here,' said Kiko.

'Then what is?' smirked Carlos.

'Or I'll just go back to the room and say I left something behind,' said Gabriela. 'With you two hovering in the background, the guard will probably let me in and out without a fuss. I'll get the Bible.'

'You're too smart by half,' said Carlos. 'Your first idea was the better one. Tomas should be brought here to see his dead mother.'

'No,' said Kiko. 'Let her get the book.'

'You have two choices, my dear brother. Go with this young woman to retrieve our nephew or go down to the lobby and sulk awaiting your beloved, so-called "son." Which shall it be?'

'I have no choice.'

'Of course not,' said Carlos. He led Kiko and Gabriela to the Mercedes-Benz. As Kiko and Gabriela got into the car, Carlos gave instructions to the driver to chauffer the two to retrieve a third person, a high-school student who must be returned immediately with them to the hospital. Carlos emphasized the word 'immediately.'

'Aren't you coming?' asked Kiko through the open door.

Carlos slammed shut the door. 'This is *your* family affair.'

Kiko anxiously looked out the limo's rear window as it pulled away. As he would later confess, he was anxious about many things. Anxious about what his brother would do. Anxious about what he'd say to Tomas and how Tomas would react. He was even anxious about this Gabriela. She managed herself around his brother better than he ever had.

The air in the rear of the Mercedes was thick with anxiety. But Kiko would only later learn of Gabriela's anxieties. Right now, neither was eager to talk.

When the Mercedes-Benz pulled up to the Icarian, Tomas was sitting between two other teenagers on a stone bench outside the main entrance. Kiko pointed him out. He was the huskiest of the three students, all in their school uniforms. Tomas was explaining something using the pad resting on his shins.

The threesome looked up as the Mercedes came to a halt. Their principal stepped out in front of them. Few were the days when one saw a gleaming *new* car in Santiago, especially a Mercedes. Fewer still when a schoolmaster was seen riding in the likes of a Mercedes. The two students with Tomas stared open-mouthed at Comrade Marquez. Tomas looked puzzled but kept a closed mouth. Gabriela noted that he had the finely sculptured head of his mother and her eyelashes to boot, but a ruddy complexion and an athletic build that must come from his father.

Kiko beckoned Tomas to approach him.

'Where were you, Papa?' asked Tomas. 'They told me you'd been taken away by state security and to wait here for your return.'

'Yes, well, good. Now you need to come along with me.'

'Where to?'

'We'll explain along the way.'

'We?' asked Tomas, looking over his shoulder at his schoolmates. He opened a palm to his buddies. They were now standing, looking puzzled. One of his buddies gave a slight wave to Tomas as he ducked into the car.

Gabriela offered a hand to Tomas. Tomas hadn't expected to be sitting between a young woman and his papa.

'Hello, my name is Gabriela Suarez Paloma. Your uncle and I met earlier this afternoon.'

'A pleasure to meet you, comrade?'

'"Comrade" if you wish,' replied Gabriela. 'My friends usually call me "Gabi."'

'Comrade Gabriela,' said Tomas, 'it's a pleasure. I'm Tomas.'

'I know,' said Gabi, nodding.

Tomas turned to Kiko as the car pulled away from the school. 'Where're we going?'

'To a hospital.'

'Is Mama there?'

Gabriela supposed by *Mama* Tomas would be referring to Pamela, Kiko's wife, whom Adriana, surprisingly, had so adored.

'No, it isn't what you might think,' replied Kiko. 'How shall I explain?'

Tomas looked intently at Kiko, but nothing was immediately forthcoming as the Mercedes made its way across Santiago. Tomas then looked at Gabriela. She cast a sympathetic smile.

Kiko noticed a button on the back of the front seats. When he pushed the button a glass pane thrust up in back of those seats, affording the backseat riders a measure of privacy.

'What is it, Papa?'

Kiko couldn't look at Tomas. Kiko churned his jaws and shifted in his seat. He looked away from Tomas. Gabriela wondered whether he'd be able to break the news to his nephew. Or would she have to lead the boy herself into the room where his mother's body lay? As the Mercedes moved away from a stop, Kiko finally opened up.

'Do you remember at all when you were brought into our home?'

'Not much. I remember going to the beach. For some reason, I remember a little red pail that Mama gave me at the beach. I remember making a castle in the sand.'

'Do you remember who helped you make this sandcastle?'

'You did, I guess, and Mama, but somehow I don't remember – I don't have an image of – you and Mama helping me. I just remember that red pail and the completed castle, where the pail itself was part of the roof.'

'We forget a lot,' said Kiko, 'but then there's much we don't want to remember when we picture the past – or present. You probably don't remember my telling you that all sandcastles eventually disappear. And that life was fuller of sandcastles than we'd like to think.

'That was big talk to a four-or-five-year-old boy, but then you were a very bright boy. Very bright and that's in no small measure why we adopted you. Maybe that was the prime reason why we adopted you.'

Tomas said nothing.

'It's good you happen to remember that sandcastle because I must tell you a sandcastle has been swept away this very day.'

Tomas asked, 'What do you mean?'

'We are going to a hospital, to a hospital room, where you will see a woman, see a woman...'

Kiko brought a clenched fist to his mouth.

Gabriela spoke. 'What your uncle wants to tell you is that we'll be taking you to a hospital room where a woman has just died, a woman who is related to you, a woman who dearly loved you.'

That's out, that's out.

'Who could this be?' asked Tomas. He looked first at Gabi and then at his uncle, who now seemed somewhat more composed.

Kiko spoke almost in a whisper. 'It was your mother.'

'My mother?' Tomas looked alarmed. He turned to Gabriela, as if to seek confirmation of what he just heard.

She nodded. 'Your mother, your birth mother, not your Aunt Pamela.'

41

Gabriela instinctively raised her right hand, beginning to offer it to Tomas. He'd clenched his eyes shut and brought his hands to cover his face. He began a rocking motion that lasted for the last few minutes of the ride to the hospital. Gabriela attempted to put an arm on his shoulder, but he shook it off. Kiko didn't try. When it was apparent Tomas would accept no comfort, his uncle looked away.

The foundations of sandcastles rest on what cannot be said, thought Gabriela. *What endures rests on truth. But what is the truth?*

When the uniformed motorcyclist at curbside opened Gabriela's door, the spell of quiet misery was broken. Gabriela got out, thankful for the fresh air. Tomas got out, his eyes somewhat reddened. He straightened his white shirt and conveyed a quiet determination that seemed to transcend his youth. He seemed to incarnate a grace and peace that could neither be traded nor cultivated.

Kiko got out on his side of the Mercedes, anxiously trying to read his nephew. He came around the car to Tomas and Gabriela and offered to lead Tomas up into the hospital.

Tomas briefly looked at his uncle. With a look of disappointment but without anger he said, 'You owe me an explanation, but not now. As for now, I will follow Comrade Gabriela. You, if you wish, may come along.'

Kiko reddened, then cast up his arms. That seemed signal enough for Gabriela. She decided to lead the way.

Tomas walked at her side and Kiko followed. *Surely, Kiko wouldn't want the students at his high school to see this.*

In the new emotional storm, Gabriela hadn't forgotten her own little voyage, which meant so much to her. She must see her brother. She hadn't forgotten, she couldn't forget, that to see her brother, Beto, she must satisfy state security. If she satisfied their curiosity about Adriana, she would see her brother. But satisfaction must come without betrayal. Was it too much to say she loved Adriana? What else could she call it? How had this love come so fast? Where would it lead? She was certain of this: she would not betray Adriana's faith in her.

She unobtrusively felt for the letters she was carrying under her dress. How could she not notice? They chafed inside her bra. With all the tumult, they'd pretty much disappeared from thought. But she couldn't forget them.

Gabriela was anxious to get to Adriana's room. When she, Tomas, and Kiko came up the stairs, they saw Carlos pacing back and forth at the corner of the corridor leading to B-153. He appeared oblivious of the patients and staff walking about. But he noticed the new arrivals.

'You're back,' said Carlos. Carlos looked Tomas up and down. 'The last time I saw you, you were a boy. Now you are no longer a boy but not quite a man.' Carlos extended his right hand to shake Tomas's right and extended his left to place it on his shoulder. Tomas did not reject either hand, but he looked his uncle straight in the eye as they shook hands.

'You may find that I'm neither fish nor fowl, Uncle Carlos.'

'What does that mean?'

'It means that I'm not classifiable. Time will tell, God permitting.'

'What's this "God" talk?'

Tomas lightened up at his uncle's alarm. 'Nothing to be alarmed about. Sometimes, new fashions are old fashions. That's all.'

Carlos looked at his brother and asked, 'Does your technical high school teach our Cuban youth to speak in riddles? I thought the Icarian was in the business of producing students who would solve riddles for the state.'

'Uncle, a riddle that I didn't know was a riddle is now on its way to resolution. I want to see my mother.'

'So, he's been told?' said Carlos.

'Yes,' said Kiko.

'Then he may proceed,' said Carlos.

'Where is the room?'

Carlos and Kiko pointed to the door of B-153. A state security sentinel stood there, the only person in an otherwise deserted corridor.

Tomas looked at Gabriela. 'You were the last to see my mother alive?'

'Yes.'

'Then, Uncle, may she come with us to the room?'

'Because you have asked, she may,' said Carlos. Then looking at his brother he said, 'My dear brother, you will stay here and stop or delay anyone who might wish to come towards the room.'

Kiko looked slightly embarrassed, but he wasn't about to say *No*. Anyway, as he later confessed, he was glad enough to be away from the accusatory eyes of Tomas. Gabriela assumed Carlos was positioning Kiko to thwart any surprise intrusions while she retrieved the *Nuevo Testamento* from underneath the vacant mattress. But then what about the sentinel? Wouldn't it help to send him away?

As if heeding this unspoken question, Carlos ordered the sentinel to join Kiko at the corridor intersection to prevent anyone from even wandering toward the room. Then Carlos waved Tomas and Gabriela into the room, while he stood at the door. Tomas took a position at the head of the bed, looking intently at his mother. Gabriela couldn't help but notice that Tomas's ears were different than his mother's. And Tomas had much broader shoulders. *But enough,* thought Gabriela. She must retrieve the *Testamento.*

She felt underneath the mattress where she'd left it. Nothing was there. She groped to the right of where it should have been. There was nothing. She felt to the left. Nothing there, too.

She stood up and lifted the mattress, but she could see nothing. How could it be missing? Possibly the

45

sentinel had taken it, but if he had he would have turned it over to Carlos. It seemed unlikely the sentinel would remove anything without direction from Carlos. Possibly some other party – someone outside the state security apparatus – had removed the book but, again, that was highly unlikely without the consent of the apparatus. Today, Carlos was the embodiment of the apparatus.

He must have removed the book. Nothing was to be gained by silence or pretending, or so Gabriela thought. She walked to the doorway, where Carlos stood watching Tomas.

'What did you do with the *Testamento*?' she asked.

Carlos was nonplussed. 'I took it and will dispose of it appropriately. Anyone who thinks otherwise is hazarding his own life. Do you understand?'

Tomas noticed what was happening in the doorway. He approached Gabriela and Carlos.

'Is there something wrong?'

'Much,' said Gabriela, 'but much we cannot solve.'

'Maybe; maybe not,' said Tomas.

'There's nothing to be done,' said Carlos. 'The comrade knows it's best to keep silent about that for which nothing can be done.'

'Is that true, Comrade Gabriela?' asked Tomas.

Gabriela looked at Tomas. 'It's true.'

Doubt clouded his face. 'Perhaps,' said Tomas. Then he walked back to the bedside. He took his

46

mother's hand. By now it must be quite cold. The pallor of her skin was darker than earlier.

'Will the staff be removing the body soon?' asked Gabriela.

'I've told them to come at 4.30. It's 4.20 now. When they arrive, we can have no further delays.' Carlos held his arms akimbo to underscore the finality of what he'd said.

What could Gabriela do? She wanted that *Testamento*. For Carlos, it was at best an embarrassment. He had no business destroying it. Gabriela was certain Adriana wouldn't begrudge her using it as a key to visiting Beto one last time. Adriana was selfless and generous. She'd testified more than once that God was generous, too. No doubt Adriana would suggest prayer now. She had been so kind and caring to Gabriela. Not that she was the first such person to Gabriela. Beto had come close to that. But somehow, Adriana had not only embodied loveliness, she had articulated it in a way to which Gabriela was receptive.

Adriana had often said we become more the image of God the more we let His love flow through us. Gabriela didn't feel any love now. She didn't hate Carlos, but she did despise him. He was so dishonest, yet so powerful and manipulative, all too much like her own father. Carlos was clever, too, but to what good? Without the *Testamento* to hand over to the local state security office, how could she hope to visit Beto? She abhorred the thought of betraying Adriana by giving up any of her letters.

Would that Adriana's God would deliver! Was that a prayer?

Tomas pulled back the bedsheet tucked up to his mother's chin. He wanted a fuller view of his mother, at least from the waist up.

'What did she die from?' asked Tomas. He hadn't asked in the car.

'Cancer, breast cancer. She had a recurrence of breast cancer that had been treated several years ago,' said Gabriela. 'She had dizzy spells when your father and mother were here in Santiago a little over a month ago,' said Gabriela. And then she realized she'd said too much.

'My father. My father is alive?'

'Yes. But I don't know where.'

Tomas looked from Gabi to Carlos, who'd been following all this from the doorway. 'I *will* find my father,' said Tomas.

'Tomas, perhaps. The state has invested much in your education. The revolution looks for medical advances from those like you who've been given your education. You will honor your birth mother more if you seek to fight the cancer that she died from than if you work out your anger at my brother Kiko. He hasn't been honest about your mother or father, but you shouldn't be angry with the revolution. No one from the party ever told him he should deceive you about your parents. On the contrary.'

'But the state approved my adoption.'

'My sister and her husband relinquished you,' said Carlos.

Tomas bowed his head. He said softly, 'She was my mother.' He turned toward the bed, looked at her remains, then leaned over and gave her a kiss on her right cheek. He turned and stretched to plant a kiss on her left cheek but lost his balance and fell across her torso.

Gabriela gasped. Carlos looked slightly disgusted. Kiko happened to enter the room, surprised at the disarray. Then Tomas stood up radiating a kind of joy.

'She's wearing something, a necklace or something. I just felt it. Comrade Gabriela, would you please remove it so we can see what it is?' Tomas asked, looking from Gabriela to Carlos. 'I assume, Uncle, that that can be done.'

Carlos shrugged. 'Go ahead,' he said, looking at Gabriela. Then he jerked his head, signaling Tomas and Kiko to join him in the hallway. They did.

Gabriela opened Adriana's hospital gown and pulled out the golden dolphin pendant that Adriana had talked about one afternoon. Gabriela wanted to examine it. *Why hadn't she asked to see it when Adriana had talked about it?*

Gabriela groped behind Adriana's neck to find the clasp. She managed to open the clasp and remove the necklace, placing it on the side table before re-buttoning the gown. No sooner had she done this than she was startled by Carlos. He plucked the pendant from the table.

'Yes, I remember this,' he said. 'It was a gift from Adan, I don't remember when. I saw it on her before.'

Gabriela went out into the hall to fetch Tomas and Kiko, who'd walked away from Tomas.

'What you felt, Tomas, was a pendant given years ago by your father to your mother. Your mother told me about it. Your uncle is looking at it now.'

Kiko followed Gabriela and Tomas back into the room. Carlos was still examining the pendant. It was a locket. Inside the locket was a picture of a three-year-old boy. Carlos had already removed something else that had been in the locket, a very small scroll.

Carlos passed on the locket for others to examine while he examined the scroll. He exclaimed, 'I can't make anything out of this. This paper's covered with lines that may be micrographics. Our experts will have to look at this.'

Gabriela asked if she could look at the scroll. Carlos seemed surprised but more surprisingly he handed her the scroll. She looked it over. There were numerous lines on its front and back, arranged as if they might be writing. If there was any writing, it was too small to be legible even under an ordinary magnifying glass.

Kiko asked to look at the scroll. Gabriela handed it to him, then peered over Tomas's shoulder as he looked at the pendant. On the back of the dolphin were Greek letters: ΙΧΘΥΣ.

'What does it say?' asked Gabriela. While she could speak and read German and French and some English and Russian, she had had no reason to learn Greek.

Kiko said, 'It reads *ichthys*. *Ichthys* is the ancient Greek term for fish. But the dolphin isn't a fish.'

Gabriela asked, 'What do you mean?'

'It's not a fish. It's a creature of the sea but neither fish nor fowl. It needs to come to the surface to supply itself with oxygen.'

'So?' said Gabriela.

Tomas said, 'There's more here than meets the eye. *Ichthys* is the old Greek for fish, yes, but it had additional uses in the ancient world.'

Gabriela was puzzled. She asked, 'Do you read Greek?'

'It helps in the sciences,' said Tomas.

'You know a lot,' she replied.

Tomas smiled shyly. 'We learn many Greek letters at the technical high school. I know of *ichthys* from elsewhere.' He left it at that.

Gabriela wondered what would be done with the pendant. As if in answer, Carlos approached Kiko.

'My dear brother, I'll take that scroll now.'

Kiko handed it to his brother.

Carlos continued, 'I'm flying to Havana this evening and will turn this over to our lab. We can all hope a microscopic reading of this scroll will provide a list of the subversives *her* husband worked with.

'Give me the locket, Tomas.'

Tomas looked up at his uncle. 'I would like to keep it, Uncle, if I could.'

'You will get it back eventually. But this locket and the scroll constitute evidence about the machinations of your father... and your mother. The scroll and pendant go together.'

'Like mother and child? Or like father and child?' asked Tomas.

'What's that supposed to mean?' said Carlos. 'Every child must eventually leave home. Your parents were criminals. Better that you left them sooner than later.'

'I still wish to see my father.'

'If you can make your way to Havana quickly, I'm sure that can be arranged.'

'Why quickly?' asked Tomas.

'Your father's trial will be this coming Monday. I doubt he'll be in Havana past Monday.'

'How am I going to get there?'

'Perhaps you'll find a way,' said Carlos smiling. He placed the scroll inside the locket and snapped it shut. 'Good day,' he said and off he went.

'I will see my father by Monday.'

Kiko looked aghast. 'Are you crazy?'

'No. And you know why.'

4.

No sooner had Carlos left then two white-jacketed men came trundling into B-153 with a squeaky metal gurney, which now plugged the doorway.

'We're here to remove the body,' said one.

'Gotta get her down,' said the second.

'Where are you going to take the body?' asked Tomas.

Neither of the jackets looked at Tomas or Gabriela or Kiko. Their eyes were drawn to the corpse.

'Down to the loading dock, of course,' said one.

'Then what will happen?' asked Gabriela.

The other shrugged his shoulders. 'They'll take it to a crematorium. Never been there, comrade. Step aside, please.'

'There should be a memorial service,' said Gabriela.

'That's your business,' said the other.

The two white jackets positioned the gurney alongside Adriana's bed. One ripped the cover sheet away from the deceased. The second grasped beneath the armpits, the first beneath the calves. They pulled the body to the edge of the bed. The one near the head repositioned himself to grasp the armpits from behind.

The second at the calves pulled the bottom of the torso so that it was partially on the gurney, then he quickly backed to the feet. From these positions, the two pulled the body onto the gurney.

Gabriela winced. The ballet she'd just witnessed suggested the two were well-practiced in removals. The thought that Adriana had become a mere carcass was one Gabriela would not live with. She looked at Tomas. How was he taking it?

She was shocked to see he was crossing himself in the traditional fashion, as the old women still did in their lonely vigils at deserted churches. Where had the boy, no, this young man, learned to do this sort of thing? Kiko seemed to read the question in her face or to be asking it himself as he glanced at Tomas. Tomas looked up at his uncle, then at Gabriela, and then at his mother being wheeled by the white jackets.

The three watched the two wheel the one through the doorway into the corridor. Their eyes were fixed on the doorway until the gurney was to be seen and heard no more.

Tomas backed to the nearest wall and slid down until he sat on the floor. In some ways, thought Gabriela, he's still a schoolboy. Yet she was hardly three years older than him, perhaps less than that.

Tomas shook his head and then looked up at Gabriela and Kiko. 'We've got to get going,' he said.

'Going where?' asked Kiko.

'Going back home. Going home to pack,' said Tomas, standing up.

'You're not coming along, Tomas. You can't. The conference I'm attending in Havana doesn't permit me to bring family along.'

'From what I've learned today, I'm no longer family.'

'Don't be peevish. Pamela and I adopted you years ago and, thanks to us, you've got a future.'

'I've lost a past. I don't know what to make of it now, Uncle. But I know I want to see my father. You will take me with you to Havana because you owe me that. I have much to be thankful for – for what you and Aunt Pamela have done for me. But you were dishonest with me. I think you owe it to me to take me along.'

'Don't force the issue.'

'I will go by other means if you don't take me.'

'Oh, you will? How will you do that?'

'That's a riddle for you to solve.'

Kiko didn't reply. Tomas got up off the floor. Then Kiko said, 'Let me think about it. It's getting late and I'm sure this young comrade wishes to go home.'

'Actually, I must first report…' And then Gabriela shut up. She didn't want to alienate Tomas or Kiko. They meant something to Adriana, especially Tomas. She didn't want to look like some toady of state security. But if she had any hope of seeing her own brother, she'd have to report to the local state security office before nightfall. That was *her* business, not theirs.

Anyway, she had no intention of betraying Adriana or Tomas or Kiko, albeit she wasn't sure about Kiko. He'd lied to Adriana's son.

'You must first report what where?' asked Tomas.

Gabriela suggested the three should adjourn to the park near the hospital. Kiko and Tomas agreed. As they headed for the stairs, Tomas ran back to the doorway of B-153. He looked around the room, then caught up with the other two as they were about to descend the stairs.

When the three were outside, Tomas repeated his question, 'You must first report what where?'

Gabriela ignored him.

The city was much busier than it had been earlier. People were traveling home from work. As always on a weekday, the homeward bustle seemed more intense.

Once the three had found a park bench, Tomas asked, 'Who are you having to report to?'

'I must report to state security,' said Gabriela. *What could be gained by hiding the fact?*

'State security!' said Tomas.

Kiko was seated between Tomas and Gabriela, otherwise, she supposed, Tomas might have edged away.

'Let me explain,' said Gabriela. 'My brother has been imprisoned at a labor station. It's called "Estacion ES."'

'What does "ES" stand for?' asked Kiko.

'I don't know,' she replied.

'Where is it?' asked Tomas.

'Near Havana. Anyway, my brother, Beto, is a doctor. My father is a doctor, too, and a party member. My father will have nothing to do with my brother. Nothing. They are such opposites. Anyway, it was my brother who got me to volunteer at the hospital. And it was my brother, unfortunately, who became politically active. He was arrested about a year and a half ago. He was convicted, then sent off to prison.'

Kiko stood up and thrust his hands in his jacket pockets. He looked at Gabriela with some alarm.

Gabriela continued, 'When Adriana was brought into the hospital, I was told I would have to gain her trust and ferret information from her if I wanted any hope of seeing Beto. The local state security men told me I must pass on any information I obtained from Adriana.'

Tomas looked away. Kiko looked relieved.

'But I've passed nothing along to state security.'

Tomas still wouldn't look at Gabriela. She wanted to tell Tomas about the *Testamento,* which he knew nothing about. What might Kiko do if she talked about it now? Would he report her talk to Carlos? Would that get her into hot water?

Gabriela said, 'I want to make sure the local state security office knows of the dolphin pendant we found. I have to report something to them.'

Gabriela knew she was pleading in effect for forgiveness. She continued, 'The pendant is now in the hands of state security anyway, so I won't be divulging something new to them. Having done my part, I'm hoping they'll let me see my brother.'

Tomas looked at Gabriela. 'Your brother means a lot to you?'

'Of course.'

'So, you too have a reason to go west.'

"I do,' she replied. 'I'm told he's very ill, perhaps dying. They won't tell me what ails him. They'd promised to let me see him Saturday or Sunday.'

'How are you going to get to Estacion ES?' asked Kiko.

'I hadn't figured that out.'

'But you'd figured out how to use my mother to see your brother,' said Tomas.

'You've got that half right and all wrong at the same time. I had little choice in the matter if I wanted to see my brother. I would never have tried to use Adriana. She became dear to me. Comrade Marquez, she left a letter for you – which I'm not reporting to state security.'

'A letter?' Kiko asked. 'Where is it?'

'I can't produce it now,' said Gabriela. What she meant was that she had no way of producing, much less finding, the letter without indecent exposure.

Kiko asked, 'Can you produce the letter soon? I'd like to see it sooner than later. If I could, I'd like to see it before leaving for Havana tomorrow. I'll be seeing my parents in Havana. I intend to be out of Santiago by five thirty in the morning and I can't ask you to get up that early.'

'You can if I come along,' said Gabriela.

'Would that be a condition of my receiving my sister's letter?'

'It can't be,' replied Gabriela. 'I promised your sister to pass along this letter. Without conditions.'

Kiko asked, 'Do you have this letter at home? I could drop you off at home and pick up the letter.'

'I don't have the letter at home.' *How true but untrue!*

Kiko asked, 'Where shall we meet you in the morning?'

'*We*?' asked Tomas.

'I thought you wanted to come to Havana with me,' said Kiko to Tomas.

'I can come?'

'Yes.'

'And this comrade?' asked Tomas.

'She can come, too, if she wishes. Do you have someone you can stay with in Havana?'

'An aunt, the twin sister of the aunt I live with here in Santiago,' replied Gabriela.

'Good, but how will you get back to Santiago? The conference I'm attending is on Monday and Tuesday. I won't return here until later next week.'

'Monday and Tuesday, in other words Christmas Eve and Christmas Day.'

'We've advanced beyond the feudal and capitalistic primitivism of Christmas,' said Kiko.

'You sound shrill when you talk that way,' said Tomas.

Gabriela didn't want to be drawn into a religious discussion. 'I'll return on my own, if necessary,' she said. 'I can stay with my aunt until Wednesday. I only need my boss's permission.' She didn't say her aunt didn't celebrate Christmas. Her boss did, quietly.

Kiko and Gabriela agreed he would pick up Gabriela in the morning at the central library. He explained he'd be driving a Volkswagen microbus recently donated to the Escuela Icarian.

How Gabriela would get to Beto's penal camp was an open question. She imagined she could catch a bus from Havana for part of the journey to the camp. A trip to Havana would be for nothing if she couldn't visit her brother.

When Gabriela parted from Kiko and Tomas, Kiko was much warmer than he'd been all day. Tomas was reserved and hard to read. He was a puzzle. *So be it.*

Securing a pass to visit her brother proved far less difficult than Gabriela had imagined. Carlos had already notified the local state security bureau of the dolphin pendant with its suspect scroll. He'd even mentioned that Gabriela had been helpful; he'd ordered that she be given a pass to see Beto. She didn't have to wait for it to be produced.

As she left the state security office, Gabriela couldn't help but wonder why Adriana's brothers were proving so helpful. Carlos had gone beyond what she would have expected (which was nothing). And Kiko seemed to have become sympathetic to her plight. At least he'd accepted her as a passenger to Havana. She couldn't afford to scorn this help, even if she'd developed her reservations about both Carlos and Kiko. And what was she to make of Tomas, the inscrutable one?

The night would be short and busy.

Autopista Nacional

5.

Kiko had underscored the need for an early start. He wanted to make the trip to Havana in one day. He'd insisted Gabriela be ready to be picked up at five thirty in the morning. Her Aunt Felisa's taxi-operating friend drove Gabriela in the pre-dawn to Santiago's central library. Cash and some homemade *pastelitos de fruta bomba* had persuaded the friend to coax his 1954 Chevrolet into service at this early hour.

Gabriela beat Kiko to the library. She didn't mind. Dawn and dusk were Gabriela's favorite times of day. She thought of them as corners of the day. They delighted her for their rich colors, perhaps all the more so since the colorations were so brief. Gabriela stood under a streetlight at the library entrance. Besides the small travel bag at her feet and a purse in hand, she'd brought along a canvas shopping bag. The bag was loaded with treats she and her aunt had made during the night.

The eastern horizon was just beginning to lighten when Kiko drove up in the Icarian's VW microbus. Its skirts were light blue; its broadsides and roof were cream white. Tomas was slouched in the back seat. *Perhaps because of the early hour,* thought Gabriela.

Kiko jumped out to put Gabriela's duffle bag in the rear of the VW. He suggested she ride up front with him. She wondered whether she'd be able to take a nap up there. She wasn't about to ask.

She took the front passenger seat, placing the shopping bag between her feet. Kiko appeared curious about the bag's contents, which gave off enticing aromas. But he was intent on getting out of the city and onto the Autopista Nacional, the trans-Cuban highway that would convey them to Havana. Arriving in Havana by the other corner of the day wasn't a certainty, even in this, the dry season.

Gabriela had never imagined taking a long auto journey with two relative strangers. *Desperation fathers new strategies, new companions, new horizons. Best to look at the bright side,* that's what her mother had always said. With that in mind, she removed the napkin from the top of the shopping bag. Besides, *pastelitos de frutabomba,* she and her aunt had fixed *frituras de ñame,* yam fritters blended with herbs and onions. They'd made *tostones,* fried green plantains, and *maduros,* fried sweet plantains. Gabriela hoped the treats would show her gratitude for being taken to Havana. She asked Kiko whether he'd had breakfast.

He hadn't, other than a cup of coffee. He was happy to sample the fare. The talk of food served to waken Tomas from his semi-slumber. He even said, 'Good morning.' Gabriela provided fresh napkins to allow the men to spread the treats on their laps. Gabriela noted that Tomas prayed and crossed himself before eating. Kiko did no such thing.

She thought of something attributed to Albert Einstein. Her physics teacher had said the great scientist had said one of the most basic decisions anyone could ever make was whether or not there was a benevolence behind the universe. If he had lived long enough, said the teacher, Einstein would have acknowledged the benevolence of the revolution. Gabriela thought revolutionary claims wouldn't have been what Einstein had in mind. He had something greater in mind. That probably wouldn't have included the likes of her transportation to Havana. Nonetheless, Gabriela was gratified for the benevolence, whatever its source.

'Comrade Gabriela, this is very good, very good. Thank you for these tasty treats,' said Tomas huskily.

Gabriela appreciated this. Did he want more? He did. So did Kiko. It was if the two hadn't eaten in days. She asked Kiko if he had any favorites. He especially liked the *frituras de ñame*. Tomas said he liked everything. Not to be bested, Kiko chimed in likewise. But Tomas said he especially liked the *maduros* and the *pastelitos*.

'So you have a sweet tooth,' said Gabriela.

Tomas smiled. *He has a sweet smile*, thought Gabriela. But then don't most Cubans have sweet smiles? What was a smile without sweetness? She looked at Kiko. She hadn't seen him smile in the less than twenty-four hours she'd known him. He was always so intense and intent. But he had a kind face. Was *kind* the framework for a smile, or was *smile* already in *kind?* What of *sweet?* If Kiko smiled, would the smile be sweet? And where would all this gymnastics land her?

Sometime later, she looked at Tomas. He'd taken up reading a book. What was it? He held it up so that she could see its title. Coincidentally, it was a book by Einstein, *Introduccion a La Relatividad Especial,* An Introduction to Special Relativity. No surprise, given that Tomas was a student at the Icarian. She was amazed that Tomas could read anything as they sped along.

She found herself becoming uneasy with Kiko's driving. She had never traveled so fast in her life. Her anxiety worked against the sleepiness that might otherwise have conquered her. On the bright side, she wasn't often able to be out in the country or, more accurately, out on a highway. Mostly, they encountered truck traffic. As the day progressed, the highway became populated with Cubans along its edge: hitchhikers, vendors, farmers, some bicyclists, all moving to their own rhythms.

In the mid-morning, Kiko brought the VW to a stop in front of a small-town gas station, where they refueled and bought cups of coffee. After imbibing the coffee, Kiko seemed not only more alert but more relaxed behind the wheel. Perhaps he was less fearful of drifting off to sleep. Gabriela felt more alert than she'd been all morning. This seemed a good time to produce the letter from Adriana for Kiko.

Gabriela pulled out the letter from her purse. Despite using an ordinary ballpoint pen and a clipboard, Adriana had produced the most elegantly handwritten letters Gabriela had ever seen. The letter to Kiko was the only one of the five she'd asked Gabriela to write. It was the last one Adriana composed. By the last she could hardly write. Except she managed to affix her signature to Kiko's letter. Dictating the letter and signing it had been emotionally taxing. Or so Gabriela recalled.

'Here's the letter I promised to pass on to you, Comrade Marquez.'

'From Adri?'

'Yes, comrade.'

'"Kiko" will do,' said Kiko glancing at Gabriela. 'Did you see the letter before it was sealed up?'

'Adriana dictated the letter to me.'

'That's too bad. She had beautiful penmanship.'

'I know,' said Gabriela. 'I've seen some of her work.'

'I remember her taking a course in calligraphy when we were kids.'

'How could she do that?' asked Gabriela.

'Our parents have both been with the University of Havana. My father still teaches there. And my mother works there part-time. Adriana took a calligraphy course at the university even though she was only ten or eleven. My parents' connections enabled her to be enrolled.'

'What does your father teach?'

'Law. He's also served on the bench. My mother has been in a statistical bureau at the university.'

'Would you want me to read the letter now or would you prefer to read it yourself later?'

'Sounds like you'd like to read it now. What do you think, Tomas?' asked Kiko. 'Tomas.'

Tomas apparently hadn't been listening. He'd taken his shoes off and had his feet up on the seat. *Relatividad* was propped against his forelegs.

'Tomas.'

Tomas responded, 'Yes, what is it?'

'Would you want to hear a letter from your mother to me? Is it of interest?' asked Kiko.

'Of course. I would like to read it myself. But if you wish, Comrade Gabriela, please read it,' said Tomas.

'Gabriela or Gabi would do,' said Gabriela.

'If you would,' said Kiko.

Gabriela nodded and opened the envelope with a small penknife. Her father said traveling with a small knife was essential. It was one of the few pieces of wisdom he'd ever shared with her. She'd taken it to heart. You never knew when you might need a penknife to open something or to help serve food or do other things.

She removed Adriana's letter from the envelope. She began, 'Dear Frederico.'

'So, she used my baptismal name, not my everyday name?' said Kiko.

'That's right.'

'I don't think she's called me "Frederico" in years. Read on, please.'

'By the time my dear friend Gabriela has provided you this letter, others will have pronounced me dead. I may be dead in their eyes or yours, but I am confident I will be more alive than ever, thanks be to our Lord. I know you do not believe that. Perhaps you never will. This, my belief in the living, redeeming Lord, is perhaps the greatest gift Adan brought to our marriage. Together, Adan and I have given our lives to a service that will outlast anything in our country or this world. Everyone drawn in service to our Lord must give up things, sometimes at great cost.'

Gabriela looked over at Kiko to see if he wanted her to pause. He was intent as ever on the road, yet all ears. He asked, 'Is that it?'

'There's more.'

'Read to the end, please.'

Gabriela did. 'Adan and I gave up our son, Tomas, to upbringing by you and Pamela. In one way or another, not a day has passed that we haven't grieved, at least in some small way, our loss. Pamela, God bless her, has been kind to me all these years, kinder than you would have ever allowed. Thanks be to her and ultimately to God, Tomas will become someone more than you could imagine, my dear Frederico. God has greater plans for him, for each of us, for even you, more than you could imagine. God's plans do not rest on slogans or fear. They are sustained by His word and realized through His love. In the Spirit of His love, I have prayed these many years that you and Pamela would grow in His grace. In parting now, I still pray that. Forgive me for my sins against you; I forgive you for your sins against me. Grow in the hope, faith, and love of our Lord Jesus Christ. God became incarnate in Jesus. Through His Spirit become incarnate in God.

'Always, Adriana.'

'She never gave up,' said Kiko. 'I take some solace she died with a measure of peace.'

'May I see the letter, Com… Gabi?' asked Tomas.

Gabriela handed the letter to Tomas. He sat bolt upright looking at it.

'I think I know the handwriting of this signature,' he said. 'It looks the same as Betty's. It can't be.'

'Who's Betty?' asked Kiko.

'Mama's dear friend, who took such an interest in me,' said Tomas. 'She would write at least once each month, sometimes twice.'

'I've never heard of this Betty,' said Kiko.

'No,' said Tomas. 'When I was smaller, Mama would read from parts of the letters. Each letter contained a chapter from the *Testamento* written out. By the time I was five or six I could read them. I practiced each night.'

Kiko frowned.

Tomas continued, 'I asked to meet the lady who sent these letters when I was seven or eight. I couldn't. And Mama said I must keep the letters and excerpts from Betty a secret... otherwise, Betty might get in trouble. I didn't want that to happen. Only in recent months when the letters from Betty stopped did I seek to find out more about her. Mama told me nothing.

'All these years, 'Betty' was my mother, my birth mother.'

Kiko said, 'I'm learning more about my family than I like. I may have to learn things about my own school I'd rather not have to learn, too.'

'Meaning?' said Tomas.

'Meaning? Perhaps you can explain,' said Kiko, 'how a photograph of the archbishop of San Salvador appeared in a restroom of the school.'

Tomas said nothing.

'Do you know anything about this prank?' asked Kiko.

'You consider posting a picture of Bishop Romero a prank?' replied Tomas.

'So, you know *who* the archbishop of San Salvador is?'

'I'm not the only student who knows. I'll wager every student at Escuela Icarian knows of Oscar Romero and who he is.'

'What's that supposed to mean?'

'It means different things to different students. For some, Bishop Romero is a curiosity. For them, he seems in the vanguard for justice, when we have all been taught here in Cuba that the church abets injustice. He's reported to be speaking out on behalf of the oppressed. Some believe he's a fool, that he will be suppressed, maybe even killed,' said Tomas.

'He will be suppressed,' said Kiko. 'You can count on that.'

'Yes, that's likely. He wouldn't be the first such priest, bishop, even archbishop to suffer for speaking out. In that way he's a fool, a fool for God. So, there are those who look to the archbishop as something more than exotic, as someone to be admired.'

'Admired?' said Kiko, turning back to look at Tomas. There was no way Kiko could see Tomas. Tomas sat right behind his uncle.

Gabriela asked, 'Would you like me to drive, comrade?' She was becoming concerned Kiko might be distracted by this conversation.

'No,' said Kiko. 'What do you mean, Tomas, by *admired*?'

'To be honored, to be worthy of imitation,' said Tomas.

'In El Salvador perhaps but only perhaps there. For all his talk, what do you think the archbishop will accomplish? Very little if anything. It would be far better if our countrymen could liberate that miserable little country and place it under a revolutionary government to accelerate the development of new norms, new institutions, and new horizons for that people. They are to be pitied. They have so much to learn from us.'

'And we have nothing to learn from them? Nothing to learn from the archbishop?' asked Tomas.

'Those are not only silly questions, they're dangerous. For all that the revolution and state have invested in your education, I would hope you'd have a more sensible, more grateful attitude. There are many who would envy the schooling you've received, the prospects that await you.'

'Oh, I'm not ungrateful. But I'm puzzled and distressed that things have been hidden from me... important things. Why did you adopt me, Papa? Uncle. Why tell me that my real parents were dead?'

'You were a brilliant little boy out of place, who in the right place would be a fruitful citizen of this country,' said Kiko.

'I wasn't looking for an answer – that answer – right now,' said Tomas. 'I don't think a real answer can be encapsulated in a sentence or a formula.'

'Well, the answer will never change,' said Kiko, 'however or whenever you seek it.'

Gabriela was both fascinated and discomforted to be listening to this conversation, marveling how she had been brought into the intimacies of a family perhaps now coming apart. What was she to make of it? What was she to do?

She assumed Kiko must be embarrassed to have these facts come to the surface, even more so with a stranger present. Yet, Tomas was perhaps as much a stranger now to Kiko as was she.

She looked back at Tomas. He hadn't re-curled himself in his Einstein. He was staring out the window as the microbus sped westward on the broad Autopista Nacional. What was to be said?

For the next half-hour, she looked at the pedestrians of every description that passed along the road margin. She decided she would count them on one side of the highway, perhaps to 100. Then she'd switch to the pedestrians on the other side of the highway, counting to 100. It was silly but it was a way of occupying the 'space' in her mind. She hated empty spaces. The counting had a soporific effect. Long before she reached the first 100, about the time they passed a farmer leading a burro, she fell asleep.

She awoke sometime later, perhaps close to noon, when she realized the microbus wasn't moving. They were at a gas station and café in a small town just off the *autopista*. With a cup of coffee in hand, Kiko was talking with the station attendant, trading comments about the winter baseball season in Cuba. Gabriela looked in the back seat. When she didn't see Tomas, she turned around to see if he might be right behind her. He was, curled up sleeping now on the shady side of the Volkswagen.

After they were back on the road, Kiko seemed eager for conversation. For starters, he asked Gabriela if she had an interest in baseball. She said she did. Her interest grew from watching her brother Beto play when she was growing up. He'd been a superb pitcher in his school years.

'This brother of yours, how exactly did he end up at a penal camp?' asked Kiko.

Gabriela wasn't eager to talk about Beto's recent past. But having learned Marquez family secrets she felt obliged to be forthright about her own family. She replied, 'He was caught handing out leaflets denouncing Cuba's support for the rebel government in Angola. The leaflets claimed this was a new form of imperialism against the Africans.'

'Such leaflets would get anyone in trouble,' said Kiko.

'It was all the worse,' said Gabriela, 'because my brother is black.'

Kiko was startled. 'How can that be? You don't look one bit African.'

'You see,' she said, 'my brother is strictly speaking a half-brother. We share the same father. His mother died from complications at birth. About a year later, our father married my mother, who had me about four years later. My brother and I have always been close. He was always so patient and kind with me. I realize now how exceptional he was and is. I can't tell you how much it hurts to know he's been imprisoned for passing out those leaflets. He would have had a wonderful career if he hadn't passed them out. Perhaps, he wouldn't be sick and dying.'

'What do you think of that?' asked Kiko.

'The leaflets... the imprisonment... the dying?'

'Not the dying. Of course, anyone would be upset by that. Do you know for a fact he's dying? What's he dying of?'

'I don't know much of anything. I do know this. I've not received any letters once he was sent off, except the one that arrived last month. He said he was very ill and perhaps dying. He didn't say from what. He said the authorities had told him one immediate member of his family could come for a visit. When I contacted the authorities, they wouldn't tell me what was wrong with my brother.

'My father has sworn never to speak again with Beto. But then he hardly speaks with me. We live apart. I live with an aunt, as you know. She encouraged me to visit Beto, if I could take time off from my work with the tourist bureau in Santiago.'

'Does the bureau know about your brother, about his being imprisoned?'

'They do. But that's offset by my father's special work as a party member. So Beto's status hasn't hurt me so far.'

'Party membership helps or more than helps. It's critical to success,' said Kiko, looking back at Tomas. Taking his right hand off the wheel, he placed it against his cheek then pointed at Tomas. Gabriela thereby supposed Tomas was still asleep.

She wondered whether Kiko wished his 'son' to be in an even deeper sleep, unaware of secrets he now knew. She supposed Kiko might be anxious about Tomas's religious proclivities. Kiko must have noticed Tomas's crossing himself.

'So, you're a party member,' said Gabriela.

'Of course. My parents are members, my brother, too. Only our late sister went off the rails. She was once a party member.'

'What happened?'

'You *are* curious. You already know much more about my family than almost anyone else in Cuba. You might as well know more about Adriana.

'Adriana and Adan were married when she was twenty-two and he twenty-nine. He was then in the Cuban merchant marine, where he served as a chief engineer. He'd traveled widely and continued in the merchant marine for a couple of years into the marriage. Then my sister and Adan volunteered for duty in Bolivia. Adan spent much of his time helping villagers dig water wells and the like. Adriana went into medical service. They left Tomas behind with my wife and me when they volunteered for service in Bolivia.'

'Why did they do that?' asked Gabriela. 'They must have been real party zealots. Why did they leave Tomas behind?'

'The state gave them no choice about going down there.'

'Nonetheless, it must have been hard for Adriana to give up Tomas,' said Gabriela.

'They went for the sake of the revolution,' said Kiko.

'And when was this?' asked Gabriela.

'A few years before Che Guevera plunked himself down in the Bolivian jungles.'

'Where he waged a guerilla war against the Bolivian government,' added Gabriela. 'What did Adriana think of Che? I can't believe she thought much of him, even when she was a party zealot.'

Kiko said, 'His activities may have inspired a number of Cubans, but not Adriana and Adan. They were never what I'd call *guerrilleros*. Adriana was a nurse, by the way.'

'She never told me that,' said Gabriela. 'I should have figured. She was so kind and selfless.'

'Those aren't necessary attributes of nurses,' said Kiko.

'No, but they're helpful,' said Gabriela.

'Yes, I suppose so. Where was I? Oh, yes, in the Bolivian jungles. When Che became active down there, our government decided to keep Adan and Adriana and other such volunteers present as reminders to the Bolivians that the Cuban government had good intentions, despite the freewheeling Comrade Che.'

'I can't imagine it was easy being volunteers down there then,' said Gabriela.

'It wasn't. These Cuban goodwill teams were under constant surveillance by the Bolivian authorities. To assuage Bolivian concerns, the Cuban medical teams were told to work with Christian medical missionaries already in the country.

'In Adriana and Adan's case, however, the Cubans were converted by the missionaries, albeit without the knowledge of the Cuban government. When Che was killed by the Bolivians in 1967, the Cuban medical missionary teams were thrown out of the country. Adan went back to serving in the merchant marine for a while but now he got involved in smuggling Bibles and New Testaments into Cuba, though I didn't know that at the time. Carlos may have suspected something. Adan was on a sea voyage when Adriana was caught up in a state security raid on a house church.'

'And that had ramifications for Tomas,' said Gabriela.

'It did. When his parents returned, he was with them only a short time before Adriana and eventually Adan were arrested. While his parents had been in Bolivia, we discovered that Tomas was a genius. He was already reading quite copiously at the age of four. I arranged to have him tested. We concluded his talents ought to be developed in science. When his parents returned, they concurred he should be given special schooling. Once his parents were imprisoned, he was returned to us to live with us.

'Imprisonment must have been hard on Adriana,' said Gabriela. 'She never talked about it though.'

'It was hard on them both, I think,' said Kiko. 'During their first prison term, they voluntarily gave up the boy in return for reduced sentences and under the condition that Pamela and I adopt him. We were happy to do so. Adriana and Adan came to regret this decision. They pleaded with me to reverse the adoption. But I wouldn't do it. Pamela especially became attached to Tomas. Anyway, Carlos forbade me to consent to any reversal. He was relentless in hounding them back into jail. They were *socially unsuitable*, he would say. And the state, of course, concurs. Adriana and Adan never had the resources or the position to get Tomas back.'

'In contrast,' said Gabriela, 'you think you do?'

Kiko appeared startled by the implied comparison. 'Perhaps, I don't. But as you can see, I'm trying.'

As they drove on, Kiko became surprisingly open about his fears and hopes. Kiko's compulsion to confess his sins before Gabriela was so at odds with the inhuman coldness of his brother. She found Kiko's vulnerabilities endearing and forgivable. But then seeking forgiveness from a stranger was easier than seeking it from family or friends, or so she thought.

Somewhere past noon, Kiko pulled off the *autopista* and navigated the streets of a larger town. He parked the VW in front of a small hostel facing a plaza. The night before, he'd called ahead and ordered some hot pork sandwiches ready for takeaway and some coffee (which he put in a thermos bottle). He said he'd learned of this place a number of years previously. The price was right, the servings were generous, food was always tasty, and no offense was taken at travelers who wanted but a brief respite from the road.

After Kiko fetched a bagful of hot offerings from the town's best public kitchen, he headed the VW back toward the highway. As he began to accelerate, he spotted three soldiers along the road, looking to hitchhike. Kiko brought the VW off to the shoulder, just ahead of the three. Gabriela wondered how all three could fit into the microbus, especially since the area behind Tomas was jammed with luggage.

Two of the three soldiers were headed to Ciego de Avila, just down the *autopista*. The third was headed to Santa Clara, further west. Kiko told the soldiers they could pile in the back seat with his son. They did. Even with one soldier sitting on the lap of another, Tomas looked scrunched. On her lap, Gabriela held the bag with the hot sandwiches. The aroma from the sandwiches was enticing, but Gabriela didn't hand them out. She didn't know if Kiko wanted portions offered to the soldiers. She thought it would be rude to pass sandwiches only to Tomas and Kiko. Perhaps to cover up his own uncertainty, Kiko chattered at a speed slightly faster than the VW. He regaled everyone with tales of his stint in the army.

As the two soldiers got out in Ciego de Avila, Tomas suggested the remaining soldier might like sitting up front with his father – the better to trade army tales. The soldier, whose first name was Enrico, assented. Kiko didn't have a chance to nix the idea. Once the soldier was settled up front and Gabriela in the back, Kiko suggested she divvy up the food. There were only three cups for coffee.

Tomas said he'd forgo the coffee. So did Enrico, but Kiko insisted he have some. Gabriela poured it out of the thermos. Gabriela couldn't remember having ever eaten in such a fashion while traveling cross-country. But then she could count the number of such trips on two hands and those trips were by bus or train.

While Kiko and Enrico chatted away up front, Tomas and Gabriela ate in silence for several miles. Then Tomas asked, 'Again, how long has your brother been you-know-where?'

She was relieved Tomas hadn't named her brother's place. The soldier might recognize the name as one associated with *the system*. Perhaps Tomas's discretion didn't matter. Kiko and Enrico shared a comradery that deafened them to the backseat two.

Gabi said, 'He's been in about eighteen months.'

'I'm sorry,' said Tomas.

'Thank you. I appreciate getting this ride. I don't know how I'd be able to make it without the help of your...' *What should she say? Papa? Uncle?* Gabriela looked at Tomas as she swirled her right hand in the air.

'My uncle,' said he.

'Your uncle,' said she.

Tomas took a big bite out of his sandwich. For another five miles or so, the two in the back spoke not a word while up front all the world became fodder for frank discussion, that is all the world except Cuba itself.

After a while, Gabi asked, 'Are you sure you wouldn't like some coffee? You must be thirsty.'

Tomas shrugged his shoulders but smiled. 'I can go without,' he said.

Gabriela took that as a signal he'd like some. She found a clean handkerchief in her travel bag, which sat atop the other luggage just behind her. She drank the remaining coffee in her cup, then wiped the edge of the cup. She poured in fresh coffee from the thermos. She handed the cup to Tomas.

He smiled over the cup and took a sip. 'Thanks.'

That seemed to break the ice. Gabriela learned that Tomas liked baseball but hadn't played baseball to speak of since he was around ten. Instead, he was on a swim team and active in an archery league. He learned that Gabi loved hiking and did some rock collecting. She'd also managed to acquire four old Cuban travel posters from the '30s and '40s. She admired their brightness, their happiness, their promise. She hoped one day to produce such posters. Of course, she'd have to work on her skills. And such posters would have to again become acceptable. Now the official preference was for photo posters. How did she know that? She worked for CubaTur (the state travel agency) in Santiago. She'd gotten the job, yes, probably in part because of her party father, but also because she'd graduated early from university with a degree in linguistics and fluency in German and French. She anticipated she'd be transferred to the travel agency's main office in Havana after a few years in Santiago.

'Gabi, I would think your career ambitions would be imperiled by your seeing your brother,' said Tomas. 'Why are you so intent on seeing him?'

'He's my brother. My dear brother.'

'Aren't we all?' asked Tomas.

'Aren't we all *what*?'

'All family in God.'

'I don't think of things that way,' said Gabriela.

'Because it would be dangerous to do so?' asked Tomas.

'Perhaps because it would be silly to do so,' said Gabriela. 'It's silly to think that God is the father of us all. It makes God far too human. There's something out there, something beyond our understanding. That I'll admit. Something started this thing we call the world. Something beautifully organizes it. But the problem with Christians, especially, is that God is too involved, too human, too personal. Not that I don't see the attraction of that. I saw that in your mother. And because of that she was very human, very loving. Like my mom in many ways. I miss her.'

'Your mother or my mother?' asked Tomas.

'Both. They both cared for me even as they cared for others, too. My father never appreciated...' *But enough.*

Tomas opened up in her trailing silence. 'The world doesn't appreciate God. God's incarnation in the world is the most flagrant affront of Christianity to the modern sensibility. You've got to ask yourself whether you've adopted a sensibility more modern than true. More like your father's or more like your mother's.'

'What does one's personality have to do with God?' asked Gabriela.

'Everything,' said Tomas.

'We can decide whether or not to be more humane, whether or not there's a God. I don't see the connection.'

'I'll pray that you do, for there is a deep connection. That's my view. That's my stand.'

'Do you always let people know where you stand?' asked Gabriela.

'Discretion is useful,' said Tomas, 'but truth is the better guide, at least in the long run. That's been confirmed for me in these last twenty-four hours.'

'Twenty-four hours isn't long run. In the long run, we all die,' said Gabriela.

'Or live forever,' said Tomas.

'There you go with the personal angle,' said Gabriela.

'Yes,' said Tomas. 'What you accept for the truth has profound personal implications.'

'Right now, the most deeply personal issue for me is to find a bus tomorrow morning that'll take me from Havana to somewhere near where my brother is,' said Gabriela.

'You'll probably have to walk out there unless you can find and afford a taxi,' said Tomas. 'I don't think they run buses to those places. You could have a lot of walking ahead of you.'

'I'm a hiker,' said Gabriela.

'Yes. At least we're not in the middle of July.'

'Yes,' said Gabriela, but she hated being uncertain how much walking she'd have to do.

Tomas went back to reading, at least until it got dark. Enrico slept for about two hours before he was let off at Santa Clara. The sun had already set when they had reached the soldier's hometown. Gabriela slept much of the distance between there and Havana. She would later tell her Aunt Florina how amazed she was that Kiko could drive the entire distance from Santiago in one day. *Coffee and determination made all the difference. That was the bright side,* thought Gabriela.

Just shy of midnight, they reached her aunt's place, which was a walk-up apartment near the University of Havana. Kiko looked fatigued. As Kiko leaned back at the wheel, Tomas said he'd retrieve Gabi's luggage. Kiko was happy to give Tomas the key to open the back door.

Tomas offered to escort Gabriela to the third-floor apartment where her Aunt Florina lived.

'That won't be necessary,' said Gabriela.

'But it's been a long day,' said Tomas. 'It's good to walk.'

Kiko chimed in, 'It's been a long drive. We're only fifteen minutes from here, but I could use a walk up, too. It'll wake me up.' He got out of the VW.

'I'm sure my aunt and uncle will be delighted to meet you,' said Gabriela, but that seemed unlikely, especially at this hour.

'We won't linger,' said Kiko.

'No, we won't,' said Tomas. 'But knowing what apartment Gabi is staying in would be helpful. Like for tomorrow morning.'

'Tomorrow morning?' asked Kiko.

Looking at Gabriela, Tomas said, 'Please excuse us for a moment.'

Gabriela was almost certain Tomas intended to put Kiko on the spot. She hoped he would. She would gratefully accept a ride tomorrow.

Tomas and Kiko walked arm in arm away from Gabriela. They talked in a whisper, stopped, disengaged, and used their arms to punctuate their points. The punctuation ending, the two walked back towards Gabriela. Kiko followed Tomas, who was all smiles. Was he happy to be of help or was he happy to have scored one against his uncle? Gabriela wondered. Kiko seemed to have pasted on a smile.

'My uncle and I will take you tomorrow,' said Tomas. 'What time should we come by?'

Gabriela suggested the two come at nine o'clock.

'Very well,' said Kiko. 'We'd better get going, Tomas. It's going to be a short turn-around and a short night. Gabriela will have to take up her travel items. She can handle them.'

Tomas looked chagrined, but he gave Gabriela her travel bag and the somewhat deflated shopping bag. His chagrin was a small price to pay for a larger victory. Gabriela wondered whether this victory would come at a far larger cost than any of them could now imagine.

La Cabeza de Cuba

6.

When Gabriela had asked her boss for permission to travel to Havana, he gave it but not without an exercise. Special favors required special exercises, *imaginative exercises* as he called them. For leave to go to Havana, she must indulge him in the exercise of nicknaming Cuba's capital region. Gabriela was game, no surprise. For starters, said she, how about calling Havana *Roma de Cuba,* Cuba's Rome? Rome was a seat of government reputed to be a feast for the eye and the palate. So, too, was Havana. Yes, said her boss, but Rome was also the seat of the Catholic Church. He couldn't publicly support the religious overtones of 'Rome.' More imaginative, he said, was the idea that Havana was *la cabeza de Cuba,* the head of Cuba. Gabriela could see that was true politically and culturally. But how else?

Imagine yourself way on high, said her boss. From where Soviet cosmonauts fly, Cuba looks to be a man whose head is tucked in as he dives into the water. His outstretched, arched arms are western Cuba. To the east his feet have just hit the water, splashing it all about Santiago and Guantanamo. Soon his whole body would be immersed. Or think of a lizard.

Gabriela could see the lizard, but even so Havana couldn't be the head of a swimmer. Yet her boss was the boss, and she wasn't about to argue with him. She could see the virtue of an anatomical makeover of Cuba. Good, he said. And with that he gave her permission to travel to Havana, albeit with the roguish admonition to give more thought to Cuba's anatomy. In her time off, she might be able to devise a real 'anatomical' campaign for winning tourists to the island. Did her boss really believe that? Or was this his off-beat humor at work?

As she prepared herself this Saturday morning, Gabriela was more than happy to allow the anatomical whimsy to color her thought. The journey to visit Beto needed a note of whimsy. Otherwise, it might be rather grim. Truly, it helped to look on the bright side of things. How else could one find one's way through life? Her father was wrong on that account, what with his relentless insistence on the 'truth.' Truth had its place, to be sure. Truth be told, there was more grimness in ordinary life than was regularly endurable. Better to look for the bright side of things. Which was one reason she enjoyed working in the travel industry.

When she heard the doorbell ring, Gabriela ran to the front window. She opened it and leaned out. Tomas was on the street below, wearing a yellow and grey pullover. Havana felt a bit chilly this morning. No surprise. But the VW microbus wasn't parked in front.

'Come on up. I want you to meet my aunt and uncle. Kiko, too.'

Gabriela and her aunt and uncle learned Kiko wasn't along. Tomas informed them his uncle was sick. He'd been vomiting since early morning. Kiko wondered whether he'd gotten food poisoning. This couldn't be, countered Gabriela. Neither she nor Tomas were sick. Perhaps yesterday's intense drive had thrown Kiko's system out of kilter. Tomas agreed; that sounded plausible. In any event, Kiko wouldn't be driving anywhere today. The trip to Estacion ES would have to be deferred. Kiko had told Tomas he'd try tomorrow. Tomas believed his uncle.

Gabriela had almost no choice. Resting on yesterday's promise, she hadn't bothered to even sketch an itinerary to the labor camp. Before Gabriela could consider her options, Tomas asked if she'd accompany him to find his father and to otherwise nose around Havana. 'Where?' she asked. She would see, he said, if she came.

Her friends might be amused if she consented to spending time with Tomas. He was still in high school. Shouldn't she spend time with her dear aunt and uncle now that the visit to Beto was deferred? Couldn't a visit to Tomas's father derail her chance of visiting Beto? One could never know. Gabriela wasn't one to court danger, but the idea of spending the day with Tomas seemed more promising, more brightening, than spending the day with Aunt Florina and Uncle Silvano.

Anyway, her boss had encouraged her to look at Cuba in foreign ways. Wouldn't a venture out with Tomas be a venture into new territory? Had it not been for Tomas and his family, she wouldn't be in Havana in the first place. She *owed* Tomas some of her time. By such thinking, Gabriela said she'd accept his invitation.

Aunt Florina smiled, then shook her head. Was Florina shaking her head on behalf of Gabriela's mother? Gabriela didn't know and only later would she appreciate the depth of her ignorance, not about her aunt but about the path she'd chosen. Eyes looking backwards see better than those looking forward, Gabriela would say. If only we could see backwards into the future from the present.

Gabriela borrowed a light pink jacket from her aunt. Tomas promised her aunt and uncle that Gabriela would be back around suppertime. Aunt Florina gave Gabriela a hug and whispered that Gabriela would be on her own for supper. 'Just don't return too late,' said her aunt.

Kiko had given Tomas money for bus fares. Tomas's first objective was to find where his father was incarcerated. Second, to find his father's brother. Kiko had divulged the existence of this brother last evening. Gabriela already knew of him. One of Adriana's letters, after all, was addressed to her brother-in-law. Gabriela couldn't help but think now was the time to tell Tomas about the other letters from Adriana. She was carrying them in her purse.

'I have something I want to share with you,' said Gabi to Tomas. The two had been walking towards a bus stop.

'What is it?' asked Tomas.

'A letter or two.'

'One or two? Which is it?'

'Maybe more. Let's find a place where you can read the letter addressed to you.'

'Letter addressed to me?' asked Tomas. 'From my mother?'

'Yes.'

'I want to see it. Why didn't you produce it yesterday when you produced that letter for my uncle? How many more letters do you have?'

'Four now. One for you, one for your Uncle Carlos, one for your father's brother, Miguel, and one for your father.'

'For my father? May I see it?'

'No. Your mother told me it was for God's eyes and your father's only. Only God, she said, would decide whether it would ever be seen by Adan's eyes.'

'So be it,' said Tomas. 'Has God no say-so over the other letters?'

'I wouldn't know,' said Gabriela.

'Me thinks he does,' said Tomas, 'but how He does is a part of life's mystery. Meanwhile, we can try to solve the mysteries that come our way... like finding out where this Uncle Miguel of mine lives.'

Gabriela smiled. 'The envelope with Miguel's letter bears his address.'

'May I see it?'

'Of course,' said Gabriela. 'Just the envelope.'

'Of course,' said Tomas. 'You are highly protective of these letters.'

'I think I'm obliged to your mother. They're not public property... as she made clear when she shared their contents with me.'

Tomas said, 'My mother must have thought highly of you.'

'And vice versa. She had a very lovely trust of me. Perhaps she had no choice.'

'I still think she thought highly of you.'

'We didn't know each other all that long,' said Gabriela.

'Some people can readily size up others,' said Tomas.

'She said I had a bit of Moses about me, which I found intriguing.'

'Why?'

'I'm not quite sure why. All I know about Moses is that he led his people from slavery into the Promised Land. But I have no people. And I'm not a leader.'

'Maybe, maybe not,' said Tomas. 'But perhaps she saw that you were a person of promise.'

'What do you mean by that?' asked Gabriela.

'I don't know. You'd have to ask her, but she's no longer around to answer.'

'You can, like your mother, say the most intriguing things,' said Gabriela. 'I can't yet give it a name.'

'Well, when you do, it'll take at least two of us to authenticate the name. That's the nature of names,' said Tomas.

'There you go again,' she said.

He nodded. The two were still walking towards a bus stop. Tomas said he didn't want to read his letter with lots of people around. It would help if they could find a church. He knew of one not far away.

The church was dilapidated on the outside and fairly dilapidated on the interior, like so much of this part of Old Havana. The church smelled musty, but the must mingled with odors emanating from votive candles. Candles were burning before a painting of the Virgin on one side of the altar and on the other before a painting (Gabriela assumed) of the saint in whose honor this church was named. A lone elderly woman knelt before the image of the Virgin.

The church interior was dim, except for a lurid fluorescent fixture right at the doorway where Gabriela and Tomas stood. It appeared there would be no better place for Tomas to read the letter. Gabriela handed it to him under that light.

'Yes, this is the same handwriting as the signature on Kiko's letter and all those letters from Betty.'

Tomas gently worked to lift the flap sealed to the body of the envelope. He managed to unseal the envelope with minimal damage. After opening up the letter, he absorbed its contents in silence. He looked up at Gabriela.

'There isn't a lot.'

'No, there isn't,' replied Gabriela. 'Your mother was getting quite weak. She told me she would trust God to supply you with the knowledge and wisdom she couldn't supply.'

'*Knowledge?* Was that the very word she used? *Wisdom* I can understand. But *knowledge?* What did she mean by *knowledge?*'

Gabriela said, 'I think she was referring to facts about yourself, about your father, about her, about why you were taken away from your parents.'

Tomas looked thoughtful. When she finished telling some of what she learned from his mother and Kiko, he added, 'I wish I'd known my mother better.'

'I wish I had, too,' said Gabriela. 'I feel closer to her than almost anyone I've ever known outside my family. I think she was a very wise person, one with a love of goodness and beauty, one with a love of a very personal God.'

Thomas said, 'I have her to thank for managing to move me to think about those ultimate things our society labels as personal delusions. She says here, quote, "I would never have given any thought to Him who transcends and yet descends had He not with His spirit moved me to see Him at work in the love and faith of others. Be a part of Him always, my son, so that you may always be a child and friend of His in this world and the next."'

Tomas looked away. 'We'd better go.'

'Where?' asked Gabriela.

'To the municipal incarceration facility. It's across town.'

Across town they went. They caught a *camello,* a semi tractor-trailer combination that served as a bus. After one *camello,* they caught another. On the first *camello,* they'd hardly said a word to one another. Tomas appeared to be thinking about what his mother had written. Several times he opened the letter to re-read it. Gabriela had decided not to interrupt his reveries. After they boarded the second *camello,* he handed the letter to her to keep in her purse. She supposed he might be ready to talk.

She didn't want to get personal. After outlining the 'anatomical' venture her boss had admonished her to follow, she asked Tomas how Cuba might look to him from outer space.

He hesitated, then said, 'I think the head of Cuba faces toward the rising sun. The island is neither man nor lizard. It is more like a dolphin that's jumped up above the water for air. And that projection where Santiago lies is a part of the dolphin's fin. Havana is way back on the tail.'

'I see how you see that, but it wouldn't work for a tourist campaign,' said Gabriela.

'No,' said Tomas. 'I suppose the dolphin image wouldn't set well for several reasons, not least because the Cuba dolphin I see has come up for air and that's not allowed.'

Gabriela wouldn't pursue this line of thought. It must surely lead in a counter-revolutionary direction. Tomas looked eager for her reply, but she wouldn't satisfy his curiosity. Anyway, he realized they'd arrived at the bus stop nearest the jail. He grabbed Gabriela's hand and the two rushed to get off.

At the jail, they learned there was no prisoner who bore the name Adan Pedro Marti Reyes. Tomas could have learned this by a mere telephone call. Was there some other reason why they'd traveled out here? Gabriela asked this as the two were leaving the grounds of the incarceration facility.

'You can't believe whatever they tell you on the telephone,' said Tomas. 'They're more likely to brush you off over the phone. Showing up as we did is costly… but the results are more credible.'

As he spoke, he looked back towards the jail, and something caught his eye. Gabriela looked in the same direction. A uniformed man appeared to be watching them. He was talking into a radiotelephone handset, which he held against the right side of his face. He wasn't wearing the uniform of a jailer. Rather he wore state security fatigues.

Gabriela gave voice to something she was sure Tomas, too, must feel. 'I wonder what that's about.'

'We've managed to arouse a sleeping dog,' said Tomas.

'Maybe many sleeping dogs,' said Gabriela.

'What they don't know is that my Uncle Carlos is a top dog in their pack.'

'Will that spare us?' asked Gabriela. As she asked, she noticed that Tomas picked up his pace. She did, too.

'Let's not wait for an answer,' he said.

Once at the bus stop, they looked back to see if anyone was following them. They were happy when the *camello* came along. After boarding, they found a few empty seats, but no pairs. That was just as well. They couldn't talk about what was on their minds in public. The *camello* accumulated enough additional riders that by the time it was passing through the tunnel under Havana's harbor there was standing room only. About the second or third stop after the *camello* emerged from the tunnel, Tomas gave Gabriela a nod, a signal they should prepare to get off. He'd already given up his seat to an elderly woman, but he now worked towards the passenger door. Gabriela did likewise. As she weaved her way among the standees, she wondered what Tomas planned to do next.

'We've got to change our clothes,' he said as the *camello* pulled away.

'Why? We've done nothing wrong,' she said, even as she knew right-and-wrong wasn't the point. They'd made themselves objects of interest. Possibly.

'You know why,' said Tomas.

'Yes, I know why, but this is the only jacket I have along. I don't need it now, but it can feel chilly at night.'

'If there's anyone looking for a couple of our description, they're looking now.'

How many agents can state security have? The street bustled with people, most walking along, while some stood in small clusters. Could agents constitute one of those clusters?

'I can take off my jacket,' said Gabriela.

'Do,' said Tomas, 'but not just yet. Follow me.'

He knows Havana?

She followed him. He spoke as if he'd heard her quasi question.

'I spent two whole summers here staying with my Uncle Carlos, when I was eleven and twelve. He and my aunt let me spend days roving the city. There's a church near here, Santo Ángel Custodio. We'll go there.'

He led the way to a church of peculiarly Gothic architecture, white in a Caribbean fashion but otherwise Gothic in style.

'This is the church where Martí was baptized,' said Tomas.

Gabriela knew Tomas was referring to José Martí, but how did he know that the famous poet and leader of Cuban independence had been baptized at this church? 'How do you know that?' she asked, as Tomas opened the door for the two of them.

They stepped inside to a much better-kept church than the parish church. Santo Ángel Custodio was bereft of anyone who might be regarded as a parishioner. A few foreigners speaking English were gazing at the Stations of the Cross along one of the perimeters. Gabriela guessed they might be Canadians. If there were any masses on a Saturday, she assumed they were in the morning and evening. Gabriela took off her aunt's pink jacket. She really didn't want to give it up.

Tomas removed his sweater. Underneath he was wearing a green T-shirt, emblazoned with the Brazilian flag and bearing the words '*Viva o futebol.*'

Where did that come from? Gabriela wondered. She asked, 'What are we going to do with this jacket and your sweater?'

'We'll leave 'em here at the church.' He placed the jacket and sweater on a nearby shelf.

'Here?'

'Yes, here. I've been here many times with my mother, I mean my aunt, no, my mother, whenever we visited Havana,' said Tomas, his voice changing timbre. 'I have two mothers to thank God for.'

'You are harder on your uncle than on your aunt.'

'Shouldn't I be?'

Gabriela didn't answer Tomas. As he was stuffing the jacket and sweater on a shelf near the entrance, he said, 'I know now why we came here so often when we visited Havana. A night or two after any visit, Mama – my Aunt Pamela – would produce a letter from 'Betty.' I suspect my real mother was at times among the women at this church when we were here.'

Tomas gazed off into the sanctuary. The Canadians were so studious in inspecting the church.

She asked, 'Do you speak any English?'

'Some,' Tomas replied.

'Do you think we could exchange jackets with one of those ladies?' she asked.

Tomas frowned. 'What would be the point? Don't you want to return the pink jacket to your aunt? Why would she want someone else's jacket?'

'I have this feeling we won't be backtracking for this jacket,' said Gabriela. 'Better to give something to my aunt rather than nothing.'

Tomas shook his head. 'I don't want to bring this church under suspicion. If those Canadians are stopped and asked about the jacket, they'll end up pointing state security back to this church.'

He was right. Gabriela just hoped her aunt wouldn't be too aggravated if her pink jacket went missing.

He removed the jacket and his sweater from the shelf. Tomas said, 'We'll leave these in the church office. I know a priest that works out of here, Father Juan. He's very friendly.'

'But this is Saturday. No one will be at the office,' said Gabriela.

'You're right.'

Tomas put the jacket and sweater back on the shelf. When they left the church, Tomas told Gabriela they might return sooner than she'd think. She didn't believe him.

The two left the church and headed for a store where Tomas said they could use his 'Kiko money' to purchase sunglasses. They didn't have to enter a store. They were in Old Havana. Even in late 1979, the area was a tourist magnet, especially attractive to party elite from the Soviet Union and Eastern Europe. Discrete entrepreneurs walked the streets looking to sell rolls of film, postcards, and other tourist baubles.

Gabriela caught a glimpse of a young man up a bystreet taking cash from a couple who'd just purchased something. Might he sell sunglasses? He did. He had just the glasses for him and her. Or so he said.

Tomas looked around. Conditions were right for a quiet purchase. The vendor was thrilled to be paid in Canadian dollars. After they had walked away from the vendor, Gabriela asked Tomas how Kiko had gotten the loonies.

'Uncle Kiko has made two trips to Canada as part of an educational team, exchanging ideas with the Canadians. Travel abroad has its privileges and advantages,' said Tomas.

'I'll say,' said Gabriela.

They were now on a busier thoroughfare. Tomas asked if she was hungry. She was. He was, too. They walked to a cafeteria serving Cuban fare. Much of the zest had been steamed out of the food. Gabriela liked the old travel posters along the wall, even if they were mixed with party posters. Tomas suggested they remove their sunglasses. The cafeteria wasn't a big tourist hangout. While some patrons might have dark glasses on, most did not. He didn't want to be conspicuous.

They practically wolfed down their food. The walkabout had stirred their appetites. As hungry as he might be, Tomas was also wary. He kept looking around so much that Gabriela began to do so, too. *Wouldn't that single them out?*

No matter. They didn't linger. Tomas wanted to find the home of his paternal uncle, Miguel. His address, he estimated, was within a kilometer or two of the cafeteria. He pulled out a city map, which he'd had in his back pocket. Rather than spend money on fares, the two decided to walk.

They'd been walking about ten minutes when Tomas caught a glimpse of two men up the street, one with a radiotelephone in hand. Tomas grabbed Gabriela's hand and led her in an about-face. They returned to the street they'd just crossed and then proceeded along it into a warren of streets where they soon realized they were getting nowhere fast. Tomas had to pull out the city map once again and ask directions.

The man who paused to help them was young and athletic-looking. He may or may not have been attached to the neighborhood. He looked a tad more prosperous than the others in this particular neighborhood, but he hadn't been bashful about offering his help. Gabriela could tell Tomas, too, had misgivings. Tomas didn't reveal where they were heading. He asked merely for directions to a major thoroughfare, any would do.

Directions were given. Subsequently, Tomas looked back as they paused before crossing a street. Gabriela asked whether they were being followed. Tomas said he couldn't see anyone.

Within a half hour, they stood before a three-story pink residence. From the center second-story window hung a Cuban flag. From the window over the offset entrance door hung a red banner with yellow lettering. The banner read: *Comité de Defensa de la Revolución,* Committee for the Defense of the Revolution.

Tomas and Gabriela looked at one another mouths agape. Could his uncle be living here, where a building neighbor was a member of the CDR, the eyes and ears of the revolution?

7.

Gabriela pulled out the envelope bearing Adriana's letter to Miguel. The address written below his name indicated he would have a second-story flat. The Cuban flag and the CDR banner hung from that very flat. Was the address mistaken or had Miguel moved without his sister-in-law's knowing it?

Tomas, too, looked at the envelope, then gave a shrug.

Gabriela said, 'Your mother never mentioned her brother-in-law's working for the CDR. Yet from what she said, I thought she and your father had been living here for several years.'

Tomas handed the envelope to Gabriela, saying, 'I guess we'll find out.'

Inside and upstairs, they went. The interior of the building, like the exterior, was rich in pockmarks and cracks. But if the walls painted aqua were viewed as a kind of geography, the down-at-the-heels appearance could be turned into a bird's eye view of a Caribbean rich in islands and sandbars. Or so Gabriela liked to think. Overlaying this richness at least on the second landing were two large posters. The posters straddled the door to Miguel's apartment. Like lions, they guarded the gates, the one on the left depicting the leader, the one on the right depicting Che.

Tomas looked at the two posters from left to right, then winked at Gabriela, supplying the lions with names: 'The Messiah and the Baptist.'

Gabriela winced. Tomas was bright, perhaps too bright. Too often he gave voice to dangerous thoughts.

Tomas knocked on the door of Miguel's apartment. Several male voices could be heard on the other side of the door.

A man in his late 40s or early 50s opened the door. He wore sunglasses and held the kind of walking stick provided to blind people. He put up his free hand in a 'stop' sign.

Out came two men athletically fit, perhaps in their 30s, dressed in street clothes akin to their countrymen but of better quality and fit than was available or affordable to the common man. The two men wore sunglasses, the kind that occluded not only the eyes but seemed to fuse into the face, creating the impression that each man was all about eying and only one eye at that. A name for the men immediately came to Gabriela's mind: the Cyclopeans. The Cyclopeans nodded at the incoming pair as they scurried down the stairs. Gabriela shuddered.

'And you are…?' asked the man in the doorway.

'Tomas, your nephew by my father, Adan,' said Tomas. 'And this is my friend, Gabriela Suarez Paloma.'

Friend.

'Ah, yes, I've been told to expect you,' said his uncle.

How could that be? Gabriela and Tomas exchanged surprised looks.

'Come on in. I'm delighted to finally meet you. Come in, come in.' He smiled without directing his face at either one.

Miguel softly shut the front door behind Gabriela and Tomas, who entered just as softly. 'Please, let me embrace you, Tomas,' he said, holding up his hands and flapping them by way of inviting an embrace. 'After all these years, I'd like to be able to size you up.'

Tomas glanced at Gabi, then accepted and returned Miguel's embrace. Tomas was taller and more muscular than his uncle. His uncle was weightier. *The tiger and the bear,* thought Gabriela. There was some awkwardness in this embrace and far less practice than at the circus. Here they were under a new tent performing what might be expected of them, but with a certain edginess that came with novelty and strangeness. As opposed to the circus, the two had never met, at least not in memory.

The two released one another.

'Come, sit down,' said Miguel.

'So, you were expecting me?' asked Tomas.

'Yes. I received a call from the very highest levels of state security last evening.'

'From any one in particular?' asked Tomas.

'It's best not to ask that kind of question, but I'm pleased we've met. Have a seat,' he said, taking a seat in an overstuffed, faded Art Deco chair. In a previous existence, it may have gloried in the lobby of one of Havana's swank Art Deco hotels.

Gabriela and Tomas seated themselves in two Louis XIV armchairs that appeared to have been reupholstered with a bright pink and blue satin. Hard telling where they had started life. Once seated, Gabriela looked around at the walls of the apartment. As elsewhere, there was an extensive jungle of cracks, plaster outbursts, and seams of underlying green showing through the fading pink paint. Overlaying this geography was a small flotilla of abstract watercolors and photos bearing calligraphic art. This must be Adriana's handiwork.

Gabriela hoped she'd have the opportunity to inspect this work. First, though, the edge of acquaintance needed smoothing. Miguel had taken a handkerchief out of his pocket and was daubing the corners of his eyes. He put the handkerchief away and spoke into the room.

'Were you there when Adriana died?'

So, there are things he doesn't know.

'I wasn't,' said Tomas.

'I was,' said Gabriela.

Miguel directed his face towards Gabriela.

'Did she die peacefully?'

'Yes. She had one hand on her *Nuevo Testamento*. I held her other,' said Gabriela.

'Thank you, my dear. Thank you.'

'She asked me to deliver a letter to you. Would you like me to read it to you?'

Miguel didn't answer.

'Would you like Gabriela to read the letter to you, Uncle?' asked Tomas.

'I heard. Whatever you hear from the pen of your mother, Tomas, it's more complicated than you might imagine.'

'Perhaps,' said Tomas, 'but I've become accustomed to complications in the last twenty-four hours, wave after wave of them and I'm still swimming along.'

'Read the letter, please,' said Miguel, facing Gabriela.

'Dear Miguel,

When you receive this letter, I'll be no more in this world. Your brother, my husband, and I were grateful for the protection you gave us under your roof for five years, even if in the end events caused you to betray us. Something had to give, and it had to be us. I do not blame – I am sure Adan does not blame – you for what inevitably would have happened.

I ask – and I'm sure Adan would – only two things. First, that you protect whatever information still lies in your home dealing with Bible distributions. Adan by imprisonment and I by death can no longer participate in that part of our Lord's work. But others can. You have always been inconsistent in your application of Communist principles. For the love of a "possible God," as you called Him, hold on to that grace. Protect others.

And second, do all that you can, such as you can, to protect our Tomas. He is now at the doorstep of manhood. Perhaps he will become a scientist or mathematician or physician. He has the talents. The state has cultivated those talents. But he has other gifts. If I know him – and I do a little (thanks be to God and to dear Pamela) – he will not rest until he fully understands his past. With that he may come to see his future in a different, God-given light. You always respected Adan's freedom of conscience and mine. All I ask is that you respect Tomas', too.

I ask you to forgive me for any of my sins against you. I forgive you, knowing the Lord God is forgiving.

Love,

Adriana'

When Gabriela finished reading the letter, she folded it and placed it in its envelope. Tomas asked to see the letter. Gabriela passed it to him. Miguel was daubing his eyes again.

'My sister-in-law not only knew the art of calligraphy, she could speak to the heart. I will miss her. Tomas, I don't suppose my brother, your father, knows yet of Adriana's death.'

'Do you know where my father is?' asked Tomas.

'Yes, of course. But I haven't visited him. You'll be able to see him on Monday. It's been arranged. His trial is on Monday. His sentencing will probably take place on Monday or Tuesday.'

'On Christmas Eve or Christmas Day?' asked Tomas.

Miguel said, 'We're living in a New Age. Relics of the Old Age have been discarded. You know that. As it has been these past several years, it'll be business as usual on Monday and Tuesday.'

'So, my parents lived up here with you in recent years?'

'Yes.'

'That seems odd.'

'Why?'

'My parents distributed Bibles, yet they lived here in the home of a member of the committee.'

'Is that the only odd thing you see?' asked Miguel.

'No, not the only.'

'You're probably wondering how someone like me, apparently blind, could be designated as the block representative of the CDR.'

'Yes, that seems odd.'

'It only makes me more frightening to others. That isn't such a bad thing. Anyway, I'm only partially blind.'

'Were you in an accident?' asked Gabriela.

'Good that you asked. Yes, I was. Tomas's father and I served together in the merchant marine. I was the one that got Adan to come to sea, which he did for several years before deciding to take up more land-loving things, like marrying Adriana and then going down to Bolivia.

'Oh, what a mistake that was! They were both such party zealots when they went down there. But when they returned, they were so changed. Among other things, they decided to formally get married. In the church.'

'Was this public or did they keep it a family secret?' asked Tomas.

'At first it was a secret, but not for long. Everything came out when they tried to regain custody of you. Your Uncle Kiko especially didn't want to give you up, Tomas. It would have been hard emotionally for your Aunt Pamela, but she probably would have given you up. Not Kiko. I think he had a hand in a police raid at your parents' home. A Bible meeting was taking place. Your mother was arrested, eventually your dad too. Your father's life has been more in prison than out ever since. When he was out, he no longer conducted study sessions. Instead, he devoted himself to Bible distribution. Adriana helped. Come see their room.'

Miguel stood up. He might be visually impaired, but he knew his own territory.

'Follow me down this hallway,' he said.

They did. The hallway led past a small kitchen, then a bedroom, and a bathroom. Along the hall were ten photo portraits of Cuban baseball giants pinned to corkboard. Elaborate calligraphy adorned each of the photos without detracting from them. Gabriela was especially drawn to a photo of the 'Immortal' Martin DiHigo. He'd died early in the decade, in 1971 or 1972 as she recalled. Miguel said Adriana had created this montage for him. He said it was his most treasured possession.

Tomas said, 'My mother created a very beautiful memorial to these Cuban baseball giants.'

'I'm grateful for it,' said Miguel. 'Would you like a memento of your mother?'

'The memento I would like would be the gold dolphin pendant she was wearing when she died. Uncle Carlos took custody of it. If you've got any leverage, I'd appreciate getting it back,' said Tomas.

'Ah, yes, I know of that pendant. I wouldn't count on my having any leverage. Perhaps you'll find something in your parents' bedroom,' said Miguel.

'Two somethings,' said Tomas. 'Because Gabi was with my mother, she should have a memento as a token of thanks.'

'That's not necessary,' said Gabriela.

'I see Tomas' point,' said Miguel. 'Come see the room.'

Adriana and Adan's bedroom was bereft of any artwork, other than one brilliantly painted piece that hung over the bed. Gabriela had once seen similar kinds of paintings at an exhibit of Haitian art in Santiago. She guessed it was Haitian. This painting depicted Christ receiving children in his midst. Everyone was black and wore contemporary clothes other than Christ, who wore a white robe.

While Gabriela's attention had been captured by the painting, Tomas had been struck by a portrait photo he'd picked up from the small dressing table.

'This is a photo of me. It was taken earlier this year!'

'Yes,' said Miguel. 'Pamela time and again sent photos of you and I don't know what Adriana passed on to Pamela.'

Tomas put a hand to his head. He shook his head, then began moving about the room as if he were looking for something. Gabriela was drawn to a set of shelves next to the dresser. The shelves held books and three cardboard boxes.

Tomas joined Gabriela in reading titles on the spines. The books bore Spanish titles. A few bore German titles. He asked, 'Does my father speak German?'

'We both speak a little, a very little. That comes from our days in the merchant marine. We frequently made voyages to Germany, mostly to Rostock in East Germany, but twice together to Hamburg in West Germany. I went there again after your dad was no longer serving at sea. I was at sea until I got this injury.'

Miguel pointed to his left eye.

'I'm completely blind in my left eye. I was working near a motor when it shorted out and blew up. I became a landlubber, came to this apartment, which I shared some years with another old mate and his wife before they broke up. After they broke up, I invited your parents in.

'Your mother was a good cook.'

Tomas had become occupied with an arc-shaped steel tube that hung around the dressing table. The tube's ends were bolted to the wall. The mid-point of the tubing hung by heavy-duty wire. Heavy black curtains hung at the wall ends of the tubing. Tomas fidgeted with the curtains until he'd fully enclosed himself and the dressing table. Then he opened the curtains.

By now Gabriela had opened up two cardboard boxes. They contained small rock samples, few of them of any obvious interest. In the third, largest box was a small black lamp with what she discovered was a black light. Under the black light she knew someone could see rock fluorescence not visible in the daylight.

'Who was the rockhound?' asked Gabriela.

'They both were,' said Miguel.

'That's the reason for the black curtain?' asked Tomas.

Miguel smiled then said, 'I've never been interested in rocks. Rocks and ships don't mix well, except if the rock's ballast.'

Was Miguel being evasive? Gabriela put the covers back on the boxes. Tomas was looking at the brush and comb and small scissors lying on the dressing table.

He turned away from the table and went to the window looking out on a back porch. Tomas asked whether they could go out on the porch. Miguel was happy to comply, opening the heavy wooden door leading to the porch.

There were potted geraniums on the porch landing. Stairs led up to the landing above and down to the landing below and to the back courtyard shared by several apartment buildings.

When Gabriela was about to ask who was so fond of geraniums, Miguel mentioned he and his brother had noted the Germans' fondness for geraniums. They were hardy in Germany and thrived all the more in Havana. Their beauty was enhanced by memories of voyages past, said Miguel. He loved the scent of them. They offered 'freshness without sweetness,' he said.

The three stepped back inside the room. Miguel shut the porch door behind them.

'I keep it locked,' he said.

'Thank you for showing us this room,' said Tomas, eyeing the one painting in the room. 'By the way, where'd the painting come from?'

'From Haiti,' said Miguel, confirming Gabriela's guess. 'Would you like to have it as a memento?'

'It's beautiful but too big for me to take. Did my dad get that for my mother?'

'I got it,' said Miguel. 'I knew a painting with children like that one would mean much to your dear mother. Don't you want it?'

'Too big,' said Tomas. 'Gabriela, have you seen anything for yourself?'

'I wouldn't think of it,' she replied.

'So I thought,' said Miguel. 'You shouldn't feel bashful. I suspect Adriana would want you to have something.'

'I have my memories of Adriana,' said Gabriela.

Tomas went for the big box that held the black lamp. He pulled out the lamp and thrust it toward Gabriela.

'Here. You're a rockhound yourself.'

'I can't take it,' said Gabriela.

'You must,' said Tomas. 'I want you to have it.'

'Yes,' said Miguel. 'Take it.'

'All right. I will,' said Gabriela.

'It's not only a good memento. It's practical and unusual. There are many unusual things residing in this apartment, Miguel. You don't have a monopoly on the unusual here,' said Tomas.

Miguel laughed. 'Come see something else unusual residing here.'

Gabriela and Tomas followed Miguel. He said, 'In the merchant marine, it's best to start a voyage with as many Cuban cigars as you can afford. There's great demand for them abroad. They make good trades. I want you to see the Advent calendar house I acquired on your dad's behalf in Hamburg after he'd turned landlubber and religious.'

'What's an Advent calendar house?' asked Gabriela.

'You've heard of an Advent calendar, haven't you?' asked Miguel. She hadn't. He explained how it was used to count down the days before Christmas. He added, 'The Advent house is an Advent calendar. It's from Bavaria and made of wood. It looks like the side of a Bavarian house with all kinds of windows.'

They were now in the tiny kitchen. On the wall overlooking a small table was the white, red-roofed Advent house. Virtually, all the windows of the house were open. At each window sat a wooden figure, more or less like classical busts, except in miniature. The figures were exquisitely carved and painted.

'This must have cost a small fortune,' said Gabriela.

'It did. My brother had seen one earlier in his seafaring days. He wasn't interested in this sort of thing in his earliest sea days. Only after he and your mother went to Bolivia did that change. He had a knack for fixing things. That's how he got the money to purchase the house. I picked it up for him in Hamburg. The house became a way for your parents to observe Christmas without the tree.'

Gabriela said, 'But I see you use it, too. I mean Christmas will be here on Tuesday. Today's Saturday and I see there are two windows with the shutters still closed.'

'I do it all for sentimental sake. I'm not a believer myself, as you can well imagine. But I always enjoyed Christmas and I've never begrudged others their religious belief.'

'How could the party abide this sort of situation?' asked Tomas.

'Oh, there are party members who are believers,' said Miguel. 'Our constitution, as you know, guarantees the freedom of private conscience.'

'But how could you *personally* tolerate my father and mother living here, especially since you apparently knew about their Bible distribution activities. How could you continue to be in the CDR?' Tomas was visibly reddening.

'How do you think, my nephew?'

'You eventually betrayed them, my mother and father, as my mother's letter to you suggests.'

'I wouldn't put it that way.'

'Say as you wish, what else am I to deduce?'

'If you only knew how complicated the facts can be. Don't judge on appearances.'

'Appearances and my mother's letter are telling in this case.'

'They don't tell everything. Let's be friends.'

Tomas said not a thing for perhaps a minute. Gabriela wondered whether she should say something. Tomas put his hands on his hips.

'I want to be convinced,' he said.

'I can't do that right now,' replied Miguel.

'Why should I put any trust in you? You've had a hand in the arrest of my father, your very own brother. How could you?'

'It's not as it seems,' said Miguel.

Tomas looked the other way. He said, 'Gabriela and I must be going. Thank you for showing us what you have, my uncle. We are not friends, but we are family. I'm not sure what kind of family. What I know of my family seems to change by the minute. Uncle, you may have gone to sea, but I'm already there tossed from wave to wave. I would like some sign of your goodwill.'

'Name it,' said Miguel.

'I would like this Advent house. It meant something to my father, probably still does. And it meant something to my mother. It may have sentimental value for you. But it meant a whole lot more to them. I'd like to have it as a remembrance.'

'You were just saying the Haitian painting was too big.'

'Yes, but this means more, even if it's too big.'

'You can't have it. I won't think of it. At least not now.'

Tomas looked surprised. 'I don't understand.'

'Indeed, you don't,' said Miguel. 'As a token of my goodwill, I'll escort you to your father's trial on Monday.'

'I don't need your help.'

'You don't know what that can be like. No, you don't. You'll be happy to have me along, especially if you hope to have any private moment with my brother. No, you had better give the matter some thought. You'll want me along.'

'Thank you for your hospitality, Uncle. I can't quite figure you out, but you've clarified some things for me. We must leave.'

'With this kind of clarity, we'll soon no longer be family,' said Miguel.

'I hope it doesn't come to that,' said Gabriela firmly. 'Family is important, very important.'

'Except when they've shown they're no longer family,' said Tomas.

Tomas and Gabriela left with a consolation prize: the black light. When they exited onto the street, the Cyclopeans nodded at them, just as they had earlier. The two men headed back into the building.

'At least they're not following us,' said Gabriela.

'No, not *them*,' said Tomas.

8.

If the Cyclopeans had followed Gabriela and Tomas, they would have noted animated gestures as the two scurried through Havana streets and byways. If they had managed to listen, they would have had much to report.

Gabriela voiced the opinion that Miguel had imperiled his position as a CDR block captain by having housed two people involved in Bible distribution.

Tomas countered that Miguel's hospitality was but a ploy to keep a close watch on the pair. Surely, he'd betrayed them long before they were arrested.

'Maybe, maybe not,' replied Gabriela. In any event, she argued, Tomas's father and mother were comfortable living with Miguel. Otherwise, they could have gone elsewhere.

'Maybe they had no choice,' replied Tomas. This was Cuba.

That's where the debate had circled several times when Tomas and Gabriela arrived at the front door of Aunt Florina and Uncle Silvano's apartment building. Would they still be going out to see Beto in the morning? asked Gabriela.

'Of course,' replied Tomas, 'provided Kiko is up to it. I'll make sure he's up to it.' He smiled for the first time since they'd left Miguel's. 'I hope you're not angry with me.'

'No,' replied Gabriela, 'but we've obviously got some differences of opinion.'

'That's probably just as well. We'll need to be on high alert tomorrow, so the more ways we're looking, the better off we'll be.'

Gabriela shared with Tomas the name – 'Cyclopeans' – she'd given to the state security agents. He didn't need to be told that the name came from Greek mythology. He said he would feel at liberty to apply the name to any of the monsters employed by the revolutionary state.

Gabriela quickly looked around to see whether they might have been overheard.

'We must be careful,' she whispered.

'Look who's talking,' smiled Tomas. 'You came up with that name. I like it.'

'Nevertheless.'

'Oh, I know,' said Tomas, about to open the front door of the apartment building.

Gabriela put a hand to her forehead. 'How could I forget? We need to get my aunt's jacket.'

'Can I bring it in the morning?' asked Tomas.

'I guess that'll do,' said Gabriela. She felt bone tired and suspected Tomas was just as ready to call it quits for the day. Tomorrow would have to do.

Tomas brought his hands together, folding them as if in prayer. He brought them up to his chin. No sooner had he touched his chin, then he held out his opened hands towards Gabriela.

This was a pleasing gesture. In response, Gabriela held up the black lamp in her right hand and held her purse against her torso with the left.

Tomas smiled. 'I give you a name if you'll take it: *Estatua de la Libertad.*'

Gabriela laughed, swinging the lamp about. 'Too long and too fixed. How about just "Libertad"?'

Tomas scrunched his nose, then made a counteroffer. 'How about "Miss Liberty" – in English?'

'Not *Senorita Libertad*?' asked Gabriela.

'Too loose for Cuba. The more I think about this, I think we must use a foreign tongue when speaking of such a thing in Cuba. But, someday...'

'If we're careful,' said Gabriela.

'Careful and wise and persistent,' said Tomas.

'Perhaps, who knows what will happen?' said Gabriela. 'But first things first. I need to get out to you-know-where by noon if I'm to see my brother.'

'Papa – Frederico – and I will be here by eight tomorrow morning. That should give us enough time,' said Tomas.

After Tomas left, Gabriela wondered whether Kiko would really show up. Her concerns about Kiko were not unwarranted, as she'd later learn. When Tomas arrived at his grandparents (where he and Kiko were staying), Kiko unleashed an anger built up through the day. He said as much. He'd gone from being worried about Tomas's whereabouts to being vexed he hadn't called to being suspicious Tomas was acting in ways that would endanger his – Kiko's – own reputation. Was Tomas so ungrateful, so spiteful of his own uncle and aunt? They'd raised him as a son. Were they of no account? Were they? And to top it all off, Miguel had called shortly before Tomas arrived just now!

'What had Miguel said?' asked Tomas.

'It doesn't matter,' replied Kiko.

'Then why bring it up?' said Tomas.

'Enough,' said Kiko.

Tomas tried coaxing Kiko to tell him what Miguel had said. But Kiko ordered Tomas away. Tomas went to the bedroom assigned to Kiko and him for their stay. Neither grandparent had intervened in the discussion between Kiko and Tomas. Tomas couldn't blame them for not wanting to.

He was hungry, as he later told Gabriela, and would have gratefully eaten a bowl of soup. He didn't want to make an issue of his hunger. And he didn't want to face his grandparents after being chastised by their son. He worried that Kiko might no longer honor his promise to take Gabriela to Estacion ES.

9.

The worry was for naught. Kiko was quite intent on getting this Estacion ES business over with. He asked Gabriela to take a backseat in the VW. He wanted Tomas up front. Tomas didn't look eager to be up front with his uncle, but he didn't argue. He opened the back door for Gabriela then got back up front for the ride out of town.

Hardly a word was spoken the first fifteen minutes. At least the VW's heater worked as intended. Kiko focused on navigating the streets of Havana leading to the *autopista*. Tomas was intent but distant. Gabriela's efforts to open conversation were met by brief answers from up front. She had no breakfast treats to help the situation.

Once they reached the outskirts of Havana, Tomas, perhaps hoping to break the ice, told Gabriela, 'I went back to the church this morning.'

Kiko exploded, 'You went where?'

'To a church,' replied Tomas. 'The pink jacket is behind you,' he said, turning to Gabriela. 'I should have gotten it for you yesterday.'

Gabriela looked behind her seat and saw the jacket neatly folded atop a blanket. 'No matter,' she said. Nevertheless, she put on the jacket.

Kiko said, 'I don't ever want you going in a church again, not ever, not unless it's part of a tour group. As long as you're living in my home, you must not visit churches.'

'Why?' asked Tomas.

'If you ever hope to be a scientist and a party member in good standing, you will not darken a church door. Church is for the childish, for the primitive urges. You know that. You've learned that in school. Nothing worthy in this life has been or ever can be grounded in religious impulses.'

'You should have seen the inside of that church,' replied Tomas.

'The architectural beauty of a church is like rouge on a pig. It cannot alter the underlying reality. Don't be lured by religious talk. Religious faith is parasitic. Look what it's done to my sister and her husband!'

'You mean my mother and father!'

'They abandoned you!' shouted Kiko.

'Or were forced to, perhaps?' said Tomas, keeping his cool.

'Not at all. They *chose* to convert, down there in Bolivia. They had no *need* to convert. How could they betray the freedom given them by the revolution, to be free from superstition and ignorance? Instead, they chose the chains, the opiate, of religion. Pamela and I

130

loved you too much to allow you to be enchained with them in their open mockery of a society governed by reason, a society ushered in by the revolution.'

'How can you, an educated man, believe all that revolutionary cant?' asked Tomas.

'And how can you have fallen into these superstitious ways? You embarrass me before my father. And your bad habits can only lead to failure, yes, even the end of any dreams you've ever had of being anybody in Cuba. You'll be lucky to be a nobody if you keep this up!'

Gabriela could feel her own innards roiling away. She would have given anything for the tranquil images and sounds of an open field on a sweet sunny morning. She wondered if there was any way she could steer the conversation onto a lighter topic. Perhaps something earthy might do the trick.

They were now traversing the farmland east of Havana. There were no workers in the fields, but an occasional *compañero* was seen walking in a field. The day was sunny, typical for this time of year, now warming up but with no prospect of rain. Weather talk wouldn't do, and farm talk would be hardly better. Gabriela knew little about farming except for what little she'd learned about sugar cane farming. She'd worked sugar harvests as a participant in student cadres.

No, earthy wouldn't do. Perhaps something transcendent. A discussion about art might be helpful, but one un-tinged by politics. Cinema would be out, censored as it was by the state. Craftwork would be out, too, exalted by the revolution. Let's see, there was sculpture, but that had become a veritable state monopoly. Sports were under the guidance of the state. Writing, well, one couldn't plumb any depth without finding markers prescribed by the revolution. So that left music. Music was hardest to tame. In Cuba, it was like a herd of horses. No, horses could be corralled. In Cuba, music was more like a herd of cats. You might capture a few, but you couldn't capture the whole lot. She wondered what kind of music Kiko liked. And what kind Tomas.

'Have you tried the car radio?' asked Gabriela.

'I have,' said Kiko.

'Is it pretty good?'

'Good enough.'

'Do you enjoy music?' asked Gabriela.

'Often, but not now,' said Kiko. 'Let's see if they might be relaying a speech from our leadership.'

'That, of course, would be music to your ears,' said Tomas.

'You think sarcasm will get you somewhere, don't you? I'd say we can just turn around first chance we get if that's the way you're going to behave.'

'No, please, I must see my brother,' said Gabriela.

'Then Tomas will know to keep his tongue in check,' said Kiko.

'Of course. It's a Cuban political habit,' said Tomas.

'A good habit,' said Gabriela.

'Thank you,' said Kiko. 'A very good habit. We must be a practical people on this grand island of ours. Actually, I've no doubt that educated people around the world envy this, the Pearl of the Antilles.'

'The pearl couldn't exist,' said Tomas, 'without the shell.'

'Yes,' said Kiko doubtfully, as if he were assessing whether Tomas was being sarcastic. 'What do you mean?'

'A pearl is a created thing, a beautiful thing. It's a kind of gift, no one earns it, but it can be found. If it's a gift, who should we thank?' asked Tomas.

'The party, of course. The dictatorship. Roll your eyes if you will, Tomas, but that's the stark truth. Oh, and I don't believe all revolutionary "cant" as you call it, but just enough to know that such cant protects all of us from sheer chaos. Once we realize that humanity is the center of existence, that we aren't creations of some higher being, then we must come to the stark realization we have only ourselves to fall back on. And which one among us should that be? Can you tell me, Tomas?'

'We are told it cannot be the capitalists, because they are greedy, supposedly at the expense of others.'

'Not *supposedly* but *always*,' said Kiko.

Tomas asked, 'If I choose to buy a banana from you, you walk away with a coin, and I walk away with a banana. Aren't we both better off?'

'Did you learn that from church, from religious literature, from the Bible?' asked Kiko.

'From common observation,' said Tomas.

'But not all can see the obvious,' said Kiko. 'Anyway, the most important things in life are not transparently obvious. They need to be taught.'

'Yes,' said Tomas, 'there is a role for the likes of the Bible.'

'That's a perverted lie!' said Kiko. 'Because that lie is based on the delusion the Bible is inspired by God. But God is a figment of humans questing for comfort in a distressing world. Our only real comfort can come in knowing there are intelligent people in charge. Obviously, they will make mistakes, too. They won't be perfect. But a beneficent dictatorship, such as we now have in this country, is the most that reasonable people can ever hope for.

'You may not believe that now, Tomas, but I can only hope you believe sooner than later. If you continue on the path you're now following, you'll head to self-destruction.'

Tomas said not a thing. And Gabriela wasn't going to bring up music again. Engine noise and passing vehicles would make for "music" in the ensuing miles. No one talked.

When Kiko turned off the four-lane *autopista*, he headed south on a much quieter but rougher two-lane road that led to the small town that Gabriela had been told was closest to Estacion ES. The silence in the microbus framed the countryside, somehow making it sadder than it needed to be. Silence was indeed a political habit in Cuba. Not that silence was all bad. Better that than living in the cacophony of civil war. Yes, silence had to be better than that. *Look at the bright side.*

When the three reached the town, Kiko pulled over to ask a pedestrian for directions to Estacion ES. Directions were provided. The labor camp lay at the edge of the wetland wilderness constituting the Zapata Peninsula. Kiko drove out of town down a pockmarked, winding road leading to the penal camp. Gabriela knew of the Zapata as a premier wilderness travel destination in Cuba. There wasn't anything particularly appealing to this entrance perhaps because she knew they were headed toward the camp. Rounding a curve, the travelers came to a wide spot beyond which the road went a kilometer arrow-straight to the entrance of what appeared to be the camp.

Kiko pulled over in the wide spot. 'I don't want to turn around immediately at the camp entrance. Someone could note down the license number. I don't need that.'

'Someone may have already done that as we were leaving that town back there,' said Tomas.

'I have a pass from the highest levels of state security,' said Gabriela, 'but I don't mind walking. The fresh air will do a lot of good.'

Gabriela opened her door. Tomas opened his. 'I'm coming, too,' he said. She left the pink jacket behind. It was warm now.

'There's only a pass for me,' said Gabriela.

'I'll wait for you at the camp entrance,' said Tomas.

Kiko said, 'I'm not going to wait here. I'm going back to the town and poke around there. Plan on meeting me back here at four o'clock. I'll pick you up then.'

'So, I can go with our *compañera*?' asked Tomas, as if he'd been anticipating opposition from his uncle.

'This is a free country,' said Kiko.

'Yes,' said Tomas, shutting the front door.

As Kiko swung around and drove off, Tomas and Gabriela headed towards Estacion ES. The two looked back once at the VW kicking up dust.

'My uncle was right about one thing. Once humanity and humanity alone is in the human equation, there can only be dictatorship or chaos. He's right about that. In such a world, labor camps and prisons are like temples for humanity freed from God.'

'I don't think your uncle would agree with that,' said Gabriela.

'Don't you?' asked Tomas.

10.

Estacion ES had a squat grandeur. A hundred-meter-wide swath of clearage skirted the camp. At least by appearance, the camp dominated the land. Two large buildings, each topped with a canopied observation post, straddled the main road at the camp entrance. A guard manned one of these posts. There wasn't any barbed wire festooning the camp perimeter. The camp's swampy surroundings seemed fit enough to contain the sanctity of the camp labors.

They walked for a while in silence, then Tomas asked, 'Is it what you expected?'

'I hadn't given it much thought,' said Gabriela.

They picked up their pace but continued in silence. In the last meters before the gate, Tomas asked, 'They arrested your brother for handing out political pamphlets, right?'

'Yes, and for belonging to a group that openly discussed issues from non-Marxist perspectives,' said Gabriela.

'So, he was sent here for social correction,' said Tomas.

Gabriela replied, 'It probably didn't help matters that he's black.'

'Black? But you're not black.'

Gabriela had forgotten she'd had this conversation with Kiko in the VW when Tomas was asleep. 'Same dad, different mothers,' she said. 'After his mother died, his father – our father – married my mother.'

'I see. Because he's black and we live in a revolutionary state, he's supposed to be especially devoted to the cause, of course.'

'Yes.'

'So, he was sent to this temple for cleansing and purification,' said Tomas.

Gabriela and Tomas looked up at a banner hanging between the guard buildings.

'Purification and perhaps sacrifice,' added Tomas.

The banner proclaimed: *El trabajo restaurará el espíritu revolucionario*, Work will restore the revolutionary spirit.

As they looked at the banner, a uniformed guard approached them. The man in his 20s appeared to be an officer. He exuded an efficiency that this temple, too, exhaled.

'If you would follow me and step inside,' he said.

'Yes,' said Gabriela. She followed the officer. Tomas followed her.

The officer led them to a small office just beyond the entrance. He waved them inside. When they were all inside, the officer turned to Gabriela and asked somewhat doubtfully, 'Are you Prisoner 875763's sister?'

'I don't know,' said Gabriela.

'She doesn't have his number,' said Tomas.

The officer glared. 'Only *she* may speak. I speak of Roberto Suarez Montarra.'

'I'm his sister, his half-sister,' she replied.

'You have an identification card?'

'I do.' She produced one from her purse. After the officer examined it, he handed it back.

'And you? Who are you?' asked the officer of Tomas.

'He's a friend,' said Gabriela.

'And?' said the officer.

'I've just come along.'

'His family helped bring me here,' said Gabriela.

'You do not have a permit to visit,' said the officer, looking at Tomas.

'No, I do not.'

'Then you will have to wait out on the road. On the road.'

Tomas later admitted he didn't like the idea of waiting. He'd forgotten to bring a book.

Gabriela would have to see her brother alone. She found this somewhat intimidating. *At least he'll be in the infirmary.* Or so she thought.

After Tomas exited to wait, the officer directed Gabriela's attention to a counter where a guard had swiveled around a large logbook. She was asked to enter personal data and then sign her name in the book. The counter guard demanded custody of her purse. Gabriela was reluctant to hand it over. The officer said she'd have to give it up. The counter guard sneered when she handed him the purse. He had rather long, dirty fingernails. Gabriela shuddered. But she managed in that instance to give him a name: Prince Charming.

The officer asked her to follow him. She did. After walking along two corridors, they exited the building, crossed a small, bare yard, and entered a non-descript building. The officer asked Gabriela to take a seat in a chair next to a window. The window afforded a view of another bare yard, bordered by a building without windows. She assumed that building must be a supply shed.

As she sat waiting, she could hear the sounds of a baseball game. She heard the crack of a bat against a ball. It was Sunday after all. It was good the men were given the opportunity to play a game. She assumed the players were inmates. By the time she'd heard perhaps a dozen cracks, she wondered how long she'd be kept waiting. She looked at her watch. She'd been waiting at least fifty-five minutes. She wondered what Tomas was doing. She wondered about her brother. What could be taking so long?

After another ten minutes, the officer returned, escorted by a guard.

'Follow me,' he said, leading Gabriela out to the shed she'd observed. The officer, Gabriela, and the escort went around the shed to a side where there was a door. The officer opened the door, looked at Gabriela, and once again said, 'Follow me.'

He led Gabriela a short distance to another door that led to a bright yet airless room. The room was bereft of furnishings except for a table with one chair facing her and three chairs facing that chair. A number of uniformed men already stood in the room. They would be in back of Gabriela once she was seated. She was asked to sit in the middle of the three chairs facing the chair across the table.

All of the chairs were wooden, heavy duty, equipped with armrests, and highly polished. The table, too, was polished. This wasn't the kind of rough-and-ready look one might associate with a labor camp. The chair felt cool and comfortable. The goings-on were discomforting. Why were the men standing in back of her? She looked back at them and noted two men were setting up a television camera on a tripod. Where was her brother? Gabriela looked toward the officer, who now stood at one end of the table.

He caught Gabriela's quizzical look and waved a hand back and forth in front of his mouth before putting his index finger against his lips. He had no answer, and she must have no question.

A door was opened nearby. One guard pulled and another pushed a gurney bearing a load. The guards wheeled the gurney to the chair facing her chair. Each of the guards bent down. Gabriela guessed they were engaging wheel locks to prevent the gurney from moving. The two guards, the officer, and two other guards then carefully lifted a body that was her brother's. From the gurney, they placed him in the chair. Someone even placed a pillow behind his back. He was wearing a clean, starched long-sleeved dungaree shirt.

Meanwhile additional lights, very strong lights, were turned on. Gabriela looked back and noticed there were a half dozen lights mounted on tripods. Whatever was going to happen now was surely not for her benefit or for her brother's. This would be for the revolution. Except what was she supposed to say? And what would her brother say? She had no script. Or so she thought.

But a script was provided. The officer handed her a neatly typed sheet of paper. It bore four questions.

'These are the questions you may ask. These are the questions you must ask,' said the officer, placing the script in front of her. He took a seat in the chair to her left. No one sat in the right-hand chair.

Gabriela read the questions to herself. '(1) Why are you sick? (2) Have you been treated well? (3) Have you regained your zeal for the revolution? (4) What would you say to those who stand against the revolution?'

'Will I be permitted to tell him anything about home?' asked Gabriela. 'Or anything else? Or ask any other questions?'

The officer shifted in his chair, then looked at her like an affectionate uncle correcting an under-aged niece. 'We must stick absolutely to the questions today.

If you wish to send a letter with other things, you can always do that later.'

The officer turned his attention to the prisoner seated across the table. Gabriela looked at her brother. He was much thinner than when she'd last seen him, the day before he was arrested a year-and-half ago. There was another difference. His head drooped to one side. His eyes were barely opened. He appeared exhausted. Two guards stood close behind, perhaps ready to catch him if he should begin to fall forward. Indeed, a third guard and a fourth appeared with a rope. Below the level of the table, the two looped the rope around Beto's torso and the back of the armchair.

Beto shot a sad smile at his sister.

'Is the prisoner ready this time for the questions?' asked the officer.

This time. What other times were there?

Prisoner 875763 nodded.

'Please respond verbally,' said the officer. 'Speak into the mic.'

A microphone had been placed in front of Beto and another in front of Gabriela.

'Yes, sir,' said Beto with a slight slur. He had straightened up a bit.

'Very well. Then we may begin. Your sister, as you know, has some questions. She will ask them now.'

Gabriela cleared her throat.

'Beto, why are you sick?'

The officer spoke. 'I must ask you to repeat the question but without the name. There must be no deviance from the questions if you would, please. Absolutely none. Understand?'

'Yes, I understand.' Gabriela wet her lips, then spoke into the mic, 'Why are you sick?'

'I contracted hepatitis some time ago and just recently I've come down with a viral infection of indeterminate origin.'

Hepatitis weakened him and the new virus will kill him unless he can receive better attention. Dare not raise that now for the trouble...

'Your next question,' whispered the officer.

'Have you been treated well?' asked Gabriela, speaking into the mic.

Beto spoke with great labor. 'I have been treated well, very well considering my circumstances. Everyone has gone the extra distance. I am grateful to the one to whom we truly should be grateful.'

Can that be believed? Grateful truly to whom?

Gabriela read the question she wouldn't have asked in a thousand lifetimes, but here she was asking it: 'Have you regained your zeal for the Revolution?'

'Absolutely,' said Beto. 'Absolutely, without question. I now see it as the hope of the people, my hope, and the hope of my family. Those who pursue anti-revolutionary or non-revolutionary dreams will only make nightmares for themselves and for others along the way. The story of the revolution is the story of humankind; to break shackles and set humankind free. May the revolution embrace all mankind!'

The officer coughed and cleared his throat. Beto appeared ready to say more but he stopped. The officer tapped the tabletop.

Gabriela asked the last question. Given what her brother had just said, she now had a genuine interest in his answer. 'What would you say to those who stand against the revolution?'

He spoke now with a slight slur. 'They are worms, nothing but worms. And as worms, they can be of no good to anybody. They will be crushed as they should be crushed beneath the heel of the revolution. When I have attained my restoration through labor, I will return to society and do all I can to crush the earthworms. There is hope, as in me, that the worms can become butterflies. To do that, they must repent and turn themselves to their only hope. *Viva el Revolucion! Viva!*'

Beto slumped forward before the guards caught him.

Gabriela stood and cried out, 'Beto!'

'Enough,' said the officer. 'Get him *pronto* to medical attention, *pronto.*'

The officer took Gabriela by both arms, standing behind her, as she watched the guards work to untie her brother from his chair. She wanted to go around the table to help, but the officer held her back. 'No, no,' he said softly.

The guards lifted Beto onto the gurney. He appeared to be unconscious. Someone had already cut the lights on the tripods. Someone else was gathering up the microphones and the video tape recorder. As soon as Beto was removed from the room, the officer let go of Gabriela.

'We must go,' he said softly.

'Yes,' said Gabriela. *But earthworms don't become butterflies. Not even when you look at the bright side.*

11.

'Where will he be taken?' asked Gabriela.

'To the infirmary,' said the lieutenant.

He led Gabriela out of the Building of Four Questions, as she now thought of it. The lieutenant led her across the small yard she'd seen while waiting. He led her into a building she'd not passed through when he'd led her to the visit. *No, not a visit*, she thought. *More like a canned interview.*

After going through what seemed like a maze of corridors, the lieutenant and Gabriela were back at the office where she'd first signed in. The lieutenant assisted her in signing out. When she'd finished signing, she looked across the counter at the guard who'd taken custody of the visitor's log. He was looking at her with a kind of leer as he handed her purse back to her.

'Lieutenant, I'm off duty in five minutes. I could take the *compatriota* into town.'

'No, that won't be at all necessary,' said Gabriela.

'I would very much like to convey you,' said the guard.

'Thank you, sergeant, but I will assist the *compatriota*,' said the lieutenant. 'Please follow me, please.'

Gabriela was more than happy to follow the lieutenant. When she glanced back, the counter guard was staring at her. She quickly looked away. She hated the fact this man now had before him her home address in Santiago. What might he do with the information? He gave her the creeps.

It felt good to be out in the sunshine. Gabriela looked through the gate and saw Tomas getting up off his haunches.

Nodding toward Tomas, the lieutenant said, 'I'd be happy to take you and your companion into town, even further. I've got to take someone else that way, too.'

Gabriela didn't know what to make of this offer. She felt almost guilty in being so ready to accept it. After all, this officer had been a party to the production just put on, the show in which she and her brother had been given the speaking parts. How was this lieutenant to be trusted, but not the guard at the counter?

'If you wish not, you need not,' said the lieutenant. 'You can think about it while I bring my jeep around.'

She thought. Tomas walked toward the camp entrance, perhaps wondering why she'd not yet passed through the checkpoint.

When the lieutenant pulled up in his jeep, another man sat in the seat behind. She'd noticed this man in the Building of the Four Questions. He'd been with the technicians setting up the lights, the microphones, the TV camera, and recording equipment. He wore dark fatigues. Under his cap, he wore thick dark glasses.

Another Cyclopean. This one had a finely chiseled cheekbone. She assumed his left cheekbone was as pronounced as his right. She couldn't know for sure because he wasn't looking at her and would never look at her. *He only looks through people; that's what he's been told to do.*

The camp entrance guard raised the black-and-white pole used to control vehicle traffic.

'We only need to go to that spot about a kilometer away where the road widens for cars to turn,' said Gabriela. 'Someone will pick us up there,' she said.

'As you wish,' said the lieutenant. 'I'll drop you off there.'

He waved Tomas over to the jeep.

'Hop on in; hop,' said the lieutenant.

Tomas looked at Gabriela for direction. She jerked her head toward the jeep. Tomas got the message. Tomas walked around to the passenger side of the jeep. He clambered on board, sitting in back with the dark man. Gabriela stepped up to the front passenger seat.

As soon as she sat down, the lieutenant put the jeep in drive. They quickly traversed the open skirt of land that surrounded the penal camp. The fresh air felt good. Getting out of the jeep felt better. Tomas and Gabriela thanked the lieutenant for the ride. The dark man clambered around to the front passenger seat. He never looked at Gabriela or Tomas. In his own way, the Cyclopean seemed as bound as her brother had been. *The Revolution works that way to make the New Man.*

When the jeep headed away, Gabriela broke down crying. Waves of sadness and guilt and anger lapped against her. She covered her face in shame, helpless before the knowledge she'd somehow been used against her brother. Her brother wasn't dead. It was worse than that. He was among the living dead.

Tomas looked on in anguish.

'Please don't mind me,' she said, wiping her tears. 'It was too much.'

'Gabi, what happened?' asked Tomas.

She covered her face again. She cried. He approached her and tenderly put his hands on her shoulders. She didn't resist.

'It was horrible, horrible, Tomas.'

Tomas squeezed her shoulders. A pick-up truck was approaching them from Estacion ES.

'Let's get off to the side,' said Tomas, leading Gabriela to the small ditch at the roadside.

The truck halted in the middle of the wide spot, its trailing dust momentarily engulfing them all. As the dust cleared, the lone driver became apparent. It was the counter guard.

'Who's your chum?' he asked.

Gabriela didn't want to reply. He had no business asking, no good business.

Tomas replied, 'I have an uncle who is in state security.'

'I'm not dumb enough to believe that, but you're dumb enough to say it. She shouldn't have to spend the evening with a dumb kid, when she could have me instead. I can help her brother.'

Tomas turned to Gabriela and in a low voice asked, 'Is *he* the one who made it so horrible?'

'It's more than that,' she whispered.

Tomas took Gabi's hand. 'This way!'

Gabriela followed him, jumping over the ditch into the woods.

'Where are we going?' she asked.

'Away from him,' said Tomas.

'We could get lost,' said Gabriela.

'We'll try to stay parallel with the road,' said Tomas. 'We can't stray too far because of the swamp.'

She looked back to the truck. Prince Charming was running toward them. He hadn't bothered to slam shut the door.

'Quicker,' said Gabriela.

For the next ten minutes, she and Tomas navigated through the dusty green forest that lined the road. Gabriela kept looking back. She couldn't see far, but neither, she guessed, could the prince.

When they came to a small clearing among the trees, there stood the grim counter man. Tomas and Gabriela ducked, hoping he'd not seen or heard them. The country was alive with birds. A slight wind rustled the leaves, so perhaps he'd not heard them. How had he gotten ahead of them?

Tomas pointed in the direction of the road. Gabriela nodded in agreement. She would rather take her chances out in the open. In the woods, Tomas might get murdered and worse happen to her.

Getting to the road took longer than expected. They had unknowingly veered away from it, but they managed to get back. Because of a road bend in the direction of Estacion ES, the truck wasn't visible.

On the road, Gabriela and Tomas walked briskly toward town, all ears and eyes scanning the woods on the west side of the road, where the guard might be waiting. *He's more animal than man.*

Gabriela began running. Tomas followed her lead. Every meter closer to town was a meter closer to safety. A shout from behind startled them. Coming out of the woods onto the road behind them was their nemesis. Prince Charming looked slightly worse for wear.

Tomas trotted to the side of the road. Gabriela stopped, breathing heavily.

Catching her breath, she asked, 'What are you doing?'

'I'm looking for a stone,' yelled Tomas, dashing into the woods.

Gabriela started running again along the road, looking over her shoulder again and again. Would she be able to outrun their nemesis? And what of Tomas?

After looking back several times, she saw Tomas running on a hummock that paralleled the road. Prince Charming wasn't far behind. As he ran, he was tugging at the pistol on his right side.

Tomas took a leap across the ditch lining the road. The nemesis, rather than leap, attempted to run down the hummock. He stumbled and came crashing head down. The counter guard hadn't managed to disengage his arms to break his fall.

Gabriela stopped in her tracks when she saw the man fall. She was almost out of breath. So was Tomas when he came alongside her. Tomas looked back to see what she saw. The man lay still by the road.

'What happened?' asked Gabriela.

'I don't know, but so far he's not getting up.'

'Should we go back?'

Tomas didn't answer immediately then said, 'It would help matters – I think – if Frederico came along.'

'What if he already came along, while we were in the woods?'

'That's what I mean. Frederico might be back towards the labor camp in the turning spot waiting for us.'

'What time is it?' asked Gabriela.

'Almost time for him to show up. I know him. He often runs early.'

'We have no choice but to go back,' said Gabriela, 'but then there's *him.*' *He* lay inert. Was he hoping to spring on them?

'Let's go,' said Tomas.

The two approached their late pursuer. He'd fallen face-first onto the road, his lower torso and forelegs forming a broken bridge over the road ditch. His knees, like his face, were well set in the dirt.

In fumbling to un-holster his pistol, the counterman had failed to break his fall. A swelling was obvious at the man's neckline. He seemed to have broken his neck. Tomas grabbed a shoulder and turned the man over so that he was face up. He cleared gobs of dirt out of the man's mouth. Blood streamed from numerous cuts on his face.

'He's not breathing,' said Tomas.

'What are we going to do?' asked Gabriela.

'They'll never understand,' said Tomas. 'Never. Help me pull him off into the woods.'

'For real?'

'Do you have a better idea?' he asked.

She shook her head.

Tomas grabbed the man by the armpits to pull him headfirst into the palm and brush forest. Gabriela straightened out the legs. Neither bothered to check the gun holster. Tomas tugged the body. Gabriela came alongside him to help pull. The running had depleted their energy. They managed to pull the body perhaps a hundred meters into the woods, near the edge of a wet area.

'Are we just going to leave him here?' asked Gabriela.

'We've got to get back out on the road to meet Frederico. As a man, he deserves a burial; as an animal, he'll be devoured; and before God, we are innocent.'

'Do you believe that?' said Gabriela.

The counter guard's holster was empty. The gun had fallen out during the dragging.

'We've got to find the gun,' she said, frisking the dead man's pockets. Frisking didn't make sense, but she did so in a spirit of thoroughness.

'Forget it, Gabriela. We wouldn't want to keep it if we found it. It would only tie us to this man's death. It would be the death of us both. I don't want the gun. Come on. Let's go.'

'Are you sure?' asked Gabriela.

Tomas nodded a 'yes' and started walking to the road.

Gabriela knew she wanted a gun or something that might be helpful. Anything. As Tomas headed towards the road, she felt a large metal object in the man's leg pocket. It was a knife, a Swiss army knife, of all things. She took it and put it in her purse. She ran to catch up with Tomas. He was following the track they'd made dragging the body into the woods.

'He had designs on you,' Tomas said.

'Yes, I know that. Thank you for saving me from *him*.'

'Thank Him up above and may He guide us, for I'm sure this won't be the end of this matter.'

She shivered. She knew Tomas was right.

'Keep your eye out for the gun!' he said.

'So, you've changed your mind?' asked Gabriela.

'Maybe.'

They were back at the edge of the road. Tomas looked about his feet.

'There it is,' said Tomas.

The army-issue pistol was lying in the bottom of the ditch.

'Don't touch it,' said Tomas. 'I'll get a stick and some leaves. Stand by the pistol. If you see someone come along, use your feet to cover the pistol with dirt.'

Gabriela stood over the pistol while Tomas ran up to some nearby foliage, yanking off leaves.

'What are you going to do?'

'I'm going to heave that thing away from the road,' said Tomas.

He returned with some leaves. He wrapped them around the gun.

'Stay here,' he said as he took off into the woods with the pistol. He'd been away about three minutes when Gabriela could see a vehicle coming from town. It was the VW microbus.

'Hurry up,' shouted Gabriela. 'Your uncle's coming.'

Before Tomas returned, Kiko pulled the VW to a halt alongside Gabriela.

'Where's my son?' he asked after rolling down the passenger side window.

'Over there,' said Gabriela, nodding towards the woods.

'What's he doing there?' asked Kiko.

Best not to say too much. 'What do boys do in the woods?' she replied.

'I see, well, you might as well get in,' said Kiko.

'Thank you,' said Gabriela.

She decided riding up front was best. For one thing, she'd want to persuade Kiko not to continue to the spot where the late counter guard had left the truck in the middle of the road. The truck would be visible just around the next bend.

'Can you turn this VW right here in the road, while we're waiting for Tomas?' she asked.

'What do you mean "can you"? Can anyone or can I personally?' asked Kiko.

'You, personally. Are you that skilled?'

'You ask and I'll deliver,' he said.

He turned on the ignition and proceeded to stir and saw the VW so that it was pointed back towards town by the time Tomas appeared.

'What were you doing in the woods?' asked Kiko.

'A job,' said Tomas, sliding in behind his uncle.

'Well, I hope Mother Nature is satisfied,' said Kiko, laughing.

'She can be easy to satisfy in the right places,' said Tomas.

'I guess so,' said Gabriela.

Kiko gunned the VW once Tomas was aboard. Kiko had become a bit of a show-off, pleased to bring easy satisfaction to his somewhat captive audience.

As far as Gabriela was concerned, Kiko's charms now were just fine. It was good to be in the VW. She looked back and noticed Tomas also looking back. What had just happened wouldn't be so easily 'satisfied.' No, nor would others. She knew that.

12.

When Kiko and Tomas dropped off Gabriela at her aunt's place, she was relieved the day had ended. Or so she thought. Tomas had wanted to escort her up to the apartment, but she had resisted. She knew she'd be tempted to unload on Tomas. She had a cargo of accumulated emotions. Better to unload them before her dear aunt rather than a stranger-not-a-stranger-anymore. What was Tomas to her? She wasn't sure. Unlike the dead man they'd left out in the woods, he resisted labels.

So did Tomas' father or, rather, his uncle. Tomas had stopped referring to him as 'Uncle,' simply using his first name, Frederico. Gabriela still thought of him as Kiko. When they'd returned to Havana, he'd treated Tomas and her to a well-known restaurant that specialized in serving hard-currency tourists. He had the Canadian loonies to pay for such a meal. Gabriela guessed Kiko wanted to shower attention on Tomas. She guessed Tomas wouldn't be swayed by a thousand meals. Nonetheless, she was grateful to be well-fed. She had hoped the meal would somehow bury her emotions. She'd had her fill of death for one day. Now she wanted a good night's rest. As Tomas left, she promised to call him in the morning.

When she came to her aunt and uncle's door, she knocked as a prelude to opening it. Aunt Florina had told her to just walk on in. As she opened the door and unzipped the pink jacket, she looked up. There stood Carlos, where her aunt or uncle might have been. Why would Carlos be here? Where were her aunt and uncle?

'Come in,' said Carlos.

Another man walked over to the door, lest she be tempted to turn around. This man stepped around Gabriela and closed the front door. She recognized the man. He was one of the Cyclopeans she and Tomas had seen at Miguel's apartment.

'Where are my aunt and uncle?' asked Gabriela.

'Why do you assume they're not here?' replied Carlos.

'Are they?'

'No. They're enjoying the evening out, no doubt.'

'Enjoying,' said Gabriela doubtfully.

'Yes. They're at a recital of pieces from *La Forza del Destino*; not the opera, just a recital. We provided the tickets. Have you ever been to the opera?'

'Once,' said Gabriela.

'Did you enjoy it?'

'I did.'

'Good. Well, I can't offer you opera tonight but you, too, now have an encounter with destiny.'

'I'd rather not,' said Gabriela. 'I don't believe in any such nonsense as destiny. Life is full of choices. Often we seem to make the wrong ones.'

'You are a good student of life. Life can be operatic, but it's much more than opera. That's why you'll cooperate and come along with me. Choices lead to consequences. And sometimes they lead to accidents.'

Gabriela nodded a silent assent. Carlos nodded at the other man. He had her travel bag in hand. It appeared to be loaded.

Pointing at it, she asked, 'What's this?'

'Your luggage, of course,' said Carlos. 'You'll not be coming back here.'

'My aunt and uncle will be alarmed if I'm not home when they return.'

'That's considerate,' said Carlos, 'but rest assured they won't be alarmed. All will be taken care of. Please, follow our comrade.'

Our comrade, my eye!

She followed the comrade. Carlos followed her, closing the door behind. Kiko and Tomas were no longer in front of the building. Instead, another gleaming black Mercedes stood at the foot of the curb. The man who led her down opened the car's rear door and signaled with the luggage that she should step inside. Carlos walked around the car and took the seat next to her. Gabriela guessed the driver was the other Cyclopean from Miguel's.

When his partner settled in the front passenger seat, the driver started the car. They were soon weaving through the streets of Havana. Gabriela asked no questions and Carlos made no small talk.

About a quarter hour passed before they arrived at their destination, a dimly lit outlook over the sea. Gabriela could hear the waves as soon as one of the men opened her door. When she got out, she was thankful she was wearing the pink jacket. The jacket wasn't adequate against the bluster of wind coming off the water. She shivered.

'You are cold, yes?' asked Carlos, now standing next to her.

Was the shivering that visible?

'Yes,' she said. 'Can we sit in the car?'

'Perhaps,' said Carlos. 'The north wind is like the hand of death. You may try to hide from it, but you either face it or you pretend it's not there. What shall it be for you?'

'The wind or death?' asked Gabriela.

'Both,' said Carlos.

'What do you want from me?' she asked.

'Now we're talking. A heavy jacket for our guest,' said Carlos.

One of his men opened the trunk and retrieved a jacket, which he handed to Carlos. Carlos asked Gabriela, 'May I help you?'

'Yes,' she replied, quickly shedding the light jacket and taking the other that Carlos handed her. It was a down-filled jacket, not typically found in Cuba. Was it reserved for occasions such as this when a 'guest' was brought to a fabulous overlook to make a 'choice'? And what would that choice be?

'What do you want from me?'

'Cooperation, of course,' said Carlos. 'Think of your brother. Think of yourself.'

'Yes, but apparently you're thinking of something else and what is that?' asked Gabriela.

'I'm thinking you had a disappointing visit with your brother today.'

'I wouldn't call it a visit.'

'No,' said Carlos, 'it was more like a rehearsal. Once you got the hang of things, you did a wonderful job reading your script.'

'And my brother did a fabulous job on his end of things.'

'We mustn't get sarcastic. Sarcasm blinds the beholder.'

'What do you want?'

'Information,' said Carlos.

'About what?'

'About the distribution of Bibles here in our homeland.'

'I know nothing.'

'You were with my sister as she lay dying in Santiago.'

'I already gave you the *Testamento*. And you took away the dolphin pendant. What more can you expect?'

'There must have been more.'

Gabriela swung to walk away from Carlos. What was she to say?

Carlos took one of her forearms and led her to the edge of the slope that dropped off to the waves below. The wind was quite brisk, almost howling.

'This is a place favored by suicides,' shouted Carlos, 'but you're too smart for that.'

She shouted back, 'I hope so. There *was* more. There were letters. There was one for your brother, one for Tomas, another for your brother-in-law, and one for you.'

Carlos led her away from the precipice. In a measured tone, he asked, 'Was that all?'

'I don't know how much your sister had to give away. She seemed to be a giving kind of person.'

'Do you have the letters with you now?' asked Carlos.

'Yours. Kiko and Tomas and Miguel have already received theirs.'

'Where's mine?'

'In my purse in the car.'

They returned to the car. Carlos opened Gabriela's door. She took a seat inside. He shut the door. While he walked around to the other side, she frantically tried to bury the Swiss army knife under a flap at the bottom of the purse. She tried, too, to identify Adan's letter. *Mustn't give that to Carlos.* It was in the larger of two envelopes she was carrying. She felt for the envelopes. The size difference seemed hardly discernible. An error would be costly, but Adan's must not remain in the purse. She plucked what seemed the larger of the two and tucked it inside her blouse just as Carlos took his seat next to her.

She was thankful he closed his door. The escorts seemed oblivious of the cold. They were wearing heavy suit jackets as they leaned against the car smoking cigarettes.

When Carlos sat down, he switched on a reading light mounted on the rear dashboard. He pulled and adjusted its caterpillar steel neck, so he'd be able to read the letter in his lap. He asked, 'Where's the letter?'

She retrieved the remaining envelope in her purse. *It had better be the right one otherwise he'll soon be pawing in the purse.*

Carlos took the envelope from her hands and ripped it open, placing the letter under the glow of the lamp.

Gabriela was relieved. It was the right one. The letter was very short, something like this as she remembered:

My dear brother,

The most important choice anyone can make in life is the choice you, too, must make: to be of our Lord's fold or not to be. By God's grace may you choose wisely.

Your Adriana.

Beneath that appeared the 23rd Psalm. Adriana had been able to dictate it to Gabriela from memory. For Gabriela, the psalm was a series of images and the one that came forward now was the image of a 'table prepared before me in the presence of mine enemies.'

Perhaps that very image had hit home with Carlos. His response to the letter was to rip it to shreds while sputtering a string of expletives. Rather than leave the shreds on the back seat, Carlos gathered them up in a tight ball. He opened his door, walked towards the slope, and attempted to hurl the ball into the sea. But the wind carried it back almost to his feet. He tried hurling it again with a similar result. After the second failure, he instructed one of his men to incinerate the paper with a cigarette. That done to his satisfaction, he returned to the car, resumed his seat, and shut the door.

'We've got some unfinished business. Enough about my sister. She's dead. If you're not careful, your brother could soon be dead.'

'He's almost dead now,' said Gabriela.

'There's always your father and your aunts.'

'My father's a party member in very good standing,' replied Gabriela.

'So what? Anyway, your aunts are nothing, nothing at all. They are something to you but nothing to me.'

And, likewise, your own family.

'I want information about Bible distribution activities. Now.'

'I don't have any.'

'Then you're going to acquire some. As of this moment, if you have any care for yourself, for those you love, or for your country, you'll begin gathering information.'

'What kind of information?'

'Anything connected with anti-state activities.'

'I'm not involved in any groups like that.'

'You're traveling with my brother and our nephew.'

'Your brother is a party member.'

'That proves nothing. And, anyway, a real poison seems to be brewing with my nephew… not to mention others. I want you to learn all you can and quickly. My family has been a millstone around my neck for too long. May my wretched sister rot in hell!'

'You believe in hell?' asked Gabriela.

'Of course not, but it's a model destination for those who oppose the revolution. Is it the destination you choose?'

'No,' said Gabriela.

'Good, then you can begin working for the revolution or count yourself among the living dead.'

'Where do I go from here?' asked Gabriela.

'I will deposit you with my brother-in-law Miguel, where my sister and her husband lived. You've been there. I know.'

'Yes, I have.'

'That's where you'll stay.'

'For how long?' asked Gabriela. 'I don't really know him, I mean Miguel.'

'You'll get to know him, along with others. That's what you've chosen for the sake of the revolutionary state.'

'Yes.' *But where was the bright side?*

13.

The bright side was this: Gabriela wouldn't be spending the night in some dank, rat-infested cell. Carlos wanted to place his newest agent elsewhere. Miguel was caught off-guard. When he appeared at his door, he wasn't wearing dark glasses. Just a stained T-shirt and baby blue pajama bottoms. He looked vulnerable, maybe because she felt vulnerable.

Was Carlos expecting her to become 'available' for Miguel? Surely that couldn't be expected. How could she protest? She was now an agent of the state. For once she wished her father were alongside. *Surely, he would protect her.* Or would his ambition know no bounds? Best not to think of it.

She was about to beg Carlos to take her to jail when Miguel spoke, 'Excuse my appearance. I was about to go to bed. This is all rather surprising. What is it, comrades, that you call on me at this late hour?'

Carlos said, 'You've met this young woman when she and Tomas visited recently.'

'I have trouble seeing her, but I detect the perfume. Yes, this is the one. Gabriela, yes?'

'Gabriela,' she replied. *What can he be thinking?*

'I want her kept here overnight. In the backroom. She'll stay with you until we retrieve her,' said Carlos.

One of the Cyclopeans shoved Gabriela in Miguel's direction. The other threw her travel bag and pink jacket onto the floor.

'Is she under arrest?' asked Miguel.

'Obviously, not,' said Carlos, 'but almost so. Be a good host.'

'But…'

'No *but*,' said Carlos. 'Take off the jacket.'

Gabriela realized she was being spoken to. She removed the down jacket and handed it to a Cyclopean. Carlos wheeled about and his men followed, slamming shut the door. That and the racket on the stairs must have awakened all the tenants, or so Gabriela thought.

'I'll show you to the room. There's a toilet at the end of the hall. Follow me.'

She did, grabbing the bag and the pink jacket. Miguel left her alone in Adriana and Adan's room. She felt exhausted. Even more, she was bewildered. She felt abandoned and entrapped.

14.

She'd not been forgotten. Tomas had wanted to talk more than he and Gabriela had allowed themselves to talk with others around. When he and Kiko had arrived back at his grandparents, he'd resolved to sneak out and retrieve Gabriela from her aunt's place. Before he even tried, Kiko received a telephone call from Carlos. His brother told him he'd placed Gabriela in the protective custody of Miguel. Kiko told Tomas and said he'd be wise to keep his mouth shut about this.

Mouth shut; Tomas was relieved. He hadn't any idea how he'd retrieve Gabriela from her aunt and uncle's apartment. But at least he'd walked from front to back at Miguel's. He guessed she'd been put in the back bedroom.

No one objected when Tomas said he was going out for a walk. It took about twenty minutes of brisk walking to reach Miguel's. When Tomas arrived at Miguel's place, he went around the block seeking an alley that would connect to the back courtyard. He wasn't disappointed. But in the courtyard, there was no streetlight. How to tell one apartment building from another?

He remembered the potted geraniums. Once his eyes had adjusted to the poor light, he looked for Miguel's geraniums. Most of the landings had potted flowers backlit by light coming through the windows. There were several second-floor landings that appeared to have potted geraniums. His rough calculation of distance and direction led him to guess the most probable set of stairs to Miguel's back-porch landing.

At the second-floor landing, he had a choice; knock at the door or knock at the window. He could hear mellow Caribbean steel drum music coming from a radio. The casement window was slightly opened inwards. Bars covered the window. The door was a heavy wooden door. He'd probably have to pound on it to be heard and the noise might disturb more than Gabriela. If indeed this was Miguel's.

Tomas squatted down at the window and gave a low whistle, then loudly whispered 'Gabi' several times. The steel drums kept drumming away from the radio.

Tomas reached through the bars and tapped on the windowpane. He tapped again. 'It's Tomas,' he whispered loudly.

'Tomas,' came two whispers, hers then his, again.

'What are you doing here?' Gabriela asked, crouching down to his level.

'I wanted to know you were OK.'

'I'm OK, more or less. How about you?' she asked.

'I'm OK. Why'd they bring you over here?'

'Maybe I should come outside. Let me get dressed. We can walk around. There're some things I want to tell you about.'

'Yes, we can walk… over to the church.'

'I'll get dressed,' she whispered. She rapidly changed into day clothes and put on the pink jacket.

She was about to open the landing door when she heard a pounding at the door between her room and the rest of Miguel's flat.

'Gabriela, what's going on? Let me in.' It was Miguel.

He couldn't just barge in because the door was equipped with an interior lock. In fact, when he'd helped her settle in, he'd shown Gabriela the lock as an assurance of her privacy. Adan had installed the lock.

If Gabriela let in Miguel, he'd have a host of questions. Why was she wearing day clothes and the jacket? Was there someone on the back porch? Who? She would have her own questions of Miguel: How had he heard anything? Was state security already on the way? But the most important question was one only she could ask and answer: Was she prepared to run with Tomas somewhere? And was *he* prepared to run and where? *Ah, yes, and that, too.*

She wished that God were personal in the way Adriana viewed God, in the way that Tomas seemed to view God. Prayer made sense if there were such a god. How could she pray? She'd never been taught.

'Let me in, Gabriela. Don't stretch my hospitality,' said Miguel.

This is hospitality?

She went to the window and whispered, 'Run. Come by in the morning. Run.'

'I will,' she heard.

What is to be said to Miguel?

Be honest, be honest.

'I'm coming,' said Gabriela.

She unlocked the door.

'What took you so long?' asked Miguel. He, too, was now wearing street clothes.

'Tomas was at the window,' she replied.

'Aye, yi, yi, yi, yi,' he said. 'A rendezvous, eh?'

'I wouldn't call it that,' said Gabriela. She felt herself blushing. 'I wouldn't make anything of it like that. No, I wouldn't.'

But there might have been some small part of *that* there. Yes, there could be. But to reduce everything to *that*, well, that was simplistic and stupid. *Perhaps that's just as well right now.*

Miguel said, 'I wouldn't blame you. Reminds me of my youth.'

'You may no longer be young, but you've not lost your hearing,' said Gabriela.

'No, I haven't,' said Miguel. He walked to the back door, opened it up, looked around the porch, then shut and locked the door.

'I have supernatural hearing,' he said.

'Courtesy of state security?' she asked.

'That's for me to know and for you to wonder about,' he replied. 'There are more eyes and ears hereabouts than you'd want to know about.'

'To make the godly people living in this room quake in fear?' asked Gabriela.

'You're bold,' said Miguel, 'like my brother and his wife, but let me tell you. I'm speaking not as the local representative of the committee but as an old sailor. Don't rock the boat. Don't rock the boat.'

He wagged a finger in the air, not just anywhere, but directly toward Gabriela.

'Tomorrow's Adan's trial. We all need to get some sleep.'

'Tomorrow's Christmas Eve,' said Gabriela.

'I know, I know,' said Miguel. 'But the state must roll on and the party washes over everything. Everything.' His voice seemed to trail somewhere between dismay and disgust.

'In some ways you surprise me, party member that you are,' said Gabriela.

'I wouldn't make much of it and as I say, don't rock the boat. Then you'll survive. Good night.'

'Good night,' she replied. She locked the door once he'd gone toward his room.

She walked over to the radio and turned it off. She undressed and got under the bed covers. She was too tired to look for 'bugs' in the room. She had little to hide anyway, not at this point. As she drifted off to sleep, an image of the Advent house came to mind. It seemed silly, but the image was comforting. All things considered, that image was a good cap to an awful day.

El Corazón de Cuba

15.

Gabriela ate breakfast alone but ready to hit the street. Miguel had gone out on a 'run of errands,' as he'd said in a note left on the kitchen table. The note invited her to whatever was in the refrigerator. The pot of coffee on the stove could be heated. Cups were in a cupboard by the sink. The note enumerated a half dozen items and their whereabouts. It ended with Miguel's promise to return by nine a.m. It was now about eight fifteen.

When she had realized she was alone, she took heart. She might be able to walk away. Her look out the front window proved otherwise. There, down on the street, stood a young man in the well-dressed casual clothes typical of non-uniformed policemen. The back of the flat had been equally disappointing. Another young man stood in the courtyard below. So, there was no going anywhere.

Why hadn't Carlos simply put her in jail? Did he want to keep her out of state security hands because of Adriana? Because of Tomas? Or was this attention coming for other reasons? Had the counter guard been found? Found or not, had his disappearance been connected to her? Was there some reason unrelated to yesterday's events that prompted Carlos to put her under guard but out of jail? Or had Miguel summoned the Cyclopeans?

These questions hovered over her breakfast: coffee with milk and a banana. As she sat at the kitchen table, she looked at the Advent house from Bavaria. There was only one window whose shutters were still closed this morning. That was the window over the door to the house. Inscribed on one of its shutters was '24.' Today was the 24th. Shouldn't the shutters be opened?

She opened the shutters. Behind that window was a figure wearing a red turban and robe. The base of his pedestal bore the inscription 'Balthasar.' She had no idea who this might be. She noticed for the first time that the house door, really double doors, could be opened. She opened the doors. Behind them was a manger with the baby Jesus in it. In the window to the right was a carved lady saint in blue robes. This had to be Mary. To the left was a man saint. It must be Joseph. She looked at his pedestal. It bore the inscription 'S. Josef.'

All the saints – they must be saints – had been arranged so they would face Jesus. Each of the carved figures had round bases sitting in round holes. Miguel could have left them facing any direction. Yet he'd troubled to insure they'd be facing Jesus when the doors were opened on Christmas morning. Indeed, he could have simply left the whole affair in storage. Or translated the house into black-market cash.

Gabriela closed the Jesus doors. She closed Balthasar's shutter. It was Miguel's job to open it. *Miguel has a warm streak.* Such knowledge was a sweet savor against the sourness of being under watch.

While washing the morning's dishes and cups, she heard a knock at the front door. The kitchen clock was ten minutes shy of nine. With a dishtowel in one hand, she used her free hand to open the front door. There stood Tomas.

'Good morning,' he said somewhat sheepishly.

'Morning,' she replied. 'Come in.'

'Is Miguel here?'

'Not that I know of,' she replied, pointing with her right hand to her right ear and with her left flittering about toward the bounds of the room.

Tomas nodded, acknowledging he understood the room was bugged. He said, 'I came by because I wanted to ask whether you'd accompany me...' and then his voice trailed off as he looked about the room. When he spotted a radio near the front window, he went over and turned it on, volume high. The voice of the leader could be heard, seemingly recorded from a recent speech. Under this din, Tomas and Gabriela whispered.

He said, 'I've learned my father's trial starts at ten. Frederico got a call this morning. Someone provided him information on the trial location.'

'Someone? Who?' asked Gabriela. *Perhaps Miguel?*

'Frederico wouldn't say. Will you come with me?'

Tomas saw her hesitation. 'If you don't wish to come, you can stay here. I'll come back later.'

'No, I think I'll go. I think I must. Yes, let's go. That would be the thing to do. But we'll be lucky if we manage to get beyond the men guarding this building.'

'I saw them, but I don't believe in luck. Randomness, but not luck,' said Tomas.

'You're confident,' she said.

'We'll get out.'

She hung the dishtowel to dry, then went to the back room to retrieve the pink jacket and purse. As she slung the purse over her shoulder, she wondered if she should remove the Swiss army knife and the penknife. Guards might search Tomas and Gabriela at the courtroom. Her purse would be an obvious search target. She decided to leave the knives in Adriana's dresser. She opened the dresser drawer. There in the drawer lay what appeared to be a house key with a blue plastic pendant emblazoned with the Bolivian flag.

She placed the knives in the drawer. She felt drawn to taking the house key. At least it seemed to be a house key. She closed the drawer. No, the key might come in handy. She opened the drawer, plucked out the key, and thrust it in her purse. Of course, to arrive at the courtroom they'd have to get around the men guarding Miguel's building.

'How are we going to get out... do you know?' whispered Gabriela when she'd returned from the bedroom. 'I have *this*.' She showed Tomas the key.

He frowned, then pointed up. Gabriela knew sometimes you could go from one rooftop to another. Would it be possible now? How could they get access to the roof? She wanted to ask. But Tomas opened the door leading to the front stairwell. There stood Miguel.

'Good morning, my friends,' he said. 'On your way somewhere?'

'We're on the way to my father's trial,' said Tomas, not in the least flustered by the appearance of Miguel.

'I'll join you there later,' said Miguel.

'So, you know where the trial is,' said Tomas.

'It comes with my territory.'

'Yes, I suppose so in the CDR. Perhaps you can tell me whether it would be best going upstairs or down to depart from this building.'

'Down would be safest, of course,' said Miguel. 'Isn't that obvious? Now that I'm here, *she* may go. You, too. I'll join you at the trial.'

'Don't feel obliged,' said Tomas. 'My father must embarrass you.'

'Oh, he's caused enough trouble for the revolution and me. But I'll come. I may be of help. The revolution has always been about helping people, ordinary people.'

'So they say,' said Tomas.

'So we know,' said Miguel. 'A car is waiting to take you.'

'A car!' blurted Gabriela.

'It was sent to Tomas' grandparents. When the driver learned you'd come over here, Tomas, he came here. You should be grateful. And you shouldn't wander about.'

Tomas said, 'I'm uneasy around government angels.'

That said, Gabriela and Tomas didn't linger in Miguel's apartment. They were taken away. As they traveled through Havana, they said almost nothing to one another. Gabriela assumed the car was bugged. Tomas must have shared the assumption. The trip wasn't without communication. Tomas handed Gabriela the letter from his mother that Gabriela had given him.

My dear Tomas,

From a distance, I have watched you through the years. I am thankful for your second mother, dear Pamela. She has been helpful to me. She has been a servant of God.

You are now a young man. Though unlikely, you may have an opportunity to become acquainted with your true father. Whatever happens, you must look elsewhere for a model of your humanity. Christ is our king and our model, for man or woman.

Nearer at hand you must look further away. You must look abroad. Abroad there is Archbishop Romero (whose photograph Pamela passed on to you). May he be a near inspiration to you. And may you grow in the grace of our Savior, Jesus Christ. Forgive me for not being the mother I could have been.

Adriana, your mother always, by the grace of God.

Handing the letter back to Tomas, Gabriela was moved to ask, 'Does the archbishop mean anything to you?'

'He does,' said Tomas. 'He's a model voice for Cubans, too.'

'But our situation is so different here,' said Gabriela.

'You think so?' he asked.

'Socially objectively speaking, it is,' said she. That was cant, but what was she to say? Someone might be listening in on the conversation.

Tomas placed his mother's letter in its envelope. He placed the envelope on his lap and produced a ballpoint pen. On the back flap of the envelope, he wrote this: Florida.

Tapping that word, he said, 'Would you like to meet her?'

'Her? You mean—'

Tomas put a finger to his lips, taking the air out of what Gabriela was about to say. Could Tomas be thinking of escaping to Florida? Was he somehow receiving support to go there? What could Florida have to do with the archbishop of San Salvador? Must she report any of this to Carlos and if so, how? She'd rather report nothing, but she had no wish to imperil her aunts or Beto – if Beto were still alive.

Carlos had others to do his bidding. Why her, too? She knew the longhand answer, but not then the short. Where would this all lead? She could hope this would lead to a brighter future, a bright land far from intrigue. Then came the thought out of nowhere that went straight to her heart: *In Cuba, betrayal is darker than a moonless night and more numerous than the stars.*

16.

Adan's trial would take place in a colonial era building. The exterior was charming. Gabriela knew older meant more charming in Cuba. CubaTur posters didn't feature Soviet-inspired Brutalist buildings except by accident.

The proceedings were to be conducted in a room below street level with high-set windows. The windows were at the bottom of light wells. The room was rather warm and stuffy. There wasn't any obvious reason why this was so. Nothing could be done about the unseasonable warmth; the windows were sealed shut. This would not be paradise.

The room was small by comparison to the courtroom Gabriela once visited as a schoolgirl. A raised platform with a table would accommodate the judge. A seal of state gleamed on the wall behind the platform. Directly beneath the judge's table was a table and chair for a court reporter. The reporter was already at her station. She would be the only woman in the courtroom beside Gabriela. Wooden benches with slatted backs looked like they could accommodate 150 spectators. These benches were taken up entirely by men of two types. They either were quite young, wearing army, police, or state security uniforms or

wearing the crisp casual of the undercover types —
except no one was wearing dark glasses here. Or they
were grey-headed men in civvies, probably pensioners
called out to duty. Tomas and Gabriela and Miguel
(once he arrived) would have to stand at the back of the
room, which was permitted. At least the guards were
courteous.

The main actors in the proceedings would occupy
the furniture between the judge and the spectators. A
team of three prosecutors, two in business suits and one
in an army uniform, entered and took their places up
front. When they took their places, the chatter faded.
Adan's entry into the court with uniformed escorts
prompted catcalls and whistles followed by a hush. One
of the guards stepped in front of the judge's table and
gave the 'All rise' as the judge entered from a side door.
The judge smiled and looked more like an uncle than a
judge. He took his seat. The rest of the assembled did
likewise.

After everyone was seated, a guard at the front of
the room identified the court case and read off the
charges. Adan was accused of distributing religious
literature without a license, conducting religious
services in unauthorized locations, participating in a
network of implicitly anti-revolutionary zealots, giving
comfort to anti-state agents and saboteurs, enticing and
corrupting the youth of the nation, and subverting the
public order and tranquility in order to sow anarchy.

'How does the accused answer these charges?' asked the judge, looking over his spectacles.

One of the men in suits stood up. Apparently, he'd been assigned to defend Adan.

The suit said, 'Guilty on all counts, your honor.'

'Innocent,' shot back Adan. 'Innocent, your honor.'

Catcalls and whistles erupted. 'Order in the court,' shouted the head guard. The room quieted down.

'Innocent, you say,' said the judge. 'Innocent, yet your own legal counsel has pled "guilty" on all counts on your behalf.'

'My counsel is an atheist and therefore unequipped to speak on my behalf, to speak to charges that arise because of my religious faith,' said Adan.

'There is not a word about this man's faith in any of these charges,' shouted a spectator.

'Hang 'em,' shouted another. Another shouted, 'He's a liar.'

'Order,' shouted the chief guard.

The judge spoke to the spectators. 'The people's perceptions of the character of the accused are no doubt true, but the people's government has invested me with the primary responsibility for administering justice in this case. While your fervor for justice sustains the revolutionary state, I must ask you to withhold further comments about the accused until a judgment has been reached. Otherwise, we may be here all morning when higher duty calls all of us elsewhere.'

Looking at Adan, the judge continued. 'Now the charges against you are not against your faith. You have, of course, complete and total freedom of conscience in matters of faith. That is guaranteed by the state. But no state can give its citizens complete freedom of action. You cannot steal. You cannot murder. And for the sake of all, each of us must submit ourselves to a regimen of regulations designed to make the best society any reasonable man could ask for. Am I not right?'

'No doubt, your honor, but even so I am innocent.'

'Even so? These are very serious charges leveled against you. The maximum sentence under the worst of these charges is thirty years' imprisonment. If you are adjudged guilty of all these charges, I could choose to impose the sentences sequentially. You'd never again be a free man.'

'Before God I am a free man. Without God, no human freedom is possible.'

'That is, of course, a deluded lie,' said the judge, 'a religious delusion, merely a quirk of conscience if kept to yourself, but a dangerous poison if shared with others. I'm sure all the adults in this room share with me the knowledge that our freedoms are granted and insured by the state. Thanks to the revolution, you live in an imperishable state that is rationally and scientifically based, assuring you the maximum freedom possible. You choose to spurn the plea offered by your court-appointed counsel just as you choose, apparently, to spurn the reasonable, protective embrace of our revolutionary state.'

'Of that, I am accused,' said Adan. 'The protective embrace of the state is a farce. No freethinking man or woman wants it. Only religious zealots who worship at the altar of the state want that.'

The judge laughed from shock. Some nervous titters could be heard around the courtroom.

'Religious zealots, altar of the state, huh? You must like million-peso phrases, but I've got my feet on the ground, and you've got yourself in the docket. These proceedings must move along. I gather you deliberately choose to reject the legal counsel the state has provided on your behalf.'

'I do.'

'Are you able to hire your own legal counsel?'

'I have none.'

'You have none. Is it your intention to act on your own behalf?'

'I have no choice but to do so.'

'Be it entered that the defendant rejected the legal counsel afforded him by the state and that the defendant claims complete innocence on all charges.'

'So entered,' replied the court reporter.

'Thank you. Now, ordinarily, I would ask the prosecutors to elaborate on the written charges submitted to the court. But given that the defendant has spurned competent legal counsel, I will, as it were, tie one hand behind the prosecution's back out of a spirit of fairness.'

Murmuring swept the spectators. The judge continued.

'Let us get to your defense. Do you have any witnesses on your behalf?'

'God is my witness that in distributing Bibles, as I'm proud to say I've done, I have never intended to harm the state.'

'You may behave like a child,' replied the judge, 'but legally you are an adult. You cannot pretend ignorance of regulations pertaining to the distribution of political and religious literature. Are you ignorant of these matters?'

'No, your honor.'

'Then how is God going to help you? Do you have his address?'

The room erupted in laughter.

'God forgive you, your honor.'

'You presume to say that in this courtroom! I could hold you in contempt of court.'

'Forgive me, I spoke out of place,' said Adan.

'Indeed,' said the judge. 'Is it your only sin?'

'I have many sins.'

'I'm sure you do.'

'We are lost sinners, all but for the grace of God,' said Adan.

'There you go again. You're engaging in religious proselytizing in this very courtroom. If you could, you'd corrupt everyone in this courtroom to your way of thinking. And then what? You'd have us set fire to sugar refineries and sling around outrageous lies about our state leadership. You'd gather people in unsafe buildings to hear you rant and rave about heaven and hell, I suppose. And then what? You'd claim your own country was a hell on earth. You've done as much, haven't you? And before you know it, the most gullible and suggestible would be out stirring up others in so many ways: spreading lies about our state leadership, impugning the motives of high-minded servants of the state, even destroying wherever possible the property of the state: ports, sugar refineries, you name it. And what can you say to all this?'

Adan hung down his head.

'Nothing, is that it? You can say nothing. You are making a case against yourself, bereft as you are of competent legal counsel. Out of the mercy of the court I give you the extraordinary opportunity to reconsider your intemperate rejection of the counsel graciously provided by the state. Will you accept that counsel?'

'I cannot, your honor. God is my only help.'

'*That* is no help at all. If you were a child, this intemperance, this petulance, would be forgivable perhaps,' said the judge, who was visibly reddening. 'But you are not a child, and I must treat you and judge you as an adult. Do you understand?'

'Yes, your honor.'

'Very well, then the court will adjourn for thirty minutes to consider the facts presented in the state's documents and as made evident in this morning's proceeding.'

The judge stood up. The chief guard shouted, 'All rise.' Once the judge had exited the side door, the room broke out in talk, largely joyous talk as the spectators shared their thrill with the superb legal skills of the judge. Some expressed relief the case was in such sure hands.

Adan was led by two guards through the center of this good feeling to the corridor. Gabriela couldn't help but see the resemblance between father and son, each with deep-set eyes and prominent cheeks. Adan appeared undaunted by events, but Tomas appeared dismayed. She and Tomas went out into the corridor in time to see Adan being taken into a room down the hall.

The crowd from the courtroom surged into the hall just as Miguel arrived on the scene. The tapping of his cane could barely be heard except to those close at hand. The cane seemed not to find a way, but rather to make a way. The crowd parted for Miguel, who took Tomas by the arm.

'Follow me,' he said. 'You, too, Gabriela.'

17.

Miguel took Tomas and Gabriela to a room that was an anteroom to another room. A guard stood in this room. He was neither surprised nor perplexed when Miguel whispered something in his ear. The guard nodded and Miguel beckoned Tomas and Gabriela to head into the room beyond.

This room had a high-set window. A table with four chairs, two facing two, took up the small floor space. Adan was seated at the table. A guard stood over him. Miguel took the chair next to Adan. He directed Gabriela and Tomas to sit in the chairs opposite. He handed the guard a piece of paper. The guard read it, grunted, then exited to the anteroom, where he joined his comrade.

Adan looked at Tomas, then Gabriela, then Miguel.

'My son has seen where we lived?' asked Adan of Miguel.

'He has,' replied Miguel.

Adan smiled and extended his hand across the table. 'My son,' he said, 'forgive your mother and me. This may be the only time you ever see me. Despite what you may have learned, your mother and I have always loved you dearly. Please, let us at least be friends.'

Tomas reached out and grasped his father's hand. 'More than friends, I think, Papa. More than friends.'

'How so?' asked Adan.

Miguel held up his right palm as a kind of stop sign, then swiveled his hand as a kind of caution sign. Was the room bugged? What was Miguel warning against? Whatever, Tomas heeded the warning.

He plunged his left hand into a pocket from which he retrieved a wallet. He opened the wallet and fished out a folded piece of paper. He unfolded the paper to reveal a reproduction of a photograph of the El Salvadoran archbishop, Oscar Romero.

'Do you know of this man?' asked Tomas.

'Of course,' replied his father. 'He's an inspiration.'

'Exactly,' said Tomas.

'Then you and I are more alike than I could have ever hoped, thanks be to…' Adan's voice trailed off.

'Somehow, the mango remembers the tree from which it came,' said Miguel.

'I think it's more complicated than that, my brother,' said Adan. 'I see the hand of God and his servants.'

'Wherever his hand,' said Miguel, 'he won't be stopping time or staying the decision of this court. Don't waste your minutes.'

'No, my brother. Does anyone have a pen?'

Gabriela was the first to retrieve one. She had a pen in her purse. Next to the pen was the letter Adriana had written to Adan. Should she hand that to him? She handed Adan the pen. There would be another time to hand over the letter… hopefully. This wasn't the time or place.

'Forgive me,' he said. 'We've never met, and we've not been introduced.'

Miguel spoke. 'Adan, would you have ever thought you'd be meeting anyone now, much less your son? This lady is a friend of your son I've just recently met. Perhaps I can explain later, but there's very little time.'

'My name is Gabriela Suarez Paloma,' she interjected.

'A companion in the faith?' asked Adan, smiling at Gabriela.

Gabriela shook her head.

'Perhaps someday,' said Adan. He took Tomas' paper and turned it over, so the photo of Oscar Romero was face down. He rapidly penned a note, then refolded the piece of paper and handed it to his son. He handed back the pen to Gabriela.

When Tomas began opening the paper, Adan shook his hand. 'Later,' he said, looking to the guards at the door.

They were chattering away. Miguel repeatedly turned his head towards the guards. Gabriela wondered whether his one semi-functional eye functioned better than he let on.

Suddenly, Adan stood up and pushed back his chair. One of the guards looked back into the room.

'I want to bless my son,' said Adan.

'Bless him? What do you mean?' asked Miguel. 'We can't have any religious ceremonies here.'

'This won't be a religious ceremony, merely an act of faith,' said Adan.

'Please, Adan, you've never known when to quit. Please, just sit down and talk while you have the chance.'

The observant guard was coming into the room.

'I will bless my son,' said Adan.

'Shut up and sit down,' said the guard.

'I must bless my son. I only wish to lay on my hands.'

'Sit down,' said the guard.

'Sit down,' said Miguel.

Adan sat, then pulled the chair up to the table. Extending his hands across the table, he said, 'Take my hands, son.'

Tomas extended his arms across the table. The two clasped hands. The guard looked perplexed.

'No funny business,' he said. He walked up to Tomas.

Gabriela put a hand on Tomas's shoulder.

'Comrade,' shouted the guard to get the attention of his partner.

Tomas looked his father directly in the face, not the least distracted by the commotion now taking place.

Adan said, looking straight at his son, 'May our heavenly Father bless you now and forever, by the power of his Spirit leading you away from harm and into life that day by day you may grow in the grace and discipleship of Jesus Christ, our Lord and Savior.'

The first guard pulled Tomas' chair away from the table. The second shouted to Adan to stand up.

'No funny business,' said the first guard.

'Take the prisoner back into the courtroom,' said Miguel. 'My brother has abused the mercy of the state. Take the prisoner away.'

'We shall. You are being generous, comrade,' said the first guard.

'The revolution is merciful,' said Miguel, 'infinitely merciful.'

'This way,' said the second guard, leading Adan from the room.

Tomas looked up to see his father being led away. Gabriela took one of Tomas' hands and squeezed it.

'We'd better return to the courtroom,' she said, releasing his hand.

'Yes,' he said, standing up.

Miguel was already at the doorway. 'Let's go,' he said.

When they returned to the courtroom, a seat was available for Miguel. As before, Tomas and Gabriela stood at the back of the room. And as before when the judge entered the room, all those in the courtroom stood and then reseated themselves once he had taken his chair. The judge spoke.

'The achievements in human progress and social justice attained by the scientific, socialist state are apparent to all decent humanity. Our new state for all the world to see has reduced criminality to the hard-core misfits and social parasites which perhaps, like disease, will always be with us. Beyond the obvious hard-core, though, there is a flesh of softer but equally perverse sort that together with the hard core form a poison fruit in the heart of any socialist paradise. We may be distracted when looking at this fruit to admire its beauty. When faced with a case such as this morning's, one cannot help but admire some aspects of the defendant.'

A murmur of denial met the assertion. The judge continued.

'Bear with me, please. I can't help but discern a certain integrity in the defendant. He has been in the business of distributing Bibles, an activity that he has not disavowed or denied before this court. Consistent with that accusation, he has pled belief in God, as if it were a requisite to the defense of his case. But God has not shown up.'

The courtroom burst into laughter.

'Nor is God a citizen of Cuba.'

There was a round of titters.

'Yet for all the obvious dangers of doing without legal counsel, the defendant has chosen to repudiate court-supplied counsel. This has been foolish bravery, to be sure, but bravery, nonetheless. Bravery is admirable. Coupled with this bravery has been perseverance. This perseverance would be worthy of emulation were it not perseverance for a perverse cause. Alas, this court duly notes the numerous previous engagements of the defendant with the authorities of the state. Again and again, the defendant has been arrested or cited for such things as illegal gatherings, illegal pamphleteering and publishing, incitement to fraudulent social objectives, debasement of youth, and so forth. Perseverance in personal conscience is no longer a virtue when it becomes obsessively destructive of human safety and the social fabric. Perseverance in pursuit of delusions is just another form of stupidity. If it became widespread, such stupidity and perverseness would greatly harm society.

'No objective, rational, scientific observer can fail to note the poisoned fruit that comes from the defendant's delusions. That the defendant has willfully rejected the competent legal counsel granted him is, however, no reason to treat him as a child. In the absence of such counsel, I shall not call for the defendant to sum up his defense. The court has already heard the defense and the defendant's implicit confession of guilt. Under the circumstances, there is no need for the state to sum up its accusations. The court shall now render its verdict.'

The chief guard bellowed out, 'The defendant shall rise.'

Adan stood. Four guards nearby rose to forestall any potential anti-judicial motions by the defendant.

'On the first charge of distributing religious literature without a license, the court finds the defendant guilty as charged. On the second charge of conducting religious services in unauthorized locations, the court finds the defendant guilty as charged. On the third charge of participating in a network of implicitly anti-revolutionary zealots, the court finds the defendant guilty as charged. On the fourth charge, giving comfort to anti-state agents and saboteurs, the court finds the defendant to be a veritable Petri dish for anti-state viruses and, hence, guilty as charged. On the fifth charge of enticing and corrupting the youth of the nation, the court finds the defendant guilty as charged. Be it noted that the defendant engaged in such activity on these very premises, as was reported to me in chambers during the court's recess.'

Murmuring swept the crowd. A catcall was hurled at Adan.

'Order in the court,' bellowed the chief guard.

'On the final charge, of subverting the public order and tranquility in order to sow anarchy, the court finds the defendant's behavior this morning to be obviously anarchical. The defendant is guilty as charged.'

The courtroom broke into orderly applause. A few moments later, the chief guard bellowed for quiet. One guard meanwhile had handcuffed Adan behind his back.

'There can be no conceivable reason for delaying sentence for the party now adjudged guilty on all counts. Were the guilty party meted out sequential sentences, he would spend the rest of his life incarcerated under the law. But the revolutionary state has always cried for mercy wherever mercy could be justly applied. Under these sentencing guidelines, the court hereby judges that the guilty party will serve concurrent sentences of punishment. The maximum such sentence is thirty years. Thus, in our mercy, we sentence Adan Pedro Marti Reyes to serve thirty years without any possibility of parole except under clemency granted by the president of the state. In the spirit of mercy and constructive social education, the guilty shall serve his first four years of service under conditions of hard labor.

'The court orders that the guilty party be delivered as soon as feasible to the requisite penal authority so that the party is protected from the just fury of the public that he has so obviously despised and afflicted. This court is now adjourned.'

The chief guard bellowed, 'All rise.'

The judge stepped down from the bench and left the courtroom. His exit set off a barrage of invective, heckling, and whistling directed at Adan. The guards could have led Adan out through the same door as the judge. But Adan was not to be provided a quick exit. The fury of the audience needed service. Two guards led and two followed Adan down the mid-courtroom aisle. The guards kept their distance from the prisoner.

A baptism of spit began to rain on Adan from the cloud of catcalls. And then came the crack of belts lashing at his head, his arms, and his back. It seemed many of the spectators had removed their belts in order to pummel him with their indignation. Of course, Adan couldn't raise a hand in defense. He was handcuffed. When he attempted to run forward to escape the lashings, he was cuffed by the forward guards. They shoved him back to the center of the storm. When he ran in the other direction, the other pair of guards was equally loyal to the storm. Once Adan realized there was no escaping, he got down on his knees. He kept repeating 'Forgive them, Lord, forgive them.' Off to the edge of the storm stood Adan's brother listening, both hands on his cane, and his head slightly bowed, listening, listening.

The blows continued for perhaps five minutes or so. Gabriela could scarcely take it all in. She wanted to escape. But she noted some men began to slacken in their fury. Some even appeared somewhat ashamed, or so she thought. Waning energy or waxing shame, there's a time and a season for everything. The guards knew their job. After a few minutes of somewhat diminished zeal, a guard shouted 'Enough!' The tumult ceased.

Another guard produced a terry cloth towel. He used it to wipe the tobacco-stained saliva and blood from Adan's forehead, cheeks, and neck. Blood kept flowing from several wounds even after the wiping. The guard with the towel gave up wiping the worst wounds. He used the towel to brush Adan's mop of hair into some kind of order. Someone else would have to bandage him up, if ever. The guards had come prepared for their job, but there was only so much they could do. So had the crowd. They had delivered as much justice and mercy as they could, as Tomas later said.

While his father withstood the blows, Tomas looked on in horror. When the towel was produced, he grabbed Gabriela's hand and led her out to the hallway. Gabriela could see his tears and feel the anger in his fist.

'What is it?' asked Gabriela. *What does he intend to do?*

Tomas clenched his teeth and his eyes seemed about to pop out of his head. If the guards noticed his rage, they might both be arrested. Apparently, the guards didn't notice. They were preoccupied with hustling Adan to a place forbidden to the public.

Tomas took hold of himself within seconds of his father's removal. He turned to Gabriela, releasing her hand.

'I must leave the building at once before someone else decides otherwise. You can stay, go on your own, or come with me.'

Tomas was giving Gabi a choice.

'Lead the way,' she said.

18.

When Tomas and Gabriela reached daylight, she asked him where they should go. And what about Miguel? They'd left him below.

'So, what!' said Tomas. 'He's with his kind.'

'And what kind is that?' asked Gabriela. 'He helped us get here this morning.'

'For this travesty of justice,' said Tomas.

Gabriela looked around to see whether others might have heard. Someone, a well-dressed young man wearing sunglasses, was walking toward them. *He must be a Cyclopean.*

'Are you coming with me?' asked Tomas. He was pulling out the paper with his father's scribbled note. She was about five paces back.

'I think so,' said Gabriela. 'But I'd like to know where.'

'I'm still thinking,' said Tomas, resuming his reading. Then he folded the paper and put it back in his wallet. 'I'm going.'

Gabriela hesitated. Tomas walked away, but he stopped and looked back. He looked determined. He had a smile on his face, a pasted smile perhaps but a smile nonetheless. Tomas didn't just want to walk away.

Was it the smile that brought her alongside him? Gabriela was never sure when she looked back, but she deliberated for what seemed eternity. All she had to do was walk to her aunt's. And whenever Carlos would come by – and, surely, he would – she could tell him honestly she'd last seen Tomas when he walked away from the courthouse, destination unknown.

But what would she say to Adriana if she were still alive? Gabriela owed nothing to her now. The letters had been delivered, except for the nearly impossible-to-deliver letter to Adan. Like it or not, she knew Adriana would want her to help her son Tomas. Why? For love's sake, really for God's sake. Like it or not, she couldn't shake off Adriana. Or Tomas. She realized she didn't want to. Yet each step she took towards him was still steeped in hesitation and doubt. She looked back for the Cyclopean. He had disappeared.

'Thank you,' said Tomas. 'You're coming.'

'I am, I guess,' said she. 'Where're we going?'

'Time will tell better than I.'

She managed to keep up with Tomas, as they retraced the route they'd ridden to the courtroom. Tomas, she concluded, must have an almost photographic memory. Either that or he'd really remembered well from those summers spent in Havana.

About twelve thirty, Tomas suggested they find a place for lunch. He had money for lunch? He did, more hard currency, Canadian dollars supplied by Frederico (no longer 'Papa'). For Tomas, there was no Papa other than the one they'd left just minutes ago. *Him and the one in heaven,* came the thought.

They stopped for sandwiches at a hotel with tables outside under red umbrellas. There were many to choose from. Few patrons remained. Gabriela heard one couple speaking German and a threesome speaking French. Tomas asked for an isolated table at one end of the array. She ordered *huevos rancheros*; he had a pork roast sandwich. What a privilege, thought Gabriela, to be able to patronize an establishment reserved for tourists and hard-currency party types. The food was excellent.

Tomas seemed inclined to linger. The meal's initial conversation had skirted the courtroom proceedings. Gabriela thought Tomas was too grieved to want to talk about the proceedings. She was wrong.

'It was a travesty of justice,' said Tomas, finishing his sandwich. 'What I don't understand was the point of it.'

'You mean having the trial?' asked Gabriela.

'Yes. The outcome was pre-ordained. It wasn't an open exercise in inquiry, not like science,' said Tomas.

'At any one time is science open to every question?' asked Gabriela.

'No, not in the mainstream. If you have questions that are too out of line, you must pursue your explorations on your own and keep quiet until you have an unimpeachable case. And sometimes even that won't work. That's my reading of science.'

'Well, in a scientific society such as ours, Tomas, you're either in the mainstream or you aren't. The current is governed by the revolutionary state. If you try to act in the mainstream against the mainstream, you're going to get caught. You're going to get pulled down working against the current, say, in distributing Bibles. For the sake of those in and out of the mainstream, the current must be evident. It must prevail. We were shown the current this morning. And so were all those state security men. For them, it re-affirmed their muscle.'

'Gabriela, that's one way of putting it, the *natural way* you might say. You've got me thinking in other terms,' said Tomas.

'I have?' said Gabriela with a laugh.

'Yes. We were attending a mass this morning of the revolutionary state, a communion in which all of those gathered – or most of those gathered – were reassured they were cleansed and made righteous by a sacrifice. Not the sacrifice of Christ but of a sinner. The state needs its sacrificial victims.'

'But not everyone hauled into court is a victim,' said Gabriela. 'In fact, most people hauled into court are probably guilty to some extent.'

'If the state is merely a state and not a religion,' said Tomas. 'But states have so much power and men worship power. We must admire the likes of an Oscar Romero, who calls power to account. In a country under the rule of law, ordinary mortals and organizations can check unbridled power. But where the rule of law is weak, we need an Oscar Romero.'

'You really admire the man,' said Gabriela.

'He has become a saint who speaks out. I intend to go to El Salvador to learn from him.'

'How can you do that? None of your uncles would approve that: Frederico, Carlos, Miguel. None. Where would you get the funds? The visa?'

'Those details can be worked out,' said Tomas.

'A visa won't get you into Florida. Any visa anywhere is a pipe dream.'

'I know.'

'Have you mentioned any of this to anyone?' said Gabriela.

'Only to you.'

'Why me?'

'I trust you, Gabi.'

She shook her head. *Like mother like son. If Carlos knew of this conversation, what would happen? And if he didn't know, what would happen to her?*

'Which is why I want to show you something,' said Tomas.

He pulled out his wallet and retrieved and displayed the image of Oscar Romero. He turned over the paper and shoved it towards Gabriela.

'Read it,' he said. 'Read what my father wrote.'

Tomas. Please do this: remove the Advent house calendar you must have seen at Miguel's. If possible, pass it to Father Juan Valores. Otherwise, see to its destruction. In Christ's name, your papa. P.S. Destroy this note.

When Gabriela had read the note, she shoved it back towards Tomas. He took it, then excused himself to use the restroom. When he returned, he reported that the paper had been flushed. *Why had he shown the note? If Carlos knew... Must he?*

'Let's go,' he said.

'Where to?' she asked.

'To Miguel's.'

At Miguel's, Tomas knocked at the apartment door several times. No one answered. Was Miguel still at the courtroom? Had he managed to secure another visit with his brother? Was he attending to party business elsewhere? Was he working overtime to restore a reputation sullied by his brother?

No matter. They would enter Miguel's apartment. Gabriela produced the key she'd found earlier in Adriana's dresser.

Tomas said, 'I *knew* there was a reason why you must be along.'

The key worked. Gabriela didn't mind being resourceful, but she hated the idea that such resourcefulness might be labeled 'criminal.'

When they opened the door, Tomas put a finger to his mouth then pointed around the perimeter of the room. Gabriela frowned. Did Tomas think she'd forgotten about the bugs?

He didn't say. He pointed twice toward the kitchen, then pointed at Gabriela. He wanted her to head to the kitchen. As for himself, he headed to Miguel's room.

Gabriela found the Advent house had been removed from the kitchen wall. *Crime or resourcefulness?* She went around the apartment looking for it. She couldn't find the Bavarian miscreant. When she came to Miguel's room, she found Tomas fiddling with what appeared to be a shortwave set. A set of earphones lay next to the set along with some wires.

'I think I got everything,' said Tomas. 'This radio set was in fact a listening center. I heard some conversations in some other apartments. I heard you rattling around in the back bedroom. I think it's safe to talk now.'

'Unless there's a secondary listening service,' said Gabriela, 'listening to your Uncle Miguel.' She laughed.

'How much listening must we have in Cuba?' asked Tomas.

Gabriela couldn't tell whether he was disgusted, angry, or merely showing despair. She hadn't meant to provoke him.

'The questions are two,' said Tomas. He spoke without whispering. 'Who removed the house? And why?'

'A criminal, perhaps, but that's too convenient. I'd say Miguel, but that seems too obvious,' said Gabriela, not whispering. She went over to Miguel's radio set and turned it on and up. Music, she hoped, would drown their conversation to listening ears.

'I think it's too convenient a theory to suppose that Miguel removed the house,' said Tomas.

'But it may still be true,' said Gabriela.

'Why?'

'I don't know why. Advent is over today.'

'When the sun goes down in a few hours,' said Tomas, 'it'll be Christmas, but that's hardly a motive for removing the Advent house, even here where we don't celebrate Christmas.'

'Tourists come to Cuba to celebrate Christmas,' said Gabriela, 'but I guess that's irrelevant.' She felt foolish.

Tomas said, 'I've not forgotten your work for CubaTur.'

'Forgive me for reminding you... and myself. Anyway, with everything that's gone on today, where would Miguel find the time to bother with the house?'

'Forgive *me* for suggesting lunch,' said Tomas. 'By stopping for lunch, we gave someone time to come here and remove the house.'

'Miguel is too obvious,' said Gabriela.

'A thief could have absconded with it,' said Tomas. 'An idiot thief.'

'Who but an idiot would choose to rob the flat of someone obviously with the CDR?' said Gabriela.

'There are idiots,' said Tomas, 'but that answer seems too convenient.'

'It does,' said Gabriela.

'How about someone from state security? How about my Uncle Carlos? There may be several people at state security with an interest in Adan and Miguel. They each might have their reasons for wanting to retrieve the Advent house.'

'You make it sound like someone in state security would be watching Miguel. Miguel is one of them almost. Carlos, for one, felt comfortable in demanding that Miguel accommodate me last night.'

'That reminds me,' said Tomas. 'Get your stuff. I don't think you should stay here another night. Perhaps neither Carlos nor Miguel had much choice about housing you.'

'I don't think *I* have much choice. I—'

'You'll stay at my grandparents.'

'That's for you to say?'

'My grandmother will approve.'

'That's good, but I'm more worried about state security.'

'Get your stuff,' he said.

She did. As she stuffed her travel bag, she thought to retrieve the Swiss army knife as well as her trusty penknife. They were still in the drawer, which pretty much ruled out the possibility a petty thief had entered the apartment. Not that they'd really considered a petty thief. What mattered was the state security apparatus. Sometime soon, she'd have to tell Tomas she was beholden to Carlos. If she told him, how might he react?

Would it make a difference? Probably not for her brother. He was as good as dead. As for her father, she knew he was beyond harm. He was one of *them,* a brother of oppression. Not so her aunts. The thought of bringing harm on them weighed on her.

As she looked in the mirror, she hated to admit she wasn't entirely motivated by high ideals. She didn't want to hurt herself. *So far, I've done nothing wrong, well almost nothing. Best not to think of Prince Charming.* Like it or not, she was already on Tomas' train.

'Where are we going now?' asked Gabriela as she locked the apartment door.

'I said my grandparents,' said Tomas, descending the stairs.

When she turned around to follow, she saw him standing before the two Cyclopeans they'd seen the first time they'd visited Miguel's. One of the men nodded to Tomas to walk through the front door. Tomas looked back up the stairway to Gabriela.

'I'm… coming,' she said hesitantly.

Tomas walked on through the door. When she reached the front landing, one of the men came up to her and said, 'Follow me to the car.'

She followed. She caught Tomas' bewildered look. A black Mercedes was just up the street. Behind it sat a white Toyota. The man escorting Tomas took him to the Toyota. The man escorting her opened the rear door of the Mercedes. She got in.

Carlos was waiting in the back seat. He got right down to business without so much as a 'hello.'

'How did the night go at Miguel's?'

'It was satisfactory,' she replied.

'No funny business?' he asked.

'None that I can recall,' she said.

'Good. Did you leave the apartment at all during the night?'

Should she mention Tomas's showing up?

'No. I did not,' she replied.

'This morning, you appeared at my brother-in-law's trial with my nephew. Did anything extraordinary happen at the trial?'

'I'm surprised you ask,' she said. 'Surely, you must have had observers there. The courtroom was packed.'

'The other observers don't count now. Only you, my dear. Only you. You're sure nothing extraordinary happened?'

'No, nothing extraordinary in our revolutionary state, I suppose. Well, I guess I should mention there was a recess in which your nephew was able to visit briefly with Adan.'

'And?' said Carlos.

'And his father performed a blessing. I'd never seen it done before... but my family was irreligious.'

'A blessing. And what did Adan say?'

'I don't remember exactly. He didn't say a word of any political import.'

'Nothing?'

'Nothing,' replied Gabriela. Strictly speaking, he'd *said* nothing of any political importance. And the paper was now lost to history.

'You witnessed this with your own eyes?' asked Carlos.

'Yes,' she replied.

'What of Miguel?'

'He was there during the blessing. He never left.'

'He watched the whole thing?'

'One can't tell with Miguel. He does have some vision. That's obvious. You must know. He gets around too well to rely on the stick alone. But how much vision; do you know?'

'I ask the questions,' said Carlos. 'Where are you two headed now? You seem to have become a pair.'

'*Seem* perhaps, but in fact less like it. We were headed to his grandparents, your parents.'

'For my mother's traditional Christmas Eve dinner?'

'I don't know. She fixes one?'

'Even though she's a Communist from way back. Is she expecting you to stay overnight?'

'I don't think so.'

'But you have your bag.'

'I do.'

'You have my permission to stay with my parents tonight. In fact, you *will* stay with them. But I won't be taking you there. Watch your step and the steps of those around you. Before you know it, you might step into the same quicksand as someone else... and you might not be able to withdraw. Beware!'

'Yes, comrade,' replied Gabriela. 'May I go?'

'Of course,' said Carlos, 'and if you learn anything about that camp guard missing from Estacion ES, let me know.'

'A camp guard missing from Estacion ES. What's that all about?' she asked.

'Perhaps you'll learn. More importantly, I want to know what happened to the missing calendar house. Sooner than later. Good evening.'

She shuddered as she got out and shut the car door behind her.

Los Pies de Cuba

19.

How had Carlos known of the Advent house? Obviously, state security knew it was missing. Had Miguel told them? Or someone else? When did they learn of its significance? And what significance did it truly have? Tomas and Gabriela bandied these questions back and forth as they trekked from Miguel's place to Tomas' grandparents.

Tomas and Gabriela deduced the Advent house hid information detrimental to Bible distribution if that information fell into the wrong hands. Or useful if it were passed on to Father Juan Valores – if they could find him. Tomas said he'd first met him about five years past when his mother, Aunt Pamela, had brought him on one of her trips to Havana. She took Tomas to Santo Ángel Custodio and made a point of introducing him to the priest.

Tomas had talked with him subsequently. They'd exchanged letters when Tomas turned sixteen. The talk and letters raised matters theological, nothing political. Perhaps the priest was more than 'theological,' as it were. His father, Adan, trusted him. Finding the priest seemed a good next step. As they came to this conclusion, Gabriela and Tomas found themselves at his grandparents' door.

There would be no quick departure. Tomas' grandmother, Elena, was fully intending to observe the old Cuban Christmas custom of lavishing the evening with a sumptuous pork-roast dinner. The aroma of roast pork hit them at the door. Elena and Tomas' grandfather, Gustavo, lived in a freestanding home. It once would have housed a family and servants.

Elena had answered the door. She was surprised to meet Gabriela but invited her to stay for dinner. Little did Elena know she was expected to host Gabriela overnight. Before Tomas could broach the topic of overnight hospitality, Elena excused herself to return to the kitchen. Her elongated face and heels clicking on the red tiles conveyed an intolerance of distraction. At least this was Gabriela's initial impression.

Gustavo was as intense as his wife. As she returned to the kitchen, Gustavo rushed to introduce himself to Gabriela. He peppered Tomas and her with questions about their day and they peppered him about his. He was a volcano of words and gestures. These alone might account for his trim appearance. Except for his glasses, graying hair, and a slight paunch, he showed few signs of aging. He confirmed Gabriela's supposition that, yes, he was active in athletics, playing tennis thrice weekly.

Gustavo suggested Tomas take Gabriela on a tour of their home. As for himself, he had papers to work on.

He said there was 'something upstairs' for Tomas, then excused himself.

No one had asked about Gabriela's travel bag. Tomas suggested they put it in the room where he and Frederico had slept the night before. Tomas led Gabriela upstairs. At the top of the stairs was a landing with doors leading to bedrooms and to a bathroom. At the landing, Gabriela wondered whether they shouldn't broach the question of her staying overnight. Would Tomas' grandmother allow this?

'She'll find a place for you,' said Tomas.

'Just like that?' asked Gabriela.

'Just like that,' said Tomas. 'They are high party members. The higher one rises, the fewer the questions.' *And the more sumptuous the living.*

Tomas showed Gabi his grandparents' magnificent bedroom, then a small bedroom next to it where he supposed she'd spend the night. He put her bag down at the foot of the bed. Then he led her into a bedroom with two single beds where he and Frederico had slept the night before.

On one of the beds was a large parcel wrapped in brown paper tied together with string. A white index card taped to the parcel was inscribed with Tomas' name and his grandparents' address. He removed the paper. Inside was a red box. Atop the box was a small white envelope bearing Tomas's name. Tomas opened it and read a scribbled note.

Tomas, the house is now yours. You have what you wished for.

Miguel

Gabriela whispered, 'This could be a house of troubles!'

Tomas removed the lid from the box, exposing the Advent house. All of the shutters were closed. The house doors were also closed.

'We can spare ourselves trouble and possibly others if we get right to the business of destroying this thing,' said Gabriela.

'Is that what you want to do?' asked Tomas.

'Not entirely. I'm curious. But others are "curious," too, if I can put it that way.'

Tomas began to open the shutters on the house, revealing the wooden figures. Gabriela did likewise. They opened all the shutters and the Christmas doors. Everyone and the baby Jesus were present and accounted for.

Tomas said, 'My father's first preference is that this be passed along. I want to honor that.'

Tomas took out a figure and began fingering it. He noticed right off that the head of the piece was loose. Indeed, he easily removed it. It had been designed to that end. Within the piece was a small chamber with a scroll. Tomas knocked out and opened the scroll. Gabriela did likewise with another figure.

Tomas's scroll bore this: **6.** S. Nikolaus. Lu. 11:13. Ps 127:3. Gabi's bore this: **13.** S. Lucia. Joh 1:4-5. Ps 43:3.

She said, 'The scrolls identify the saints they belong to and here on the bases are the saints' names.'

'And numbers representing December days in Advent,' said Tomas.

'In more than one way, this whole thing represented a lot of thought and work,' said Gabriela.

'Beautiful work,' said Tomas, 'tied in with the season and Bible readings.'

'There's hardly anything here that ought to excite your Uncle Carlos or state security. In today's Cuba, someone at a folk museum might be interested,' said Gabriela.

'If it were Cuban,' said Tomas. 'There's something about all this we're not seeing and I'm not talking about folk origins.'

'It might be right before our eyes,' said Gabriela.

'Yes, before our eyes and others,' said Tomas. 'Let's put it somewhere where it can't be found.'

'Obviously, Miguel knows you have it. And your grandparents know you've got something up here even if they don't know what it is. Where're you going to put it?'

Tomas said, 'I don't know. Let's pack it up.'

They did, inserting the scrolls into their chambers, recapping the pieces, placing them in their window spots, even closing the shutters before putting the lid on the box.

Tomas said, 'Would you mind going downstairs to the kitchen? Tell my grandparents I've decided to go out for a walk. If they ask why, tell them I appeared to be upset. I mean, after all, shouldn't I be upset with what happened today? But who has time to be upset when you're carting off houses?'

'Where are you going to take it?' asked Gabriela.

'In case you're asked, it would be better if you don't know. And don't say what was in the box unless you must, if you know what I mean.'

'I know.'

'I'll be back in about an hour,' he said.

'That long? Dinner might be sooner.'

'If I'm not here, they'll probably start anyway.'

'Be careful,' said Gabriela.

'You, too.' He laughed.

They slipped down the stairs and he out the front door. She went into the kitchen passing by a library where Gustavo pored over papers, perhaps reports from the university or submissions from his students. In the kitchen, Elena was chopping onions. She was now wearing glasses, probably as protection from the onions.

'You have a mighty chop,' said Gabriela. 'Can I help?'

'That's kind of you. Yes. Take an apron from that peg over there, if you would, and work on the tossed salad. You'll find some greens in the bottom drawer of the refrigerator.'

The kitchen was equipped with a refrigerator and stove and countless other things fit for a dream house. Gabriela found her greens and made a tossed salad with the leaves.

'Where's Tomas?' asked Elena.

'He went for a walk,' said Gabriela.

'Did he see the present from his Uncle Miguel?'

'He did.'

'What was it?'

'I'll let Tomas tell you.'

'Very well. I'm surprised he didn't take you along.'

'I think he's still upset about what happened this morning. You know what happened this morning?'

'I know enough not to want to know more.'

'Yes, it wasn't pleasant.'

'His father was slime. He pulled our daughter into his pit. I will never forgive him for that. He's gotten what he deserves, but not Tomas. Tomas has so much promise... and now all this sorrow. It's his natural father's fault... but now he appears to blame the revolution. Tomas can be healed through work. Work heals so much. Sometimes, I must confess, I can't decide which is our truer savior: the revolution or work. I'm thankful the revolution resolves my indecision by glorifying work. I feel whole again.'

Gabriela found this self-disclosure somewhat charming. Somewhat. But she could no longer find it convincing. She couldn't see herself as a witless serveling of the revolution. It was enough right now to say, 'I've come down because I want to help. We knew there was work to be done in the kitchen.'

'Tomas could have offered to help, too,' said Elena. She took a mighty swing at the last of the onion. 'That's one thing that hasn't changed in our New Order, that is, in the kitchen. Not yet. But the dictatorship has liberated us from so much else. I'm so grateful to our leader. He's wonderful, isn't he?'

'He's very eloquent,' said Gabriela.

'Ah, isn't he, but I'm afraid our children nowadays don't appreciate all they've been given.'

'Do they ever?' replied Gabriela.

'A residual poison infects too many.'

'You mean your own sons.'

'Oh, not my own sons. I'm proud they live up to their names. No, I'm thinking of the next generation, yours and Tomas'. How old are you?'

'I'm twenty-one,' said Gabriela.

'Well, you're a well-preserved twenty-one.' Elena laughed. 'I hope you haven't been poisoned.'

'You mean by America.'

'No. Americans are merely bloodsuckers,' sneered Elena. 'No, it's worse than that because you can't shoo them away like bloodsuckers. No, it's deeper, more resistant, to the changes we all hope for. No, it's the poison of religious faith, especially of those Christians. Tomas has been adversely affected.'

Elena opened the oven door to check on the pork roast.

'My father is a party member,' said Gabriela. 'My mother is dead. But outside medicine – my father's a doctor – my father is totally consumed with party activities.'

'That's good,' said Elena. She looked relieved.

Gabriela couldn't resist pushing a button. 'What do you make of the likes of Archbishop Romero in El Salvador? Some, I'm told, regard him as a political progressive.'

'He's an idiot,' said Elena. 'He's eloquent, yes, and even smart, yes, but he's a total fool to be appealing to God and to the goodness of others. If he accepted the truths of Marx and Engels, he'd be leading the Salvadorians to true salvation: a bloody revolution as the foundation of a regenerative state. He should be leading the people to the barricades. Death to the capitalists! Death to God!'

Gabriela was thankful Elena no longer had the chopping knife in hand. Kiko – Frederico – entered unannounced, took his mother, and planted a kiss on her cheek. She looked pleased.

'How was your day, my son? I didn't hear you come in.'

'It was good. It's been a good conference so far. I'm looking forward to tomorrow's proceedings. Where's Tomas?'

'He's out,' replied Elena.

'For a walk,' added Gabriela.

The phone began ringing. Elena lifted the receiver. 'Hello.'

'Oh, Carlos, my dear, I was just thinking of you... Nothing bad... You have nowhere to go for supper? Julia is at her sister's?... Well, you're welcome, of course, to come here for supper. We've got plenty. And we've got some guests you'd probably like to meet... You already know them? You look forward to visiting with everyone? Well, we should have a delightful evening.'

Gabriela involuntarily shuddered and hoped no one noticed.

20.

In all of her years, Gabriela had never experienced a feast where the table could groan from an amplitude of food. That she would now be participating in such a feast was just another unexpected turn of events, set off by the wholly unanticipated relationship with Adriana. What would Adriana think of tonight's feast? What would her own grandmother think?

Gabriela's maternal grandmother had told her of Christmas Eve feasts of old. She told how the table would be laden with roast pork or sometimes roast fresh ham. The roast meat would be accompanied by roast yucca and plantains *maduro y verde*, ripe and green. As side dishes, there could be more yucca prepared in a garlic sauce, red beans, sweet rice, and sometimes even couscous. There might be a choice between a mixed green salad and a salad of banana, orange, and mango chunks. There could never be too much, said her grandmother. The leftovers would be shared with others in the neighborhood. Everyone should eat well, she said, before going to the Christmas Eve mass.

Her grandmother would get a wistful look recalling those feasts and why they were served. Alas, the mulled wine could never wash away one of the sadder aspects of those occasions. For all their bounty, said her grandmother, there were those missing from the celebration. The long gone might be missed, but not grievously. The recently dead were always deeply missed. There would be a toast in their memory and a moment of silent prayer for their souls. However, as much as the recently dead were missed, the most acute absences were those of the 'living dead,' as she termed them.

The living dead were those who by choice were absent from the table. Those at sea or in prison, who by circumstances could not enjoy the table, were of course not blamed for their absences. They were not among the living dead. But those who chose not to come, who spurned their own family, well, these absentees were accusers whose accusations were not well-received. These absences were accursed. Yet, said her grandmother, if any of the accusers had shown up, especially on Christmas Eve or Christmas day, they would have been heartily forgiven and well-received. And, of course, everyone would be well-fed.

Gabriela could see everyone would be well-fed tonight. Yet here, too, there would be absences. What would the table make of Tomas' absence? And what of Adriana's? Would her ghost be an accusing presence that Elena and Gustavo would attempt to whoosh away? What *did* Adriana's parents feel about their daughter's recent death? Elena hadn't said a thing about Adriana's death as Gabriela helped make the mixed salad, sliced the bread, and set out one thing or another. Nothing had been said. Gabriela had wondered whether she should say something. Did Elena and Gustavo know she had spent time with their daughter as she lay dying? What had Kiko told them?

Elena pulled the pork roast out of the oven. It was ready. Kiko returned to the kitchen in time to assist his mother in removing the roast from the oven. Elena looked at the kitchen clock.

'Carlos should be here any minute,' she said. 'Has Tomas returned?'

'He's not here,' said Kiko, 'we'll have to start without him.'

Elena frowned. 'I hope that boy doesn't go astray and become one of the least of the Lessers.'

Elena left the kitchen to fetch Gustavo.

'What's a Lesser?' asked Gabriela.

Kiko replied, 'That's my mother's term really for most people, those who have to be guided by the Greaters, the ones illuminated with *la Verdad,* the Truth, spelled with a capital "V."'

'I see,' said Gabriela.

'Perhaps you ought to be more cynical,' said Kiko with a pasted smile. 'Cynicism is above the truth. That has many practical advantages.'

The doorbell rang. Carlos had arrived with his two Cyclopeans. The two kept on their sunglasses despite the place and hour. Elena decided the two associates would partake of the feast in the front room. Carlos joined everyone else in gathering around the kitchen table. The aromas emanating from the food were heavenly, thought Gabriela. This heaven was not without its moment of prayer. Gustavo spoke.

'We all know this night in times past occasioned a misbegotten feast offered to celebrate the birth of a so-called "savior." We know what happened to him. He was annihilated. But some made a living of making nothing into something. A few good things came of all this, including in the far reaches of Christendom the likes of this Cuban feast.

'Our revolutionary state even now struggles against the opiate of religion. Perhaps it always will. Perhaps religious faith is like disease, a human condition that can be managed but not eliminated. As a lawyer, a teacher, and party member, I can tell you we can view our feast tonight with two eyes. Some may think we ought to do nothing on a night like tonight, but the night is still part of our culture, still part of our memory. As a legal scientist, I say we should capture the cultural moment and dedicate it to another purpose. To the north, the capitalists have captured the moment to great success for their greedy ends. We would do well to emulate them in capturing the remnants of faith, re-clothing them to serve the revolutionary state's task of transcending history to make the New Man.'

'And woman,' said Elena.

'And the New Woman,' said Gustavo. 'I think we should dedicate this night tonight and in the future in this house and in other houses all across our beautiful island to a remembrance not of the past. The past in all its ugliness must be eradicated. No, we must dedicate it to a remembrance of a future made by mankind for mankind under the guidance of the best that mankind can produce. We produce not a lowly, miserable so-called "savior." No, we produce leaders, jurists, engineers, doctors, managers, teachers, soldiers, journalists, yes, even policeman who will guide those less able among us. Together, we will be the savior state, looking out for the least among us, knowing that our knowledge will transform this mere earth into a banquet without end. We have nowhere else to look and to be gratified.

'Thank you, my dear Elena for this fine feast,' said Gustavo before planting a kiss on her cheek.

'Thank you, Gustavo, for your fitting words. Let's eat. Enjoy!' said Elena. She looked pleased. Not a word about Adriana. Elena's boys Carlos and Kiko each kissed her before taking a serving dish to the main table. The table was already furnished with place settings and bottles of wine. When it was loaded with hot foods, Carlos invited in his two Cyclopeans. He loaded up their plates for them and sent them back to the front room. Once the family and Gabriela were seated, they began loading up their plates. Elena sat at one end of the table, Gustavo the other. Kiko and Carlos sat next to each other across from Gabriela. The vacant chair (for Tomas) was to her left, Elena's to the right.

Kiko and Carlos spoke with their father but not with each other. That aside, the conversation was seasonably cheerful and at times drew in Elena. Gabriela ate in silence, thinking about Adriana, Adan, and Aunt Florina and Uncle Silvano and wondering what had become of Tomas. Carlos was sitting directly across from Gabriela. Like his minions, he hadn't bothered to remove his dark glasses.

Carlos produced Adriana's dolphin necklace, laying it next to his mother's plate. 'Do you remember this, Mother?'

'Why yes,' said Elena, wincing. 'How did you obtain it?'

Just as Carlos was about to reply, his mother raised her hand, 'No. Don't tell me. Some things are unspeakable or not to be spoken of. I don't want to know. But why have you shown this to me now? Carlos, you make me proud, but your professional activities have necessarily eroded your sensitivities. You were the most sensitive one in the family, even more than *her.* '

Gabriela assumed 'her' referred to Adriana.

'So, for once I receive a compliment, kind of, under this roof,' said Carlos. 'But I'm here less as a family member, Mother, and more as a professional. That's why I produce this now.'

'To what end?' asked Elena. Not only had Gabriela stopped eating, but so had Gustavo and Kiko.

'I need to find Tomas, the boy, the man. I believe he may have something of interest to state security. It's no longer at Miguel's. Miguel is missing. Tomas is missing. And I don't know what to make of it.

'Might you know anything, comrade?' said Carlos, directing his reflective gaze at Gabriela. She could see herself in his glasses.

'I know that Tomas went for a walk,' said Gabriela.

'I think you know more.'

'I don't know where he went. He refused to tell me where he was going. He was still upset by his father's trial today.'

Kiko said, 'He'd be well-advised to absolutely forget those who abandoned him.'

'The way you put that doesn't exactly square with the facts,' said Gustavo. 'Absolute abandonment didn't happen.'

'Can you possibly be sympathetic to your grandson's rejection of me?' asked Kiko.

'It isn't rejection of you. It's anthropological reality setting in,' said Gustavo.

'We don't have time for anthropological realities of that sort. If we're to attain the bright future you've outlined, Father,' said Carlos, 'we must lock tight that dream. We must ensure that everyone in the present contributes to the inevitable best future of all.'

A nightmare, thought Gabriela.

'You must help me find Tomas.'

'What can we do, Carlos? I don't think any one of us knows where he is,' said Gustavo.

'Here I am,' said Tomas.

21.

'Forgive me for being late, Grandma, but I *am* hungry, and I know you're the best cook in Havana.'

Elena smiled. Gustavo looked puzzled. Kiko looked alarmed. Carlos was expressionless. Impassive facial features were a plus in a policeman, thought Gabriela. Surely, he must be surprised. *Every next moment brings a wonder.*

'You've worried us, Tomas. You shouldn't have taken off,' said Kiko.

'The young man's here now. That's the important thing,' said Elena.

'Maybe,' said Carlos.

'Have a seat,' said Gustavo.

'Let me go wash up, please.'

Tomas left the room. So did Carlos, presumably to order his associates to take up positions in the front and back of the house. Then he returned to the table. Elena was filling a plate for Tomas.

Tomas took the empty chair next to Gabriela. He looked Gabriela in the eye as he sat down, as if he were signaling some kind of intent. But what?

Flight seemed impossible. State security was in their midst. Deceit was also impossible. State security wouldn't go off on some wild goose chase. Dishonor seemed impossible. Would Tomas choose to betray his father? Delay would only work so long.

But delay would do, so it seemed. Tomas was very hungry. While others had finished, he worked through his first plate, then asked for another.

Uncle Carlos asked Tomas if he knew anything about the Advent house that had been at Miguel's place.

'I do,' said Tomas. 'It once belonged to my birth parents. I've given it to Father Juan. Advent is over. My birth mother is dead. And my birth father, as you must know, is headed for prison once again but probably never to come out. He'll end up in a pit. I thought my parents would want someone to have it who would appreciate it.'

Kiko interjected, 'But it was at Miguel's. You can't just give something like that away. How do you know it didn't belong to Miguel?'

'I do,' said Tomas. 'If Miguel hadn't told me, I would never have known. Miguel gave it to me.'

'Who's this Father Juan?' asked Carlos.

Gabriela couldn't help but wonder why Tomas had mentioned the priest. Perhaps he figured the truth would come out sooner than later. Better to be forthright than dishonest. But honesty in this instance wouldn't honor Adan's wish. Surely, he wanted to honor his father's wish.

'Who's this Father Juan?' asked Carlos again.

'He's a priest we met at Nuestro Señor de la Esperanza Saturday morning,' said Tomas.

'Who's 'we'?' asked Carlos.

What's this?

'Gabriela and me,' said Tomas. 'We stopped there for morning mass on Saturday morning.'

Nonsense.

'You weren't along, Kiko?' asked Carlos.

'No, absolutely not.'

'But you traveled to the labor camp.'

'Not exactly,' said Kiko. 'For one thing we went on Sunday, not Saturday. I wasn't even ever exactly at the camp entrance.'

'Not exactly, but close enough. You, too, must come along.'

'Where're we going?' asked Kiko. 'I've done nothing wrong.'

'But your son… or rather your nephew…'

'Your nephew, too, Carlos,' blurted Kiko.

Carlos proceeded, '*Your* nephew – and please don't interrupt – has been involved with this Advent house calendar.'

'That's a crime?' asked Kiko. 'To deliver a religious calendar? Even those of us hoping for the death of religious faith cannot squander our energies with the likes of this. Surely this isn't a crime.'

'There is more here, I think, than meets the eye,' said Carlos. 'As soon as Tomas finishes that plate, we'll go to Father Juan's church.'

The festive mood that had ushered in the meal was gone. Hardly a word was now spoken, except for words of excuse. Gustavo was the first to leave the table. Elena asked if anyone would mind her clearing off the table. Kiko said he would be happy to help. Carlos decided there was no need for him to attend to Tomas. Carlos and Kiko discussed travel arrangements to the church. Kiko offered to take Tomas and Gabriela in the VW microbus. Carlos mulled over this offer, then responded he'd accept his brother's help because he was a loyal party member. After that, Carlos joined his men outdoors.

'You've gotten us in trouble,' said Kiko to Tomas, 'and over such a silly thing.'

If he only knew, thought Gabriela.

Kiko returned to the kitchen with another round of empty plates and glasses.

Tomas eyed Gabriela and whispered, 'When we leave, be sure you bring the travel bag with everything. We're not coming back.'

To get back to Santiago would be enough, she thought. To forget everything that had happened these past several days would be bliss, even to forget her brother, perhaps most of all to forget her brother. To forget what had been done to him. But she knew she could not forget, did not want to forget. It would be wrong to forget. It would be wrong to play the dummy, to pretend that nothing had happened. For even the state in its perverse way knew something had happened.

Accidentally, inexorably, and against her will, she was becoming identified as an enemy of the state. Not for the right reasons, to be sure. But the new label would stick to her file at state security. Somehow, the label would be right, regardless of the facts, and that's what would make it so horribly wrong. There would be no bright side to the label.

That grim prospect wouldn't make it any easier to know what to do. But the prospect made it possible for her to think of actions she wouldn't have otherwise contemplated. Like running away with Tomas, completely away. But how? *Steady, steady, steady. Focus on the now.* She got up from the table. More platters, plates, and glasses could be removed. She would help Elena. When she had finished doing so, she walked by the table, where Tomas was finishing off his meal. He winked at Gabriela as she turned to go upstairs.

When she came back down with her bag, she went into the kitchen to thank Elena and Gustavo for their hospitality. Gabriela couldn't read their moods. Certainly, they must have been upset by the turn of events. But they were stalwart party members. They gave a formal good-bye to Gabriela, to Tomas, and to Kiko and focused their attentions on their kitchen.

Elena said nothing to Gabriela about the travel bag. No one had gotten around to asking about her staying overnight. Now that she was going off with Carlos, an overnight stay was moot. She didn't anticipate returning. Kiko expected otherwise, at least for himself and Tomas. But then she was the one with the floating accommodations in Havana. Why would tonight be any different? Tomas took the travel bag in hand and gave Gabriela a nod that she should follow Kiko. She did.

The microbus was parked behind the Mercedes. Tomas opened a door of the VW and waved Gabriela aboard. He followed. The two were alone in the VW's backseat while Kiko and Carlos discussed the route to Nuestro Señor de la Esperanza.

'We're sure to hit a red at a stop light,' said Tomas. 'If we do and if we don't have a guard riding up front with Frederico, then you and I are getting out.'

'Getting out!' sputtered Gabriela.

'If not along the way, then at the church,' said Tomas.

'What about Santiago?' asked Gabriela.

'We can only dream of going home. We've lost our homes,' said Tomas.

'Not me,' said Gabriela.

'You, too. We've never had them. In the revolutionary state, only those at the top have homes and then only at the pleasure of the state.'

'But my aunts.'

'Yes, I know.'

'But I don't want them hurt. Or my brother if he's still alive.'

'That I understand. I understand more than ever,' said Tomas. 'But there's only so much we can do.'

When Kiko walked to the VW, one of the state security men came along. Kiko got behind the wheel. The Cyclopean took the front passenger seat. He spoke into a walkie-talkie, reporting that all was in readiness for a 'go.'

'Very well,' crackled the walkie-talkie. 'Get going.'

Kiko pulled out into the street and the Mercedes followed. Kiko blabbered about one thing or another, to which the state security man replied with 'Yes' or 'No' or a grunt.

Tomas took Gabriela by the hand to get her attention. Then he put a finger to his mouth to secure her silence. He opened her travel bag. The only light in the back of the vehicle was that cast by passing streetlights. Gabriela hadn't the faintest idea what he was looking for. Then he pulled out the black light lamp, the one he'd insisted she accept as a memento at Miguel's. She'd quite lost track of it in all the hubbub. Tomas hadn't. Why bother with the lamp now? He seemed to have rocks on his mind and in his head.

Tomas shook the lamp in his hand with the exultation of an athlete awarded a trophy. He closed the travel bag and by gestures conveyed the message the bag would stay but he'd take the lamp. Tomas shook his right fist with his thumb pointed to the door. He pointed to a passing traffic light, then he jabbed his thumb at his chest, then pointed at her, then raised two fingers and swished them to the door. She took all this as a signal that she should be prepared to rush out at a red signal. To follow Tomas would be crazy, she knew, but to allow others to dictate the course of events would surely lead to a Beto-zombie existence. Crazy defiance was better than living death.

When the Mercedes and VW came to a red traffic light about two blocks from Nuestro Señor de la Esperanza, Tomas shook his head vigorously and swung open his door. Gabriela followed, not closing the door behind. The two caught the Cyclopean completely by surprise.

But rather than run away from the VW and the Mercedes, Tomas chose to run *ahead* of them, towards the church.

'What are you doing?' shouted Gabriela.

'Don't fall behind,' Tomas shouted back at her. He had the black light in his right hand and his left hand extended back to grab hold of her.

Tomas looked right and left at the cross street and yelled, 'It's safe.' It wasn't safe but she took his hand. They just managed to reach the opposite curb as two cars and a truck whooshed past their backs.

Gabriela looked back and saw no one chasing them on foot. But why bother if they could follow along in vehicles? And pursue they did once the light turned green. But by then Tomas and Gabriela were running up the church steps. Inside, the church was more populated than could be expected at any other time of the year.

'Follow me,' said Tomas.

Gabriela followed Tomas from the back of the church to a doorway to the right of the altar. Tomas opened the door and jerked his head, signaling Gabriela to follow him along a dimly lit hallway. He opened yet another door that led out into a back courtyard. A grillwork door was set in the shoulder-height wall. But the door was locked.

Gabriela spotted a box in one corner of the courtyard. She removed the pots stored in the box and brought it to a spot in the wall next to Tomas. She flipped over the box. The black lamp was at his feet.

'Good idea,' he said, cupping his hands. 'I'll help you over. Step on the box then put a foot here on my hands.'

'What's next?' asked Gabriela, but she did what was needed, putting her right foot in the 'cup' and managing to swing her left leg over the top of the wall. When she swung the other foot up, she was thankful this was a church wall. There weren't any glass shards.

She looked down at the pavement on the other side of the wall. She wasn't going to jump down from where she sat.

'Can you make it?' asked Tomas.

'Of course,' she said. She looked back but no one had yet opened the door from the church. She slowly lowered herself against the wall, using her shoes as brakes. Finally, she kicked away from the wall and let go, falling toward the wall. She scratched her hands but was otherwise uninjured.

She looked up. Tomas was at the top of the wall. He had the lamp in hand.

'Here, catch this,' he said.

'Throw it.'

She caught the lamp. As she put it down on the pavement, Tomas jumped. He landed feet first but unbalanced. As he tottered backwards, Gabriela managed to catch him before they both crumpled to the pavement.

'Thanks,' he said. 'Are you OK?'

'I am,' said she. 'And you?'

'We've only just begun,' he said. 'We've got to get to Santa Catalina del Mar. That's where Father Juan is now, not this church. That's why I took so long tonight. He oversees several churches.'

Tomas stood up and helped Gabriela to her feet.

'He's got an evening mass at Santa Catalina.'

'Is that where the calendar house is?' asked Gabriela.

'Yes, and soon enough the heavies may figure that out and be there, too. We've got to get there before they do.'

'If we can avoid the police,' said Gabriela.

'We can.'

'And then what?'

'One thing at a time,' said Tomas.

God help us find the bright side! Or the brightness.

22.

Tomas and Gabriela got some distance from the church without being seen by their pursuers. Gabriela wondered whether they were even being pursued.

'They may not be after us this very minute,' said Tomas. 'But they will be. They want the Advent house. So do I.'

They kept up their pace.

In under a half hour of brisk walking and some running, they reached Santa Catalina. A full-blown Christmas mass was underway, led by Father Juan. Tomas dipped his fingers in the bowl of water set by the front doorway. He crossed himself and then waited for Gabriela to do so. She shook her head. He shrugged his shoulders.

'Follow me,' he said.

'I've been doing that for some time.'

Instead of leading Gabriela into the sanctuary, he headed to a side door. He opened the door. In a well-lit office on the top of a desk was the red Advent house box for all to see.

'Go ahead and open it up,' said Tomas, 'while I find a place to plug in this black lamp.' He still had it in hand.

'The black lamp is going to help us with the Advent house?' asked Gabriela, removing her jacket.

'I think so,' said Tomas. 'From what I could see, my parents' rock collection hardly warranted a black lamp.'

'I agree,' she replied. 'Most of the rocks were only ordinary roadside junk rock.'

'Exactly, though admittedly the ordinary often hides the extraordinary. The rocks seemed like an excuse for having the lamp. These kinds of lamps can be used to detect various kinds of invisible inks. I've wondered whether my mother's art of calligraphy spilled over into writing on those little Advent house scrolls. I think they might. We'll see.'

'I think not,' said Gabriela. She had just removed the cover from the box. 'There's nothing inside. Nothing.'

'Nothing? Father Juan must have hidden the Advent house,' said Tomas.

'Why would he leave the box out?' asked Gabriela.

'Good question.'

Tomas opened a door near the electrical outlet where he'd just plugged in the black lamp. It was a closet door. There was no Advent house behind the door.

'Let's try that other door by you,' said Tomas.

Gabriela opened the door. Behind it was a mostly darkened office.

'Tomas? Is that you?' came a voice.

Gabriela recognized the voice. Tomas came beside her. She could hear him fumbling for a light switch.

'Tomas, don't turn on the light. I'm using a black-light flashlight that I long ago bought from a Stasi misfit in East Germany.'

'Uncle Miguel!' said Tomas.

'Yes, your uncle. Close the door behind you and cut the light you just turned on. We don't need it. I'm transcribing these names and addresses into a notebook. Come on in and close the door. Your eyes will adjust. Come on. We don't have much time.'

Tomas quietly closed the door behind him.

'Uncle Miguel, what are you doing here?'

'I just told you, Tomas. Come over here. That's Gabi with you, yes? You two can help me open up these little pieces, while I note down the addresses. Or maybe you, Gabi, can write the addresses. You've probably got better writing than me. My penmanship leaves something to be desired. Not to mention my vision.'

'What would the CDR think of your penmanship right now?' asked Tomas.

'Perhaps I'll have a chance to explain sometime, Tomas, but not now. Let's just say for starters even as a Communist I always believed in religious liberty. That was a quiet little heresy on my part, but it led as heresy often does to bigger things. Your Uncle Carlos and his friends are very much on my trail. Just another reason to help me. I think we share goals here.'

'Maybe we share tails,' said Tomas. 'We just left Carlos and his men at Nuestro Señor de la Esperanza. I think they'll soon be here.'

Gabriela asked, 'Where should I sit?'

'Right here where I've been sitting.' Miguel got up. She could see him now in the dim light. She took the chair where he'd been sitting.

'The pieces on your left have been unopened. Those on the right have been opened and read. I've just finished San Juan de la Cruz.'

Gabriela looked at the open scroll under the black light. 'S. Johannes vom Kreuz,' a Psalm reference, a New Testament reference, and '14' were printed on the front. On the reverse could be seen a name and address, the writing appearing as a white ink against the background.

'What do I do with the scrolls once I've read them?' asked Gabriela. It looked like she had about ten scrolls yet to read.

'They go in the coffee cup to your right. We'll burn 'em sooner or later. Father Juan has a little stove where he burns palm fronds to make ashes for Ash Wednesday. State security will acquire a house without meaning. Tomas, you should step outside to keep an eye out. When I say "outside," I mean out on the street. If they show up, we won't have much time to get away. Father Juan showed me a way out.'

'Why didn't you hang onto the Advent house?' asked Tomas. 'Why did you deliver it to my grandparents'?'

'Because the one thing I didn't know was who you might deliver it to. I figured your father had directed you to hand it over to someone, but I didn't know who. I followed you this evening when you brought the box here. Now go on outside.'

Tomas was persistent. 'And you persuaded Father Juan you wouldn't turn him in?' he asked.

'I did.'

Gabriela wasn't so sure. But she had no idea of how she could convey her reservations to Tomas. It was too dark, and she didn't want to become vocal.

Tomas said, 'In Cuba, it always helps to know the back way. I'll keep an eye out for our guardians.' He turned and left the room, quietly closing the door behind him.

Gabriela opened up a scroll. The top of the scroll read '21. S. Peter Kanisius.' On the reverse was an address. She transcribed it from the scroll to the small notebook Miguel had handed her. He was proceeding to remove head caps and knock out the remaining scrolls.

Gabriela couldn't write as fast as Miguel could de-cap pieces. He took to replacing de-scrolled pieces in the window perches where they belonged. She transcribed as rapidly as possible, discarding the read scrolls into the cup. When she had two scrolls left to transcribe, she grabbed one and Miguel grabbed the other. He threw it into the coffee cup.

'I haven't read that one,' said Gabriela, as she proceeded to transcribe the one that she had in hand.

'Something tells me we don't have time for the last. We'll have to discard it as unfinished business,' said Miguel.

'But shouldn't we have a complete list?' asked Gabriela.

'The perfect list is known but to God,' said Miguel.

'*You're* a believer?'

'I don't know. And you?' he asked.

'I haven't been. Maybe I'm being carried along in ways…' She didn't finish the thought out loud. She was being carried in ways she'd never imagined, in frightening ways. She thought of her 'zombie' brother and was ashamed to think she'd been more zombie than he. She closed the address notebook.

'Who gets this notebook?' asked Gabriela.

'Father Juan,' said Miguel, turning on the room light. 'He apparently knows someone in the network who'll give it to the new captain, whoever that is.'

'Not Father Juan,' said Gabriela. 'He's in their crosshairs.'

'Well, hold onto the notebook. So are you. Put the Advent house back in its box.'

The office door opened a crack then all the way. Tomas asked, 'You finished?'

'More or less,' said Miguel.

'Good. They've just parked the black Mercedes about fifty meters from the church. There's a police car, too. They seem to be fanning out around the church.'

Gabriela asked, 'Still want the box, Miguel?'

Miguel asked Tomas, 'Think we have time?'

'Not much,' said Tomas before walking out.

'Box it,' said Miguel.

She put the house in the box. She scrambled to re-place the last pieces regardless of where they were meant to go. It was enough that every piece was somewhere. A sadness cut against the celerity of her scrambling handiwork.

While she labored with the house, Miguel labored to start a fire with his cigarette lighter. The lighter was a silver-plated affair probably from his seafaring days. The first scroll was reluctant to take flame. Miguel was becoming aggravated, but the scroll finally took. He placed it in the cup where its brothers and sisters lay. They all took flame. A sweet smell lingered from the brief fire. Miguel opened a window to remove the odor.

He grabbed the red box from Gabriela. She followed, putting on Aunt Florina's pink jacket.

Tomas was in the outer office. 'Quickly, follow me.'

'Follow, follow everywhere but nowhere's where we're going,' said Gabriela.

'Follow him,' said Miguel.

'I just need to get the black light we brought,' said Tomas.

'How many black lights do we need?' said Gabi. 'It seems we won't need any black lights now. Those days are over.'

'They might still come in handy,' replied Tomas.

Is this a bright idea? Gabi shook her head.

Tomas paid no attention. He led her, followed by Miguel, to a door fronting a narrow staircase. Gabriela looked back to Miguel.

'Keep going,' he said. 'Tomas seems to know the way.'

Tomas led the two down a stair into a catacomb of stone pillars, gravestones, and musty smells.

'At the other end of this thing is another set of stairs going up, so Father Juan told me. Those stairs will lead to a room with four doors. Facing the stairs, the one to our left leads outdoors. The one to our right leads back into the sanctuary of the church.'

'You're sure about the doors?' asked Gabriela.

'Pretty sure. Anyway, when Father Juan and I talked earlier he told me the sanctuary door leads right onto the altar. The state security guys aren't going to be up at the altar.'

The stairs they'd come down were a conventional, straight affair. But the stairs up were a spiral. By the time they'd reached the top of the stairs, Gabriela had lost any sense of orientation to the outside world. Apparently, Tomas and Miguel had, too. All three were flummoxed. The muffled sounds of 'Silent Night' could be heard. The walls and doors were of such thickness and resonance that none could be certain which door led to the altar.

Gabriela said, 'We'll just have to trust what the priest told you. The one on the left leads outdoors, isn't that what he told you?'

'Right now, I'm not certain what was said,' said Tomas. 'If anything, the music seems to be coming from that direction. No harm can come from trying one door or the other. There aren't any skeletons on the other side.'

No, they are down below.

Tomas partly opened the right-hand door. The room was flooded with the voices of the congregation singing 'Silent Night' accompanied by a guitarist. Tomas closed the door quietly.

'Let's go,' he said, heading to the opposite door. 'There was a state security guy snooping behind the altar. We can hope he didn't notice.'

'Let's get out of here,' said Miguel.

Gabriela reached the opposite door first and opened it to fresh air. Miguel headed out with the box and went straight for a gate set in the courtyard wall. This gate was unlocked. Gabriela was relieved. She followed Miguel out the gate. Tomas followed her, shutting it.

There weren't any policeman or security types waiting to arrest them. As they paused to take in what they could see on the street, they now heard 'Joy to the World.' Someone had just stepped out the door where they'd stepped out.

Tomas had heard this, too. There could be no dithering. 'Let's go,' he whispered. Miguel didn't hesitate to follow. Tomas started to run. He looked back to see who was following. Gabriela hesitated.

23.

She ran hard to catch up. When Gabriela looked back, she saw a man following, no doubt a Cyclopean. He was wearing dark glasses. When Tomas turned into a side street and then into a side street from the side street, she and Miguel and the Cyclopean followed. The weaving through a myriad of streets persisted in an almost game-like fashion. The Cyclopean never caught up, which seemed odd. Gabriela kept looking back over her shoulder and finally the follower was gone. Gone, yes, but that hardly helped. Havana was *their* city and Cuba *their* country, despite the travel posters.

Tomas and Miguel waited for her, panting. Miguel still had the red box in hand and Tomas the black light.

'Where do you think our police friends are?' she asked.

Tomas looked back. 'We've lost whoever was following us, I think.'

Gabriela looked back again. 'I guess so, but where are we?'

'I know the neighborhood,' said Miguel.

'Good,' said Tomas. 'Let's go back to Nuestro Señor.'

Miguel led Tomas and Gabriela back to that church. On the way, they'd seen an oncoming police car and ducked into a dark entryway. The car cruised right on by. What struck Gabriela was how agile and perceptive Miguel appeared to be. His one eye was shut, to be sure, but the other appeared to be fully functional. The partial blindness in his good eye had been a well-crafted ploy to serve the party. *Who does he serve now?* Gabriela wondered, but there was no turning back.

Kiko was sitting in the VW microbus in front of Nuestro Señor. Gabriela was surprised he'd been left unsupervised. Perhaps a state security operative lurked in the shadows. Gabriela was about to advise caution. Before she could say a thing, Miguel ran ahead to the VW.

Gabriela caught the tail-end of Kiko's bewilderment: that Miguel wasn't wearing dark glasses, that he seemed to see as well as he, and that he was to be seen at all. Where had he been? State security was looking for him.

'Never mind,' said Miguel. 'We need to get out of this neighborhood.'

'And you want me to provide the taxi service. Am I right?' asked Kiko.

'There aren't many taxis running at this hour,' said Miguel.

'There aren't many *people* running at this hour,' came the reply.

Tomas broke this fruitless repartee. 'Frederico, I speak to you as a nephew in name only. If you want me to be a nephew again, as a nephew you could regard as a son, you will get us out of here.'

Kiko looked vexed. Miguel began to walk around to the driver's side of the microbus. Perhaps he was prepared to pull Kiko from the vehicle.

'I don't like this any more than you do, Frederico, but we're desperate.'

'But the law,' replied Kiko.

'This isn't about the law,' said Tomas.

Miguel opened Kiko's door. 'Come on. Get out! You'll be clean with the law.'

Kiko got out of the VW. Miguel got in and placed the Advent house box in the front passenger seat. He slammed shut his door, rolled down the window and shouted, 'Let's go.'

Tomas opened the back door for Gabriela. She was surprised to find her travel bag still in the back seat. Tomas was surprised, too, but at least now he wouldn't have to run any more with a black light in hand. She was amazed he hadn't succumbed to the impulse to throw it away and said so. What good would it do them now? They'd had their run of invisible ink.

'No matter,' he said. 'Someone may be able to use it again in the distribution business. Put it in your bag.' There seemed no point or time to argue the matter. Gabriela would do as Tomas said.

He hopped in behind her and slammed shut the door. Miguel gunned the VW, almost drowning Kiko's plea to his nephew, 'Be careful!'

Miguel navigated through Havana streets until they'd reached the main highway heading east, the Autopista Nacional. Even before reaching the highway, Tomas observed it'd been incredibly easy getting away. Too easy to be believed.

'They've intentionally let us get away,' said Tomas.

'You think Kiko is in on this?' asked Miguel.

'Maybe. Why was he left out there in the VW all by himself?'

'They only had so many men, and they had no idea we'd find our way back to Nuestro Señor,' said Gabriela.

'No, unless you, Miguel, are part of *their* plan,' said Tomas.

Miguel looked back at Tomas with a long face. 'You're the one that suggested we come back to Nuestro Señor.'

'One of several contingencies *they* planned for,' said Tomas.

'There are so many deceptions and betrayals and so many incentives for them in Cuba,' said Gabriela. 'Right now, this brand-new VW microbus practically shouts out our whereabouts. How many can there be in Cuba? Perhaps our problem now is not deception but a lack of camouflage.'

Tomas said, 'I'd like to know where you're heading, Miguel. Just what's your plan? We've got the Advent house, but its secrets have been decoded into the notebook. By the way, where's the notebook? I'd completely forgotten about it.'

'I've got it in my jacket,' said Gabriela.

'The pink jacket. Good, I guess,' said Tomas.

'Good,' said Miguel. 'Developments prevented our passing it on to Father Juan. I did leave behind my black-light flashlight. He may be able to use it somehow. But I wouldn't be surprised if he's arrested and taken out of circulation. We can't help him now. We've got to figure out some way of disposing of the notebook.'

'Without giving it to state security,' said Tomas sternly.

'Look, you think that somehow I'm a double agent working for state security,' said Miguel.

The VW micro was now going through the outskirts of Havana. No vehicle appeared to be tailing them. At least not yet.

'You don't have to be a double agent. You've been with the CDR for years,' said Tomas.

'As one trying to help the revolution,' said Miguel, 'while also helping my brother and his wife. I saw no contradiction.'

'You're driving a contradiction now or you're playing a double game. Somehow, I think it's the latter, but I can't figure it out.'

'So how can I prove to you otherwise?'

'For starters, what's your plan for tomorrow and for the day after tomorrow? We've pretty much made ourselves undesirables to the revolutionary state.'

'Unless,' said Miguel, 'your Uncle Carlos is somehow engaged in a game of his own.'

'Explain,' said Tomas.

'When your father was arrested a month or so ago in Santiago, your Uncle Carlos paid a visit to my place. He'd never paid a call previously. We'd never met before, except at my brother's wedding. I'd reported on my brother and your mother for years. Small reports, enough to do the job but never so much as to harm their Bible work, though I knew of it. I never meant them any harm.

'The party seemed satisfied with all this. But I'm guessing someone in the party wanted to take Carlos down a notch, perhaps someone gunning for the same top spot he's wanted for so long. When my brother and Adriana were arrested in Santiago a few weeks back, I'm guessing it came as a surprise to Carlos. Perhaps someone else in the organization arranged for those arrests. Carlos had to make sure there would be no more arrests, no more street time for Adan and Adriana. Keeping a lid on the pot wouldn't be good enough any longer. The pot had to be removed from the stove.

'The twosome had to be dealt with. Along with their permanent removal from the street, Carlos has needed to show he's decisively destroyed what they were working for. He's figured out the Advent house had a role in Adan and Adriana's work. He'll do whatever it takes to get it. That's putting everything in the best light.'

'Isn't it,' said Tomas. 'But if we put things under a black light, we see things we'd otherwise miss. Like somehow Carlos has guessed the Advent house is connected with distributing Bibles in Cuba. And, somehow, he manages to keep up with us without his men having to really exert themselves. There are some dark connections here.'

'So far as I can tell,' said Miguel, 'we aren't being followed.'

'Where are you planning on going tonight?' asked Gabriela.

'There's a seaside estate east of Havana, once owned by a sugar baron but now used as a resort for party elite. It's on the north coast. For many years I've gone out there on weekends, where I run fishing charters for party members.'

'So, the party knew your good eye's vision wasn't so impaired,' said Gabriela.

'They've always known,' said Miguel. 'The cane and dark glasses were part of an act.'

'A convincing act,' said Tomas.

'I don't want to be part of the production,' said Gabriela. 'I don't want to go to this estate. Not me. I just want to go back to work at the travel agency. I want to go home.'

'You can't go home anymore,' said Miguel. 'Somewhere this evening, we've all crossed the line. None of us can go home again. We'll either be arrested, or we must leave our homeland.'

'I know I can't go home,' said Tomas. 'My mother is now dead; my father will be worked to death. For me, there's no home to go to.'

'What of Kiko and Pamela?' asked Miguel.

'I will miss her. She's been more loving to me than I ever recognized.'

'That's true of so many mothers,' said Miguel.

They were all quiet for a while. Then Tomas said, 'We have no choice but to leave. Are you ready to help us? Or are you preparing to put us in the oven so you can go home?'

'You still don't trust me,' said Miguel. 'How much running do I have to do to gain your trust?'

'I don't know what to make of you, but I don't see anyone else around that can get us out of Cuba.'

'Then you'll have to trust me.'

'That I'll do,' said Tomas. 'Gabriela?'

Gabriela winced. It was bad enough to have to rely on Miguel, but worse to leave Cuba. She had no desire to leave. She could still hope, she must hope, that her brother would leave prison, that she would see her aunts and uncle again, that she – Gabriela – would one day have a husband and children here in Cuba. These were good, ordinary hopes. But, yes, they'd become extraordinary. Beto was now a sock puppet and soon the sock would be empty. Like brother like sister, really. For both, life in Cuba was at an end. And she hadn't the wherewithal to help her aunts. *Heaven help them!* Gabriela said nothing.

Tomas asked Miguel, 'You have a boat at this party estate?'

'I do. It's ready and seaworthy. I've got all the supplies stashed around to do this. I've been getting ready for years. I would have left sooner except your father depended on me in a way. He and your mother were like the snail steadily carrying on their Bible distribution. I was their shell. I didn't want them left exposed. But she's dead now and he's beyond helping.'

Gabriela wondered how much of this was true. How much had Miguel left out? Maybe he'd supplied more information to state security than he let on. Just as she was more tied to state security than she let on. Perhaps he was somehow now double-crossing his nephew. *Oh, to be done with it.* 'I think I want out. I want to go back to Santiago.'

'Are you sure?' asked Tomas. 'Do you have a choice? I don't think you do, unless, of course, you're prepared to spend much of your life in prison. That's if you live. I wouldn't put it beyond my Uncle Carlos to shoot you. He's had enough family and the like who've caused him awkward moments. It would be nothing for him to dispense with you.'

'Are you trying to scare me?' replied Gabriela.

'I'm just hoping to aid your reflection.'

'I need a moment when I'm not in motion. That's what I need, Tomas.'

'Would you want us to drop you off somewhere?' asked Tomas.

'How can we do that?' asked Miguel.

Tomas said to Gabi, 'Perhaps at some little town here east of Havana where you have family?'

'There's no such place nearby,' said Gabriela. 'Let me off somewhere like a bus stop or train station.'

'We can't do that,' said Tomas.

'If you don't want to come, we can't force you,' said Miguel.

'Thank you,' said Gabriela, 'But I'd better give you the notebook with the names.'

'Yes,' said Miguel and Tomas.

She unzipped her jacket pocket and handed the notebook to Tomas. Then she unzipped her travel bag, thinking she'd retrieve the black light. *Tomas must plan on leaving Cuba with the stupid thing.* She fished around in her travel bag. She felt the black light. She also felt something else. It felt like a small jar of cream, except she would have kept such a jar inside the purse that she'd put in her bag. She didn't remember leaving a jar of cream in her bag. Her aunt might have slipped it in. Her aunt would do things like that. 'Little treats,' she'd call them, slipped in without notice though she always delighted in their being noticed. This must be one such thing, though Gabriela hadn't noticed it before. There wasn't much point of making an issue of the jar now. What mattered was to just get out of this vehicle to have a moment's respite.

Tomas interrupted her thought stream. 'Let's see if there's someone listed for a nearby town in the notebook. Perhaps we could entrust it to them,' he said.

'In the middle of the night?' asked Gabriela. She felt guilty about the notebook. The notebook represented a kind of nobility that transcended the mere wish to live day by day. She owed it to Adriana to see that the notebook was passed on to someone other than state security, *someone serving other than Pharaoh*. That was an odd thought.

'Do you have a better idea?' replied Tomas.

'None,' she replied absently. 'Do you want this black light?'

She felt foolish as soon as she asked the question.

Tomas laughed. 'That won't help here.' He turned on the overhead light.

Miguel turned off the *autopista*. He said, 'We're heading to a town that has a station.'

'Its name?' asked Tomas.

'Aguacate,' said Miguel. 'I'm quite familiar with this town. Once had a girlfriend here.'

'I remember there's someone in Aguacate in the distribution network,' said Gabriela.

'God is watching over us,' said Tomas.

'You're so confident,' said Gabriela.

'That doesn't mean we're beyond earthly harm,' said Tomas.

'Isn't that the truth!'

In minutes, they arrived at the Aguacate train station. Tomas asked Gabriela whether she really wanted out. Wouldn't she want to deliver the notebook to its new guardian?

She pondered the offer. Delivering the notebook would somehow complement all that Adriana had done to open her eyes to another way of seeing life. But entrusting the delivery to Tomas would return a favor to Adriana. Adriana would be so proud of her son, to know he was doing this. She was more than happy to return the favor. She more than trusted Adriana's son. 'You deliver it along with the black light lamp,' she said with a smile. 'Do you think you'll find the address in the middle of the night?'

'We will,' replied Tomas.

'As for me, I need to pause and think. Just leave me here.'

Tomas looked at the station. It wasn't especially welcoming. One fluorescent fixture lit the street-side station doorway. Two others flickered badly. Other lights were simply out of service. A husband and wife sat huddled next to one another on a bench to the right of the door. They were asleep, draped by a small travel blanket covering their shoulders down to their waists. The husband wore a turquoise-colored baseball cap.

'You want me to leave you here?' asked Miguel.

'Yes.'

'But you've no place to sit,' said Tomas.

'I just need to get out and think, maybe to look up to the stars,' said Gabriela. 'You've got the notebook and black light. You'll deliver them?'

'We will,' said Miguel. 'And if we can't, we'll come back here for you.'

'We'll come back in any event,' said Tomas.

When Gabriela stepped down from the VW, Tomas handed her the travel bag.

'I think you're making a mistake,' he said, 'but not a big mistake. We'll be back.'

'I guess I hope for that,' she said.

'Of course, you do,' said Tomas. He gave her a wink.

By now the man in the ball cap was half awake. He looked surprised as the VW pulled away leaving Gabriela standing in front of him.

The man brought a hand out from under the blanket and pointed it toward another bench. Gabriela hadn't noticed it. It was on the other side of the station door. No light shone over it. The bench was empty.

She nodded her head by way of thanks and walked to the bench. She was anxious and in no mood to sit, not even to put her bag down. *Funny, I want neither to leave nor to stay. I just want to be delivered, to be saved, from this mess, the mess of this life. I want to live.*

Gabriela shook her head and looked up at the stars. She did so for several minutes. She was looking when she heard a vehicle pull in front of the station. It was the black Mercedes.

Gabriela walked backwards as Carlos and one of his Cyclopeans got out of the car. There seemed no way of getting out of this mess.

24.

'Where are the men?' asked Carlos. 'Where's the VW?'

'I don't know,' said Gabriela. 'How did you find me?'

'I ask the questions. You should have stayed with them if nothing else for your family's sake.'

'How was I to know? How can it be... for my family's sake?'

'Not sticking with them is like running from state security,' said Carlos.

But they are running from state security.

'Whatever they're doing, I want to go back to an ordinary life,' said Gabriela. 'I'll get the next train to Santiago.'

'They're obviously running from state security. You should have stuck with them to help us.'

'I can't make heads or tails of what you're saying,' said Gabriela.

'It's not your business to make sense of things. Just do as I say. We've got important business to attend to. So, forget about Santiago... but not your aunts or brother.'

'My aunts or brother?'

'You know what I mean. Don't ever forget them. We don't.'

'How can I be of any help now? Miguel and Tomas left me, as you can see. I'm tired of running.'

'They won't run far.'

Gabriela wished she hadn't said what she'd said, but she plunged on. 'We managed to keep one step ahead of you.'

'But no more than a step,' said Carlos. 'They've become worms.'

Gabriela *wished* to be with them now. Carlos revolted her. She could never do a poster that would veneer over his suffocating arrogance, his self-righteous tyranny.

Carlos was standing right in front of her, his henchman just off to his back. Gabriela looked over at the couple. The man was fully awake. His wife still slept with her head on his shoulder. He was moving his shoulder to awaken her. He looked alarmed. But he could hardly be as alarmed as Gabriela. What was she to do?

'They were headed to an estate somewhere out here,' she said. *Did she have to say that? Who was the more despicable? The tyrant or the tyrannized?*

'Know anything about it?' asked Carlos.

Enough! 'No, not at all,' said Gabriela. 'Are you satisfied?'

She hated herself for saying as much as she had. Would it do her aunts or brother any good? Or was she merely blabbing out of base fear?

'Come on along,' said Carlos.

'I don't want to. You have no reason to bring me along. None of this has anything to do with me.'

That was a lie, but she could hope it would work. She had no wish to hurt Tomas, nor Miguel for that matter. And the whole effort to quash the Bible network seemed pitiless and futile.

'I'm not going. You'll have to arrest me.'

'Very well. You are under arrest for resisting an officer of the law and for abetting anti-state activities. Get in the car.'

As she turned to the Mercedes, the screech of vehicle brakes could be heard. Carlos and the Cyclopeans were as startled as she. Not more than eighty meters away was the VW microbus with Miguel at the wheel.

Carlos shouted, 'Get in the car.'

She did. As she got in the Mercedes, Miguel spun the VW about and headed away. The state security men shot at the VW.

Carlos jumped into the Mercedes and slammed the door. His henchman did likewise. The man at the wheel gunned the car.

'Follow them,' shouted Carlos.

25.

The VW turned a corner. When the Mercedes came around that corner, the microbus wasn't to be seen. The driver headed down one street or another, as if he knew where the VW had headed. But he didn't and Carlos told him to halt. Carlos seemed confident *he* knew where Miguel was headed. 'Head to Casa Avanzada,' he ordered.

The Mercedes was soon speeding out of town without the bucking and swerving that had characterized their tour of Aguacate. In this comparative calm, Gabriela first heard a bleeping noise. So did Carlos. He shouted at the front rider to turn off 'the homer.' The henchman reached for a black box with a red blinker. Next to the blinker was a small circular screen awash in white light. When the driver turned off the blinker, the screen went dead. So did the bleep.

'A beauty of German engineering,' said Carlos. 'Now give me your travel bag for another one.'

'Why?'

'Just hand it over.'

Perhaps that was the moment when the desire to go home completely evaporated. Without the least compunction, Carlos could require anything of her.

There was no sphere however tiny that was her own. Home in her homeland was a fragile illusion bolstered by all those who were meant to be life's dearest friends. But the state could trespass on that world, picking pockets (as now) or removing family and friends as only a tyranny can.

Gabriela let go of the travel bag, which she'd been clutching. She shoved it toward Carlos. She consoled herself that the little notebook of addresses was not there.

Carlos took the bag. He opened it. He pawed through it. As he did so, Gabriela heard a thump behind her. She made no mind of it. Carlos held a jar aloft, the very jar she'd noticed earlier. From the light of an oncoming car, she saw the look of pride on his face.

'The VoPo are geniuses,' said Carlos, passing the jar up front to the front rider.

'The VoPo?' asked Gabriela.

'The Volkspolizei, the German People's Police. You would never have been able to open that jar if you'd tried. And we would never have been able to follow you without it if we'd tried. But technology is a faithful servant of the state. Someday, we can hope to keep track of everyone that way. That sort of thing will be needed if we are to be one family united as a family ought to be.'

All the more reason to get out of this mess, thought Gabriela.

She heard the thumping noise again. It seemed to be coming from the trunk. Carlos seemed unperturbed.

'So, I was carrying a homing device? When did you put it in my travel bag?'

'Does it matter?' he replied. 'Don't waste your time trying to figure out when. You've been helpful, if only unintentionally. You must become more intentional. You wouldn't want your arrest to become a matter of record, would you?'

'What can I do?' she asked.

'For one thing, you might become helpful in every possible way about the matter of Sergeant Rodriguez.'

First the arrogance; now the oil of gladness.

'Who is Sergeant Rodriguez?' asked Gabriela.

'The missing guard from Estacion ES.'

'I only went there, as you know, to visit my brother, not to take anybody away, though I'd have been happy to bring Beto away.'

She heard another thump. Carlos said nothing. The Mercedes moved on through the night. Gabriela saw no red taillights ahead, but then they were now traversing a curvy road. It was becoming foggy. She inferred they were approaching the north coast. Wherever they were, the VW wasn't in sight.

'Your brother isn't my concern. He's now a kept man,' said Carlos. 'Forget your brother.'

So you would say, thought Gabriela. 'What about this Sergeant Rodriguez?'

Carlos said, 'He went missing about the time you and Tomas left the camp. He took a truck from the camp, admittedly without authorization of the camp commander. Be that as it may, he left the truck in the road within two kilometers of the camp. The key was still in the ignition, but the motor turned off. The driver-side door was open. He apparently got out of the truck and walked to the side of the road. Footprints lead from the truck to the roadside. From there the trail goes cold. So far, the authorities haven't called in the search dogs. Right now, we can't be sure where Rodriguez went. Did he go into the thicket? If so, why? Or did he walk along the side of the road into town? If so, why? All in all, it seems more likely he went into the thicket. But what prompted him to take the truck only to abandon it so close to the camp?

'He was a quirky guy, so they say, transferred from another camp where he'd gotten himself into some trouble because he was sexually too forward with female guards and prisoners. You may have aroused the beast, Comrade Gabriela. The camp authorities have wondered as much.'

'That's nonsense. There was a camp officer with me at all times so whenever I may have been with this Rodriguez, I couldn't have done anything to arouse him.'

'I didn't say that. The beast may have been aroused by the mere sight of you. Let's be honest.'

The direction of this conversation was making Gabriela rather uncomfortable. She hoped they'd soon arrive at the estate.

'So, you have nothing to say about this?' asked Carlos.

'I don't know what I could say at this point,' replied Gabriela. 'This Sergeant Rodriguez was apparently more beast than man, and I wouldn't know who he was on that account.'

'They tell me you dealt with him when you checked in and out of the camp. You would have left your purse in his custody when you entered the camp.'

'Creepy,' said Gabriela, 'but somehow I think your interest in Miguel and Tomas and me has little to do with the whereabouts of this Sergeant Rodriguez and everything to do with the issues you raised when you took me on a ride to the seaside.'

'Oh, I wouldn't be so certain. There are many things on my plate right now, but you can be sure I want to be done with them to my satisfaction. I will either devour the plateful, or it will be sent back to the kitchen and the cooks. Whoever's had a hand in its preparation will pay with their hands or heads. Your pertness suggests you don't appreciate how lethally your recipe of activities reflects on you. Don't try to deceive me.'

Again, she heard a thump.

'What is that thumping noise I keep hearing?' she

asked.

'You'll see,' said Carlos. 'Life brings its surprises and so does death.'

26.

The Cyclopean probe through the night halted before a massive Spanish Baroque arched gate. The gate interrupted a wall the height of an elephant. Classical gods and goddesses in statue adorned the gateway. They were necessarily indifferent to the fog and the human purposes cast beneath them. Gabriela was not.

The front rider looked back at Carlos.

'Call first, but bust it if they don't open quick,' said Carlos.

The rider got out and went to a metal box with a phone. He put the handset to his ear and dialed. About a minute passed. No conversation took place. The man placed the handset back in the box and closed it. He looked at Carlos and shook his head. The man pulled out his gun and shot at the gate lock. The phone started ringing. The henchman shrugged. He took three more shots at the lock. The last worked. He opened the gate.

'Is this Casa Avanzada?' asked Gabriela.

'They're here,' said Carlos, not bothering to answer. Gabriela assumed he was referring to Tomas and Miguel.

The henchman returned to the car; slamming shut his door. The Mercedes proceeded through the gate. The driver drove slowly on the narrow, paved road knifing through the thicket.

Perhaps a kilometer in, they came to an open area where the road was lined with royal palms. A lawn edged the road right and left. The great house, for surely there must be one, still wasn't visible. Morning couldn't be too far away. The sky overhead was starting to turn blue. Gabriela could see one star through the fog. The stars were thinning and perhaps next the fog.

Carlos spoke almost in a whisper. 'Cut the lights.'

The driver shut off the headlights and stopped the car. Gabriela heard another thump in the trunk.

'Who do you have in the trunk?' she asked.

'*Shssh!* You ask too many questions, especially for someone with so many privileges,' said Carlos. 'We'll wait here until it gets a little lighter. I don't want to use flashlights. We could become targets.'

'You think they have guns, commander?' asked the driver.

'They might. Miguel's resourceful. He's been playing a double game for a long time. So far, he's gotten away with it. I want to capture him alive. He may have a good deal of information. As for the youth, dead or alive, it doesn't matter. He's a goner anyway. I want that Advent house.

'What do you know about that thing, Gabriela?' asked Carlos.

She replied, 'I don't give it much thought.'

'So you say,' said Carlos.

Gabriela could see him peering up to the sky. Unlike earlier, his shadowy appearance wasn't lit by the glow of the front instrument panel.

'Let's get out. You, too, *compatriota.*'

She could hear the click of the master door lock. The door locks had been disengaged. Should she run for it? If so, where? There were no signs of Tomas or Miguel or the VW microbus. It was one thing to run away. It was another to run *somewhere*.

Gabriela got out and slammed shut her door. She looked up at the palm fronds crowning the roadway. The smell of the seashore mingled with the sweet odors emanating from night-blossoming flowers. Bats were still flitting about. She could hear the cooing of some kind of morning bird, some kind of early riser, no doubt. She envied the bird, since she'd slept not a wink all night. The morning would soon display its splendor. All she wanted was to sleep. That was reason enough not to run. She wouldn't have the energy to escape.

The front rider signaled for her to walk to the back of the Mercedes. The driver had already opened the trunk. He asked, 'Should we untie 'em?'

'Both,' said Carlos.

Both. Who?

The driver shook the body nearest the hatch. He shook it again. There was no response.

'I think he may have lost consciousness,' said the driver.

Gabriela could see the man was a priest. He was wearing a clerical collar.

'Get him out. The other's the one we must deal with now,' said Carlos.

The driver and his partner lifted the body of the priest from the trunk. She guessed it was Father Juan. The men laid the priest on the wet grass parallel to the car. The priest was bound hand and foot and blindfolded and gagged. When Gabriela started to approach the priest, Carlos held her back.

'The priest can manage on his own,' said Carlos. 'Remove the gag, men.'

One of the men removed the gag. Both returned to remove the other man from the trunk, a man similarly bound. This was Kiko. All things considered; the priest seemed a plausible prisoner here. But Kiko?

Kiko was laid in the grass, but he wasn't the inert body the priest had been. He thrashed about and emitted a noise somewhat like the cooing of the morning bird, but with anger. No doubt he objected to many things, not least the wet grass.

'Calm down, my dear brother. Calm down if you wish to be unbound.'

Kiko stopped thrashing about and stopped cooing. Carlos directed the men to unbind his brother. In moments, Kiko was unbound. With help he stood up.

The first words he blurted out were, 'You didn't need to do that.'

Carlos said, 'You have made yourself a threat by threatening to go to the authorities. We are the authorities so any such talk must be taken as counter-revolutionary.'

'Counter-revolutionary, my eye. I'll remind you I'm a party member, a party member in good standing.'

'You were until you threatened me,' said Carlos.

'Threatened! I was only defending my own, my charge, my son.'

'He was never your son, my dear brother. And even if he had been, he wouldn't be, can't be, and you know it. A child is a privilege to be trained up to serve the state. You direct a whole school in Santiago, an elite school at that. Yet you have failed miserably in training Tomas. He appears to have become a counter-revolutionary like his biological parents.'

'I don't know what happened to Tomas, but I still love him,' said Kiko. 'And if you were even half the uncle you should be, you'd give him some slack.'

'To consort with Christian zealots?' retorted Carlos. 'We have to draw the line somewhere; otherwise, too many will drink from this poison cup. You ask me to betray the revolutionary state.'

'You're more concerned about your ambitions than you are about the state.'

'You should talk,' said Carlos. 'Or rather you talk too much. You've become a counter-revolutionary.'

'No, I haven't.'

'You could prove that by helping us find your boy and Miguel. I have every reason to believe they're on this property tonight.'

'Where are we?' asked Kiko, looking around.

'One of the party retreats east of Havana.'

Kiko looked around. A saffron hue now suffused the wispy fog. The outlines of the estate house were visible in the direction of the waters.

'I recognize the place. I've been here before. Casa Avanzada, beautiful Avanzada. There's a lovely boathouse right on the water and both an indoor and outdoor pool.'

'You've enjoyed the benefits of party membership,' said Carlos.

'And you haven't?' asked Kiko.

'You've always been cynical about it,' said Carlos. 'You view the revolutionary state as a necessary evil, the best that can be had in an evil world.'

'Isn't that the truth?' asked Kiko.

'Such ornate language artfully condemns me, your brother, and pillories the state with faint praise. All your sniggering behind the curtains won't save you from this final act. You're finished, my dear brother, because you're no longer of use. He who looks to the state for insurance must acknowledge the state may cancel the policy. I don't think you really want to help round up Tomas,' said Carlos.

'I don't want to see him lumped with Miguel. Miguel and Adan were poison to our sister. But I won't let my son be poisoned.'

'He's not your son. You thought of him that way, but he's not. You picked up that rot from Adriana. Her son is already poisoned.'

'I hadn't seen her in years,' said Kiko, 'not until you dragged me to see her—dead.'

'Enough. You can go see her now,' said Carlos.

'She's dead,' said Kiko.

'Of course, and that's best,' said Carlos. 'Like you, she was a traitor at heart. Get out of here!'

'What?' asked Kiko.

'You heard me. Get going.'

Kiko backed away from the state security man who stood nearest him. He looked unsure, suspicious.

'Run while you can. You've already done enough damage. Run, I say.'

Kiko turned and ran between two royal palms onto the road. He ran along the road to the edge of the forest.

'Aim for the lower back and legs. Immobilize him,' said Carlos to his men. They had already retrieved the pistols from inside their coat jackets. 'I want him to go slow.'

Four quick shots rang out and Kiko screamed. His right hand came shooting up in the air and his left broke his fall to the ground. Gabriela gasped. Kiko screamed for help, then began to moan. Except for the moaning, the world had become silent.

One of the henchmen spoke. 'Are you sure, commander? I can finish him off.'

Carlos didn't speak immediately. Nothing stirred in the thicket, neither bat nor bird. Then Carlos spoke. 'He needs to feel it as he goes. That will be his just due. Leave him. Officially, of course, he was shot as he attempted to escape. We've got more work to do. Go sweetly, my brother. Go sweetly, favored child.'

Revelación

27.

Where was the bright side? Gabriela was still alive. The driver walked over to her and nudged his pistol into her back. The state security men always seemed to know what to do next without benefit of word. But then, of course, they were gods, monster gods. Would they just shoot her at point blank range, or would she be told to run like Kiko?

'He was nothing but a thief, stealing affection from an early age, then stealing the affections of our revolutionary state. He was a parasite,' said Carlos, 'sucking all he could from the living tree of the revolution. He produced misfits like his genius "son." Well, now, we must find the "son" and his misfit uncle. For that, Gabriela, you may be of use.'

Dear life! God deliver me from this mess!

'Let's find that infernal microbus, gift of the Red industrialist. Shall we?' said Carlos, looking at Gabriela.

He walked toward the driveway, lifting his feet gingerly to minimize the effects of the wet grass. His henchmen followed. They had put on their sunglasses. *Of course.*

Gabriela looked back towards the priest. She thought she saw him move. She said nothing.

The front rider forged ahead of Carlos until he came to a fork in the driveway. He looked back at Carlos for direction. His commander wagged a finger to the left. The man nodded and went leftward.

The driveway formed a large oval in front of the house. In the middle of the oval was a concrete-lined pond. A bronze larger-than-life statue of Che Guevera stood atop a man-high limestone pedestal in the pond's middle. As opposed to the Greek gods at the entrance gate, the birds seemed to favor Comrade Che. His head was bedecked with white poop.

Gabriela counted five cars parked near the entrance to the great house. She'd never seen a private home so large or grand as this one. Three stories high, it was done in the Spanish Baroque style seen at the entrance gate. Lush bougainvillea and other flowering plants skirted the house. Except, of course, this was no longer a private home. To advertise its revolutionary personality, its entry portico was festooned with a red banner that read *¡Marcha atrás nunca!* Not one step back! *Indeed.*

While the great house was off to Gabriela's right, to her left at the lawn's edge was a collection of outbuildings amid wooden fencing. From that direction, she heard the braying of a donkey or mule. Carlos and the men began to snicker.

'It must be hungry,' said the driver.

'Something's happened to the caretakers,' said Carlos. 'This place has a family of caretakers. They didn't answer the gate phone. And that *beast* hasn't been fed. Keep your guard up, men.'

The front rider was now perhaps thirty meters ahead of Carlos, the driver, and Gabriela. He shouted back, 'It's here, over here off the driveway.'

'Let's go,' said Carlos. He began running to catch up. The rider was around the corner. The driver nudged Gabriela in the back and they, too, ran. When they came to the far end of the oval drive, they ran onto the grass to the side of the great house. The VW was parked with its nose facing towards the water's edge. It was parked between the great house and a large structure at the water's edge. Gabriela took this to be the boathouse.

The Cyclopean had already opened the driver-side door of the VW. 'There's no one here,' he shouted.

Carlos opened the passenger-side door when he caught up with his man. Then he opened the back door.

'Not here,' said Carlos. 'We've got to find that calendar house. Let's check the boats out on the pier.'

There were six powerboats and one sailboat moored alongside a floating pier that projected out into the still waters. The pier rested on pontoons and was connected to the shore by a gangway. Carlos and his henchman ran down the gangway and onto the pier, looking into the powerboats. In two instances, they boarded the boats. They found nothing. Then they boarded the sailboat, which was perhaps twelve meters in length. As the henchman began descending the ladder into the sailboat cabin, Gabriela heard a siren coming across the fog-enshrouded waters.

The driver withdrew the barrel he'd held against her back. She caught him looking off to their right. There, standing behind a balustrade, were three men staring at them. They weren't steady on their feet, but then they each had a champagne glass firmly in hand. A green bottle sat on the balustrade. The men wore white trousers and brightly colored shirts, one in golden orange, one of purplish hues, and one turquoise green. Gabriela couldn't imagine they'd just gotten up. They'd probably been up all night, but not singing Christmas carols. Or perhaps they *had* been singing carols, state forbid, and that's why they were drunk. Gabriela was thankful for their tipsy presence. Their gift might be to moderate the turn of events.

Yet help first came, albeit briefly, from the waters. Out of the fog appeared a black police boat with four men aboard. As the boat came alongside the pier, the siren was cut off and one of the crewmen jumped out with a line in hand. Soon another man from the boat had secured the boat to the pier. Carlos and his henchman jumped off the sailboat and approached the newcomers. The pistols were no longer in sight. Instead, Carlos and his front rider produced their credentials.

By now, Gabriela and the driver had stopped where the gangway came up from the pier onto the dock. She wondered if this might be her opportunity to bolt. She looked around toward the great house. The three tipsy men had apparently gone inside. Walking towards the dock was a woman in her thirties. She looked anxious.

As Gabriela would later learn, the woman was one of the caretakers. She'd heard the shots earlier, first towards the main road and then on the front grounds. Her husband had just gone out to find out what was going on. He'd called the police after hearing the second round of shots. She had decided not to come out of the house until she heard the police siren. She hadn't expected the police to arrive by sea.

A police boat, as it happened, was in nearby waters. Two marine zoologists from the University of Havana had managed to get it pressed into research service. Fishermen the day before had reported the presence of seemingly thousands of dolphins gathered in bay waters and in the nearby open sea. The university's research vessels were elsewhere. The police boat had been pressed into duty to help the zoologists see what was going on... provided the fog lifted.

Given that state security services were already represented here, it was agreed the police boat could resume its special mission. Indeed, they'd best be on their way, said Carlos. A breeze from the north was picking up. Carlos gave the policemen a hearty farewell. The zoologists, who'd remained in the police boat, got a wave, too. The two waved back. *So, there was a bright side this Christmas morning!*

In this leave-taking Gabriela, took a cue. Before her guardians could do anything, she bolted towards the great house. She wasn't sure what she'd do once inside, but she hoped to find the tipsy men. As it turned out, the lady caretaker ran to catch up with her, making it awkward for Carlos or his men to follow. On the run, the caretaker introduced herself and mentioned her husband. Her name was Maria, his José. 'Mine's Gabriela,' said Gabriela.

Maria welcomed her into the house, escorting her into the front entryway, where dual stairways framed the grand entrance. So many non-public buildings of this vintage were in sad disrepair. This one seemed well-trimmed. Gabriela complimented her guide on the building's condition, all the while wondering how she'd get out of the place or connect with Tomas and Miguel. *And what about the good father and Kiko, out there on the grass?*

Maria didn't linger. The caretaker excused herself. She said she had something to do. No sooner did she exit then señors Gold, Purple, and Turquoise walked into the entryway shoulder-to-shoulder locked in arms. They hardly batted an eye at Gabriela. Instead, they walked out the front door shoulder-to-shoulder. The door was that big and their intentions perhaps even bigger. In any event, they left the front door open. Gabriela followed.

The tipsy gentlemen went headlong to a small balustrade overlooking the front lawn. Their attention was focused out front. There Tomas hovered over Father Juan, who was sitting up on the grass and no longer gagged. Just coming out of the woods was the caretaker's husband, José. He was slowly leading a donkey towards Tomas and Father Juan. *Maria, José, and a donkey all on a Christmas morning.* Gabriela wanted to think this was some kind of cosmic joke. State security wouldn't see it that way.

Gabriela straddled over the balustrade and ran to Tomas and Father Juan. She helped Tomas bring the priest to his feet.

'Good to see you're back with us,' said Tomas with a smile. 'Where's Carlos?'

Father Juan wasn't steady on foot, and Tomas seemed all too confident.

'Where's Miguel?' she asked in a loud whisper. 'And did you see Kiko?'

'Kiko?'

'He was shot over there by the entry road,' said Gabriela, pointing in the direction where Kiko had been. He wasn't to be seen.

Tomas said, 'We've got to get Father Juan over to the VW. He needs medical attention.'

'Are you crazy?' asked Gabriela. 'You're not going to take anyone anywhere. They want to kill all of us.'

'One thing at a time,' said Tomas. 'We've got to help the good father.'

'I think I can walk,' said Father Juan. 'But I know I can't ride.'

'This is craziness,' said Gabriela.

'This will help focus our afflicting angels where we want them to focus,' replied Tomas.

'Unless they get you where they want you first,' said Gabriela.

'Can you hold him?' asked Tomas looking at the priest.

'Yes,' said Gabriela.

'I'm OK,' said Father Juan.

Tomas let go and ran in the direction where Kiko had been shot. Tomas shouted, 'There's blood here.'

He followed a blood trail into the thicket, where he disappeared. Gabriela could hear him thrashing in the thicket. Carlos came out of the great house and his Cyclopeans came around each side of the house. Tomas reappeared. As he saw Carlos running toward him, he raised a finger. Carlos stopped. Without lowering his finger, Tomas approached his uncle.

'You shot Kiko, didn't you? You shot Papa.'

'He's not your papa and I didn't shoot him. He tried to escape. He's become an enemy of the revolution. Is he over there in the weeds?'

Tomas said, 'An honest judge would convict you of attempted murder.'

'Attempted murder!' shouted Carlos.

'The attempt is obvious,' said Tomas coolly. 'I didn't manage to find the body. I thought it best to get back here to help the living.'

'You'll not help the living by accusing anyone in state security of murder. Anyone,' muttered Carlos.

By now, one Cyclopean had come over to Father Juan and Gabriela. The other had joined Carlos. No pistols were drawn.

'Get that beast over there to the priest,' shouted Carlos to the caretaker.

José lowered his head, as did the donkey.

'Put the priest on the donkey,' said Carlos, approaching the priest.

'I can walk,' said Father Juan.

'No, I want to help you,' said Carlos. 'You're obviously not feeling the best. I want to make up for how we brought you here. If you cooperate in finding that Advent house, you'll be able to return home on your own feet.'

'I've really nothing I can tell you,' said Father Juan. 'I don't know where the Advent house is. It was at the church, yes, but as you yourselves saw when we went to look, it was gone. I don't know where it is now.'

'You're a liar,' said Carlos. 'All priests are liars and as a matter of habit. Get on the donkey.'

Gabriela didn't like the trend of events.

While José steadied the donkey, Carlos, his henchman, and Tomas helped the priest mount the animal. Perhaps he'd never been atop a donkey or horse. He draped his arms around the beast's neck.

'Tomas, you walk on one side and make sure he doesn't fall off,' said Carlos. 'Caretaker, let's head for the microbus. Now.'

The henchman ran ahead to open the VW's side door. Carlos followed. José jerked the donkey into motion, leading the animal towards the driveway. Gabriela followed the donkey. The priest couldn't sit upright. He'd slumped forward and looked like he would fall off. Tomas prevented that. Gabriela could hear the priest muttering the Our Father.

Gabriela looked toward the big house and realized the procession had become a spectacle to señors Gold, Purple, and Turquoise.

'He should be sitting up on the donkey,' said one of them.

Another said, 'No, *she* should be riding the donkey with the baby, and he should be alongside.'

'No,' said the first, 'he *should* be riding the donkey, only better 'an that. He's to ride the donkey, you know, into the city.'

'Oh, it's all the same because the baby's not been born yet,' said the third.

The second said, 'Of course he's been born. It's Christmas. That's why we're here.'

The first spoke, 'But we don't have any coats for the way into the city.'

Gold and Purple began to buckle and weave and ended up pulling Turquoise down with them behind the balustrade.

In their own bumbling way, perhaps they've been helpful, thought Gabriela. At least the inevitable had been delayed. She ran to be alongside Tomas and Father Juan.

The priest may have been weak, but he was cogent. He said, 'We're never on our own, if we but seek Him. I pray we can be His hands and feet and heart now.'

'His lungs, too, Father,' said Tomas. 'You're having trouble breathing, aren't you?'

'It won't matter soon,' said Father Juan. 'Put me down on the ground, please.'

Not a good trend.

Tomas looked at Gabriela, then turned the priest about. 'Here, I'll put you on the ground but standing. We need to get you to the VW.'

The priest fell into Tomas's arms. Tomas held steady while the donkey let out a bray.

Carlos looked back. He shouted at the caretaker, telling him to scram pronto with his donkey. The caretaker and his wife, he shouted, should have neither ears nor eyes nor mouth about what happened this morning. José nodded and produced a carrot that lured his donkey into a quick pace towards the outbuildings. Rather than lead him to a stable, José removed the donkey's bridle. Then he ran with the bridle into the great house. The donkey began grazing on the grass.

Father Juan seemed to regain strength, once he was on the ground. Nonetheless, he did not resist the help of Tomas on one side and Gabriela on the other. They managed to get him to the microbus. Oddly, or so Gabriela thought, neither Carlos nor his henchman made any attempt to assist in placing Father Juan in the VW. Indeed, they moved away from the microbus. No matter, Tomas and Gabriela managed to put him into the front passenger seat. That done, Tomas opened the VW's side door for Gabriela. She clambered in.

As he was about to close the door behind her, Carlos tapped his shoulder. Tomas spun around.

Carlos said, 'I want you to drive back to the station, where we lost track of the microbus. I'll want to retrace every street and road you took, Tomas, once you left Gabriela at the station. Or you can simply tell me where Miguel left the Advent house. Don't pretend you don't know its significance beyond Christmas. I've deduced its importance to my late sister and her husband. There's no use in hiding its whereabouts, especially if you hope to distance yourselves from the disappearance of Sergeant Rodriguez.'

'Who's Sergeant Rodriguez?' asked Tomas.

'Don't play dumb. Tell me where that calendar house is.'

'Miguel knows its whereabouts, but I don't know where Miguel is,' replied Tomas.

'You're lying,' said Carlos.

'I've got no reason to lie,' said Tomas.

'Then, we'll follow you back to the station. Get up front and drive this thing. You're the genius,' said Carlos.

'If I can find my way,' said Tomas.

'Oh, you will,' said Carlos. 'Miguel's not here so you have no choice.' Carlos walked away to the Mercedes.

'What are we going to do?' asked Gabriela as Tomas climbed into the driver's seat. 'We'll never make it to the station.'

'Isn't that the truth! He's demanding I drive for a reason,' said Tomas. 'Miguel better show up quick.'

'We can't drive out of here,' muttered Gabriela.

'Agreed,' said Tomas, turning on the ignition.

'You've driven before?' asked Gabriela.

'Not very far,' said Tomas.

Father Juan spoke. 'Let's see if I can talk to these men. I'd rather have the local police involved, too.'

'What can they do against Havana?' asked Tomas.

'It never hurts to have witnesses, Tomas. Back this thing towards the Mercedes. Stop it in front of the front steps but so the VW roughly parallels the Mercedes. I'll get out on my side and you two can pile out through the driver's door. You'll have to run fast. The bus will give you some protection.'

Tomas began backing as the priest instructed. Tomas asked, 'What about you?'

'I'll be taken care of. I believe I'm called to do this for you both. But you must do as I've said.'

'God bless you, Father,' said Tomas as he braked the VW at the entrance of Casa Avanzada. He had swerved the VW so that its nose faced the front door, making the bus roughly parallel to the parked Mercedes. Tomas opened his door. 'Come on, Gabriela.'

Gabriela snaked her way between the two front seats. Tomas pulled her out the door. 'God bless you, Father,' she whispered before stumbling toward Tomas. He grabbed her before she could fall.

The two looked back to see that Father Juan had gotten out of the VW and was walking toward the Mercedes. He held out his arms in the beginnings of an embrace. Then came rounds of shots. Shot after shot whizzed around their heads. The two ducked and ran towards the boathouse.

As they reached the boathouse side door, an explosion ripped apart the VW. Gabriela and Tomas looked back to see the microbus enveloped in flame. As they ducked into the boathouse, a charred piece of metal landed just behind them.

'Over here,' said Miguel. He was in the boathouse kneeling in front of Kiko, who had a wound around his left thigh and another in his right lower chest. 'I found him alive, but he's not going to make it. I thought we could bring him along. But he's not going to make it. Bleeding too much.'

Tomas went over to Kiko and spoke to Miguel. 'Are you sure we can't take him?'

'We'll be lucky if we get out alive ourselves,' said Miguel. 'You've provided the diversion. I tried. But we've got to run.'

Kiko spoke without opening his eyes. 'Tomas, go with Miguel. Leave. Start anew. And forgive… me.'

The pool of blood around Kiko was growing larger. Miguel yanked Tomas away from Kiko.

Tomas shouted, 'I forgive you, Papa. You…'

'God rest his soul,' said Miguel. 'We've got to run.'

'Lead the way,' said Gabriela. 'The pot is boiling over.'

'This way,' said Miguel.

All three exited the boathouse and looked toward the fire consuming the VW. Miguel ran from the boathouse to the gangway leading down to the pier. Tomas held his forehead as tears streamed from his eyes. Gabriela grabbed his free hand and pulled him in the direction Miguel had taken.

'Come on, Tomas, we've got to go,' she said. The two caught up with Miguel, who stood at the head of the gangway.

'Head for the powerboat at the far end, the big one. I'm the rear guard,' said Miguel, pulling out a Lugar and looking back.

'Where'd you get that?' shouted Gabriela.

'Guess,' said Miguel.

Tomas and Gabriela scrambled down the gangway and along the floating pier. The pier rocked to-and-fro from their running. At the end of the pier, they came to a sleek powerboat with a forward cabin, about seven meters long. The motor was already chugging. In the cabin doorway stood José. At his waist two little boys'

302

faces appeared on each side of him. Maria was tucked in the cabin with her daughter.

Tomas ran forward to untie the forward line. As he ran aft to release the aft line, Miguel jumped into the boat, took the steering seat, and waited for Tomas to jump from the pier onto the boat.

Tomas jumped aboard. Bullets cut through the air as Miguel gunned the boat. Except for Miguel, everyone kept their heads down. Carlos and his men continued to shoot as they ran down the gangway to the nearest boat.

Miguel knew the channel and soon rounded a point. They were traveling through patchy fog. Fuel cans were stowed all around the boat. They'd have plenty of fuel for their escape if they managed to elude Carlos and his friends.

From somewhere, Miguel had retrieved a captain's hat. Gabriela supposed what he later confirmed. He kept it stowed on this boat, the very one he used to take party officials on high-powered fishing trips on the open waters of the Florida Straits. He never went to sea, he said, without wearing that hat, as silly as it might be. He'd purchased it in Hamburg years ago.

He purchased it along with the Advent calendar house, sitting now in its red box in the forward cabin. When Gabriela learned of its presence on the boat, she asked why he'd brought it.

'Maybe it's like this hat,' said Miguel. 'Like the hat it didn't come from Cuba, but it became part of my

Cuba, my sister-in-law and brother's Cuba, and I'm going to take it with me.'

'They want the calendar,' said Tomas.

'Too late now,' said Miguel. 'Anyway, it no longer has state significance. Its secrets are still in Cuba.'

'They don't know that,' said Tomas.

'They're too late,' said Miguel.

'It fuels their pursuit,' said Tomas, looking astern.

Miguel looked astern, too, and could see that the smaller boat was catching up with them. 'We need to head for a patch of fog.'

Miguel turned the boat toward a fog bank off to the port side. Would the bank be *there* when they got there? Toward that bank, the red and green hulls of fishing vessels were to be seen, along with a black hull. Gabriela thought the black boat was the police boat. It could be summoned to aid state security if Carlos had a radio.

'We'll make it,' said Tomas. 'I think we're blessed to live another day. To El Salvador for now, but I will come back to Cuba.' He said this looking intensely toward the receding Cuban shore and the intervening boatload of state security gods.

'Don't be crazy,' said Miguel. 'I love Cuba, too. Always will. But we must keep our ardor in bounds; otherwise, our love will kill us. You'll never find me going back.'

'I think I'm called to go back,' said Tomas.

'Nonsense. Who's calling?'

'Knowing what you know about your sister-in-law, my mother, and my father, your own brother, who do you think?' asked Tomas.

'That sort of thing doesn't run in the blood,' said Miguel.

'No, you're right. You're very right,' said Tomas.

'Carlos is closing in on us,' said Gabriela. 'Perhaps we could slow him down.'

'How?' asked Miguel.

'Throwing the Advent box in the water,' said Gabriela.

'Never,' shouted Miguel, 'not until Gabriel blows his horn.'

'I'm blowing it for him,' said Gabriela. 'But just the box, not the contents.'

'She's got a point,' said Tomas, heading down the ladder into the cabin.

'Is he getting the box?' asked Miguel.

Gabriela looked in, then said, 'Yes, just the box.'

'OK,' said Miguel, as if Tomas were waiting for his uncle's approval.

Tomas lifted the box onto the quarterdeck then scrambled up the ladder. Miguel had cut back on the engine speed. The boat surged along from momentum. Miguel put the thing in reverse. Between them and the fog bank, about hundred meters away, was a veritable pandemonium of dolphins in a school so thick and numerous it seemed impossible to go forward.

Gabriela had never seen such a thing in her life. Nor had anyone else. Maria and José stood halfway up the cabin ladder looking out over the churning waters. The kids had come up all the way.

'We can't make any progress,' said Gabriela.

'All the more reason to give up the box. It'll buy us a few minutes,' said Tomas. He was standing on the stern deck that formed the aft perimeter of the quarterdeck well.

He waved the box to-and-fro with his right hand. 'They must see it hit the water,' said Tomas.

He continued to wave the box to-and-fro.

'Throw it in the water and get down, Tomas,' shouted Gabriela.

As soon as she said that the first bullet hit Tomas. He lost his footing and spun into the water. The box fell in with him.

'Throw him the lifebuoy,' shouted Miguel.

Where could it be?

'It's right there,' said Miguel, pointing to a spot behind Gabriela.

She removed the ring from its clasp and threw it toward Tomas. Miguel began bringing the boat around to pick up Tomas.

'Keep going, keep going,' shouted Tomas. 'I'll head for one of those fishing vessels.'

'That'll do you no good,' shouted Gabriela.

'Don't worry about me,' shouted Tomas.

Carlos's boat was about two hundred meters away and closing. The box seemed to be drifting toward the pursuers, towards Cuba. Tomas had managed to swim to the life ring, which he clasped with his left hand.

The nearest fishing vessel was at least two hundred meters away. And the dolphins were as frisky as ever. They had come to surround Miguel's boat. They looked to be surrounding Tomas. Would that help? Or would the ring of sea creatures merely enable Tomas to be captured?

Miguel could slip into the fog bank. It was less than fifty meters away now. The fog seemed to be moving toward Cuba. But the revolution was moving again. Carlos and his men had retrieved the big red, empty box. They now headed to Tomas. He was sure to be a goner. The dolphin swarm seemed to be moving shoreward, toward Cuba. There was now mostly open water between Tomas and Miguel's boat.

Bullets whistled overhead. The state security gods were now dead in the water, thanks to the dolphins. Miguel closed in on Tomas. Thirty meters. Twenty meters. Ten meters.

Miguel handed Gabriela a grappling hook affixed forward of the boat's steering station. He shouted, 'There's a Jacob's ladder right aft. Throw it over the side.'

Gabriela had never heard of a Jacob's ladder, but she figured it was the rope ladder that lay on the fantail, just about where Tomas had stood when he got hit. She cast it over, then stretched across the fantail holding the grappling hook out towards Tomas. Bullets were flying overhead. One hit the deck beside her, churning up small shards of wood. How long before one hit the mark?

Tomas was kicking with all his strength. Gabriela was reaching with hers. Finally, he grasped the hook. She pulled back on the hook. Another bullet hit the deck beside her. Should Tomas even dare to climb the ladder? He would be a standout target. As Gabriela was about to shout to Miguel, the fog enshrouded the vessel. Miguel cut the engine. He and she pulled Tomas aboard.

Tomas lay on the deck, shivering. 'There're blankets below,' said Miguel. 'And sheets for wrapping up that wound.' Blood was flowing from his right upper arm. Maria appeared from the cabin with a cloth towel, which she helped Gabriela tighten above Tomas's wound.

Miguel gunned the boat.

As the boat headed deeper into the fog bank, Gabriela, Maria, and José removed Tomas to a cabin bunk. They removed his wet clothes and bundled him under blankets. When Gabriela tried speaking to Tomas, he didn't respond. She assumed he had lost consciousness. She and Maria elevated his legs. Gabriela gave him a kiss on the forehead and started rubbing his legs. Perhaps it didn't do any good, but she felt impelled to do something. José joined her.

Life went on around them. Maria broke open a packet of crackers. The kids apparently hadn't had breakfast. They devoured crackers while watching their father and this unfamiliar lady rub the legs of the man who'd fallen into the sea. When the man started mumbling, the lady went topside.

Topside, Carlos and his boys were nowhere to be seen. Miguel was heading the boat, he said, to Key West. Gabriela came back down into the cabin to find Tomas's cheeks aglow, a good sign she thought.

He awoke for a moment, very sleepy eyed. 'You've been through a lot with me,' he murmured to Gabriela.

'Look who's talking,' she said.

'Come closer,' he said.

She did. He attempted to lift himself up. He brought his good, left hand around and touched her right cheek. He was smiling, but now he looked quite pale. He fell back. He had a vacant stare, then his eyes shut. His breathing became quite husky. His skin felt clammy and cold. Gabriela had spent enough time as a volunteer to recognize shock.

She elevated Tomas's legs even further using blankets from the other bunk. She went topside to explain what had happened. Miguel didn't seem especially perturbed.

'We're in luck,' he said. 'First the dolphins, then the fog bank. And the third time will be a charm. Turn around and look on the horizon. What do you see?'

Gabriela turned around. On the horizon was a ship heading west. Miguel had the boat headed to intercept the ship.

'You can see the ship?' she asked. 'Your good eye proves it's the best eye around.'

'Not really. I can't see the ship. A blip this size on my radarscope tells me it's a ship.' Miguel tapped the radar screen. She hadn't really paid attention to it.

'Can we overtake it?' asked Gabriela.

'We can. We'll have to hope it's a friendly ship.'

'Meaning something other than Cuban?' asked Gabriela.

'Cuban or Soviet or East German or Polish, you get the idea.'

'I do.'

'If it's Commie, we'll keep heading for Florida,' said Miguel.

'Shouldn't we just head to Florida anyway?' asked Gabriela.

'There's not always a friendly reception from the authorities there. I'd rather take my chances with the right ship at sea. We can eventually get to Florida. Can you see the flag she's flying?'

'I can't make out the flag yet,' said Gabriela.

Miguel had the boat going full throttle. Gabriela looked astern again and again, but not once did their pursuers come through the fog. *Fitting they got hemmed in by the fog and dolphins*, thought Gabriela.

Then she recognized the flag fluttering high above the ship now three hundred meters away. It was a German flag, the West German flag.

'The German flag, meaning the flag of the Federal Republic of Germany, not the German Democratic Republic, which is neither democratic nor a republic. Are you sure?' Miguel asked.

'Sure, I'm sure,' replied Gabriela. 'I'm in the travel business.'

'West German or East German?'

'West German.'

'Very well. We'll go for it.'

And, so it was they came alongside this stranger in the Florida Straits that did them the courtesy of taking them aboard. The ship, the *Westerwelle*, was heading to Veracruz, Mexico. Several in the crew spoke Spanish, which meant a lot to Miguel, whose German was fractured and finite. Gabriela was pleased to be able to brush the rust from her German.

She was with Tomas when he woke from what had been a long sleep. He'd been put in the ship's sickbay, where the orderly had treated and bandaged his entry and exit wounds. Tomas had been lucky. There didn't appear to be a bullet lodged in his body.

When Gabriela told him where they were headed, his eyes lit up. 'Mexico's better than Florida. Closer to El Salvador.'

'You would count that as an advantage,' said Gabriela.

'Would you come with me?' he asked. 'As a friend, just a friend, a very good friend.' He held out his hand and smiled.

She hesitated then took it, saying, 'I don't know how this could be arranged. I don't have any family in El Salvador.'

'Christian missionaries can help us. We'll be volunteers.'

'Things are happening too fast,' said Gabriela. 'Just days ago, I was holding your mother's hand as she lay dying. Now I'm holding yours as you come alive.'

'Who would have imagined?' said Tomas.

'Yes. It's extraordinary. I wouldn't have ever imagined this.'

'No, the ordinary hides the extraordinary and that's cause for hope,' said Tomas, 'real hope.'

'You have a point,' she said. 'Let's take ordinary days one at a time if we can find them somewhere.' She shook his hand.

'Agreed,' said Tomas. 'At least, we're headed for Veracruz.'

'I'll have to do a travel poster,' she said. *And much, much more.*